THE CROSS
OF LAZZARO

THE CROSS
OF LAZZARO

John Harris

A WILLIAM SLOANE ASSOCIATES BOOK

Published by William Morrow & Co., Inc.

New York, 1965

c. 3

THE CROSS
OF LAZZARO

1

If he hadn't been there—personally—Henry Chappell would never have believed it. But he saw it with his own eyes, coming up through the drifting rain like the miracle they later tried to say it was.

He was standing with Caporelli on the slopes above the lake where they could see both the town and the dam. Cadivescovo lay just below them, a collection of wooden and stone buildings around the Church of Lazzaro di Colleno, full of narrow streets and flowered balconies with Gothic lettering and dark frescoed arcades. It was a narrow little town of carved doorways and decorated shutters, its thick roof tiles weighted by stones against the sudden winds that could blow down the Val Caloroso off the Catena di Saga, sited where the Latin and German cultures of the South Tyrol overlapped, and still more Austrian than Italian, its roots way back in a culture from which it had been wrenched in 1918 when it had been ceded with the rest of Trentino to Italy. Beyond it the water of Lake Colleno was

the silver gray of steel, flat calm and stretching across to the misty fangs of Monte Cano at the other side, half hidden in cloud—standing among the slender spires and imposing towers of the Cano massif like a rampart above the meadows.

But there was no mist over Cadivescovo and the water that morning. The drizzle was lifting gently on the breeze, falling across the lake, it seemed, in ripples—almost like the shot silk of corn in a summer wind. Overhead, a hawk was circling slowly on curved wings and below, the *Citta di Trepizano,* the lake ferry, was just coming into Cadivescovo from Trepizano at the other side where the houses speckled the shadowed mountainside. A few tourist cars stood alongside the pier where the ancient high-funneled ship called, and a few more were jockeying for places on the narrow Via Colleno that ran around the lake from Trepizano. But not very many, because the unsettled weather was still keeping them at home and the season had just started. The geraniums packed onto the balconies of the public buildings were still in bud and the painters were still busy picking out in black paint the sharp-edged words carved lovingly into the façades of dwelling houses—*Klein aber Mein,* and other such sentimental mottoes. Even the brass band that had been playing waltzes in the Piazza della Citta beneath the statue of the Tyrolean patriot, Andreas Hofer, had looked stiff and uncomfortable in uniforms only recently taken from camphor-smelling oak chests and from behind cottage doors.

The water of the lake was clear and still, except in front of the Punta di Vescovo where they'd been exploding small charges in the water. There was still a flurry over the surface around the cluster of boats where they'd detonated the last one. They'd been at it for weeks, Caporelli said. The European Universities Underwater Exploration Group, they called themselves, though they were mostly English, with an odd Frenchman or American or German or Italian, and they'd been looking for the lost city of Arcuneum most of the summer. Two or three

8

of them were standing at that moment on the beach near the mounds that marked all that was known of the ancient city, pacing out the distance with tapes.

From where he stood with Caporelli, Henry could see the remains quite distinctly. Cadivescovo had once been known as Arcono and before that as Arcuneum until an earthquake had submerged it beneath the lake in the year 547 A.D. A medieval *castello* stood near the dug-out ruins of a Roman fort, and it was possible to make out quite easily how the straight muddy mounds just below the surface of the water connected with the earthworks. It was clear there *had* been a city there, but archaeologists had been searching on and off for forty years now without ever discovering anything beyond a suggestion of a broken wall.

Another small explosion in the shallows threw up water in a low mushrooming heave on the surface of the lake, rather like a small depth charge, and they could see the archaeologists —mostly students and members of skin-diving clubs who enjoyed the adventure of swimming below water as much as the search for archaeological treasures—lining the sides of the boats, peering downward, rather as though they expected to see fragments of statuary come floating to the surface.

Caporelli shook his head and lit a cigarette.

"They'll never find Arcuneum that way," he said. "They'll have to find the remains of Bishop Lazzaro's barge first. It's down there somewhere."

"Why?" Henry asked. "Why there?"

Caporelli shrugged. "He was Bishop of Colleno, and he'd founded a monastery at Arcuneum. When the town disappeared in the earthquake he came to see what he could do for the survivors. Unfortunately there was a storm."

"And?"

"And the barge was a bit top-heavy. He always had a great wooden cross on the bow to warn the Barbarians of the wrath

9

of God. So! It capsized and in the rush no one thought to rescue Lazzaro. Hence Cadivescovo. Casa di Vescovo. The home of the bishop."

And Punta di Vescovo, Henry thought. And Via Vescovo and Piazza Vescovo. Everything about the place was redolent of the life of the dead bishop. Ninety per cent of the wood-carvings done in the town and by the shores of the lake and half the paintings daubed by the artists struggling to make a living in Madonna del Piano on the hill were of Bishop Lazzaro's death.

"The way they're going on," Henry commented, "they'll have blown the barge to bits before they find anything."

Caporelli turned and smiled, small and squarely built before Henry's lankiness, thick-necked and earthy-looking against Henry's lean scholarliness.

"Doctor Cappell—" he began.

"Chappell," Henry corrected him absent-mindedly, and he smiled and nodded.

"Of course," he agreed. "Shappell! They say, Doctor Shappell, that Labbaro's cross marks the site of the city and that when Lazzaro decides it's time to discover Arcuneum he'll give a sign."

"Sign?"

Caporelli gestured. "If I didn't know he was in the crypt of the Church of Lazzaro di Colleno," he said, "I might expect them to blow him to the surface with their explosives."

"Why explosives?" Henry asked, staring downward. "It's a funny tool for an archaeologist to use."

"They're very good at it," Caporelli pointed out, a note of respect in his voice. "I know. I was a Partisan, wasn't I? I used to use explosives a lot myself. Plastic in small cans. That's what they've got. Pentolite or hexogen. It's very well restricted. They fire them with a car battery."

"But why?"

Caporelli grinned and indicated the stream that ran over its bed of multicolored granite and dolomite pebbles down the mountain, past the carved crucifixes that were a reminder of the Catholic faith in an area that had been part of the Holy Roman Empire for a thousand years. They could just see where it entered the lake in a brown cloud of mud which the rain had washed off the mountain.

"The water has piled soil and gravel where they think the walls are," Caporelli said. "It's formed a hard crust. They decided that small planted charges dug into it would loosen it enough for them to wash it away with pressure hoses. They will then find Arcuneum—they hope."

"And when they do?"

"*Ecco!*" Caporelli grinned again. "Another Pompeii!"

He came toward Henry and leaned on the wall alongside him, peering over it toward the lake. His manner seemed flashy against the reserve of the taller, fairer Northerners of Trentino. He was a Neapolitan in his early fifties, and to Henry's certain knowledge, before becoming a soldier and finally a hotelier, he'd studied engineering and medicine. He was a long-nosed, broad-shouldered bull terrier of a man with a dry sense of humor, curiously unemotional for a Southerner, perhaps because he'd spent some years in America and had even hawked plaster saints among the devout Irish in Dublin.

His hotel, the Stettnerhof, as it had still remained across the years in spite of Mussolini's insistence on the use of Italian in Trentino, standing on its little ridge of rock above and outside the town, was the best on Lake Colleno. The Underwater Exploration Group had made it their headquarters and filled the bar below the gilded Austrian eagle every night, arguing and quarreling among themselves as they grew more despondent at their failure to find anything exciting.

"I often wonder," he said, pointing downward in the direction of the old round hump where the Roman fort had stood on the Punta di Vescovo, "why they always search there. Why do they always assume the old town ran from the fort toward Cadivescovo? It could just as easily have run the other way toward the Punta dei Fiori." He gestured toward the shallow end of the lake where the swallows whirled in graceful arcs over the reedy patches of marshland. "After all," he went on, "that's where the stream came out originally, isn't it? Down the Val Caloroso and into the lake there—before they built the dam and drove it through Cadivescovo."

Henry turned from the wall and stared behind him at the dam, a tall, thoughtful-looking man with an intelligent, precise manner. He could see the dam around the shoulder of the mountain, gray and gaunt and wildly out of place among those high Dolomite peaks above Lake Colleno. Even from where he stood, he could see it was sway-backed in the middle, an ugly flat surface among the strange, beautiful rock spires of yellow and gray that were streaked like banners with black and purple and red.

"Why *did* they build the dam and drive the water through the town?" he asked.

Caporelli laughed. "Because the Von Benedikts, who were lords and masters of Cadivescovo, or Arzen, as it was then, didn't like the drive around the lake to the other bay when they could just as easily put up the sawmills here in Arzen. So they built the dam and stopped up the stream." He indicated the barrack-like structure near his hotel. "That's the sawmill there. It's the Orphanage of St. Francis now. When it happened, the village by the Punta dei Fiori became deserted and vanished, and everyone came here to Arzen, and the water was directed down an artificial channel through the town. That's what brings the mud down they're trying to get rid of. The channel's full of mud now. The walls have fallen in and it's all overgrown. If the water had to come down that way it'd flood the town. Blame it all on the Von Benedikts. They built it." He caught the look on Henry's face and frowned. "Why?" he asked. "Something wrong?"

Henry rubbed his nose and glanced up at the dam again. "Well," he said, "your friend, Von Benedikt, didn't know it then, but he was very probably building a bomb. That dam's lethal now."

A flicker of anxiety sped across Caporelli's face. "Lethal?"

"It should be strengthened," Henry said. "I can see it from here. I'll bet the blasted thing's sprouting leaks like a colander."

He fished in his pocket and, producing his glasses, put them carefully on his nose and glanced at the notebook in his hand. He had the whole history there, taken from the thick file Caporelli kept in his office. The dam that old Von Benedikt had built had been nothing originally but an earth wall, but as the sawmills in Cadivescovo had grown bigger and bigger, so had the dam been pushed higher and higher, and wider and wider, with more thought to increasing the output of the mills than to the safety of the town. It was now nine hundred feet wide and two hundred feet thick at the base. There was a road running along the rim, though it hadn't been used by anyone except the mountain people for donkeys' years. The gray wall, which had been added to strengthen it in the nineties, rose a hundred feet over the artificial stream bed that Von Benedikt had had dug and to which it was anchored.

Caporelli was squinting upward at the dam, too, now, following Henry's eyes. "It was the winter," he said slowly. "It was quite a winter here."

"It was quite a winter in England."

"The frost got into it. It opened it up. Nothing's been done to it since 1920 when the government took it over."

"Why *did* they take it over?"

Caporelli grinned. "A lot of strange things happened here in 1919 and 1920 when the Alto Adige was becoming Italian," he said. "Everybody was still in the process of changing nationalities and people took advantage of the language problem here on the lake. There was a lot of political unrest."

"There still is," Henry reminded him gently. "They're still blowing holes in the railway. I was held up myself on the way here." He stared upward, his eyes narrow. "Why the hell didn't they do something about it?" he asked.

Caporelli shrugged. "Because Mussolini was too busy rebuilding the Italian state," he pointed out. "We'd been cold-shouldered at Versailles, and Italy was anxious to prove she was as good as anybody else. It was more important to build monuments to Italian glory than to restore an old dam which nobody ever saw. After all, it had functioned perfectly well for sixty years."

"It won't function much longer," Henry said shortly. "I'd say there are nearly two million tons of water behind that wall. Doesn't everyone down in Cadivescovo feel as though they're living under a rickety water tower that's going to burst its seams? If it went, it'd be like Niagara pouring down the valley for twenty minutes. It's five hundred feet higher than the town. Nearly two hundred meters. That's a hell of a drop."

"O.K., I know," Caporelli said, his face hardening. "Give me a chance. I've only had this thing in my lap for a fortnight—*this* year. Sister Ursula from the orphanage was the first to notice it. They take the children picnicking up there, and one of them pointed it out to her. She saw it was different from last year." He paused and looked squarely at Henry. "Tell me, what do *you* think about it—truly?"

"I've only just seen it," Henry said. "I've not had time to form an opinion."

"You stayed here last year—in my hotel. That's why I remembered you when I wanted advice."

"I was on holiday then." Henry gazed up at the dam again, speculatively. "I'll have to check closer."

14

Caporelli looked disappointed. "You won't commit your-self?"

"I've only just arrived. You dragged me up here almost be-fore I could draw breath."

Caporelli shrugged. "O.K.," he said flatly. "I must wait. Will it burst this year, that's all?"

"Dams don't burst these days. We stop them in time."

"That's what everybody says to me. But it's not really true."

He was quite right, of course, Henry knew, but no engineer worth his degree could panic over possibilities.

"I'll have to check," he said again.

Caporelli pulled a wry face. "O.K., I understand. I just wanted something to offer to the Provincial Council, that's all."

"I can't give you anything—not yet."

Caporelli smiled. "Dr. Cappell, you don't give much away, do you? Just tell me this, though—is the town in danger?"

Henry shrugged. "The Tower at Pisa's been leaning for centuries."

"It's in danger of falling now, I hear. What about the dam?"

"It needs repairing."

Caporelli banged his fists together. "I want more than that, Dr. Cappell," he insisted. "I have got to persuade them to spend money on it that they haven't got. Even emptying it costs money."

"Look," Henry said. "That dam wasn't *designed*. It just grew. Nobody ever provided a proper means of letting the water out of it in case of trouble."

"It's got plenty of discharge pipes."

"Twenty-four inches wide," Henry said contemptuously. "And at a guess mostly jammed with mud and rubbish. It wants a good spillway to stop it overflowing, or a decent outlet pipe or gate. There should be one in the stopper wall on the east side. At the other side of La Fortezza." He gestured toward the fang of rock that towered over Cadivescovo like a rose-pink

15

spire in front of the flat faces of the Catena di Saga. "If there were, it could be drained then, down the old stream bed, and come out by the Punta dei Fiori where it originally ran into the lake. That'd harm nobody. It *could* be done. It *ought* to be done. *Now.* There are only forty feet of water in it now. If it reaches sixty feet, it's only a question of time before it makes a cut. There was one once before while it was still in use. They had to repair it. I've seen the reports."

There was another small explosion in the water off Cadivescovo and they both turned and stared down.

"I sometimes wish," Caporelli said gloomily, "that we had some of that pentolite up here. Then we could simply blow the gate out of the stopper wall altogether and take the weight of the water off the main wall—for good."

"That's what you'll have to do eventually," Henry said. He squinted again up at the ugly gray wall peeping around the shoulder of La Fortezza. For years it had moldered away up there in the mountains, visited only by nature lovers and climbers on their way up to the rock faces of the Catena di Saga. And the years had not been kind to it, and behind it there was a lake two miles long and a mile wide in places, and here and there the water was a hundred feet deep.

"I'm surprised someone hasn't blown that gate out before," he said thoughtfully. "There seems to be no shortage of explosives these days around here among these—what are they called?"

"Montanari—mountain men. 'Andreas Hofer's' terrorists."

"Call 'em what you like," Henry said unemotionally, uninterested in the politics of the area. "They've had a go at more than one hydroelectric plant, I know. I've read it in the papers. They even had a go at the Simplon Express. O.K., why not this?"

Caporelli smiled and spread his hands. "Because it was built by the Austrians," he explained quietly. "And the Montanari claim to be Austrians too. And because it wouldn't hold up any trains. Nobody would be inconvenienced. It's better when you're trying to convince someone that you're a persecuted minority, to stop the traffic or cut the electric light. Draining a dam that ought to be drained anyway wouldn't do a scrap of good."

There wasn't much that Henry could say because Caporelli was right. His own train had been held up because someone had blown a span out of a bridge and the railway had had to lay on buses to take the passengers, Henry included, to the next station.

"It wasn't like this last year," he said.

"There was no 'Hofer' last year," Caporelli pointed out in a flat voice. "But it started years ago. In 1919. There were isolated incidents even then. It grew worse when the Fascisti settled the place with Southerners to Italianize it. Then the war gave the young men ideas and the old Tyrolean feeling revived. The signs the Germans had put up were retained and a German press was started. Now Tyrolean irredentism wants self-government."

"Will they get it?"

Caporelli shook his head. "There's too much Italian feeling after all these years," he said. "So we get 'Andreas Hofer' and bombs. Since he started operations, civil war's come to the lake."

Henry nodded. The first thing he'd seen in the paper as he'd sat over his cold meat and salad at the Stettnerhof the night before had been a story of explosives stolen from a quarry on the Via Colleno and pictures of the inevitable note signed in the name of the Austrian patriot. There'd been road blocks outside the town as he'd arrived and queues of cars, and policemen searching boots and suitcases and pushing through the buses to examine passports, and an atmosphere of tension ever since, as those who knew the methods of the Montanari and the

17

mysterious "Andreas Hofer" who led them waited for the inevitable bang.

Caporelli was turning up the collar of his coat now, his face twisted in disgust at the weather. "Let's go back to Cadivescovo," he suggested. "I'm hungry and it's wet up here."

He glanced up at the sky. Vast thunderheads of clouds were butting against the mountain walls, rolling along their faces like great armies of gray soldiery.

"It's going to rain again," he said. "The forecast was rain. It's been a bad spring. I expect it'll be a bad summer. Get into the car, Doctor. I could do with a beer."

They walked back toward the big Alfa Romeo Caporelli drove, with the drizzle lifting into their faces as it blew from the northern tip of the lake.

"Austrian rain," Caporelli said with a grin. "The rain and the tramontana come from Austria." He pointed toward the south. "The sun comes from there. The sun's Italian."

It was approaching noon now and the larks were singing in the drizzle above the fields and the new wines that were starting in the vineyards toward the villages of Madonna del Piano and Trepiazze, whose yellow-tiled campaniles stuck out of the folds of the valley to the east. The sound of the bells hung in the air, trembling over the tombs of dead priests and forgotten soldiers, as heavy in the damp atmosphere as the boots of the forgotten armies that had tramped past the lake on the way south to Rome or north to Vienna.

As Caporelli opened the car door for Henry, they noticed that the two boats on the surface of the lake had moved further toward the Punta dei Fiori and, as they watched, they seemed to up-anchor and move out toward the center, in the direction of Monte Cano on the other side.

"They're going to let off another one," Caporelli said eagerly. "Wait a minute. I like to watch them. I like the simplicity of explosives. With explosives you can so easily remove so much

18

that's dangerous and ugly and make room for something new and graceful and of value."

They stood by the wall, staring down, while the thin mountain grass bent and quivered in front of them and the tops of the twisted pines and the acacias and wild laburnum on the slopes above Cadivescovo sprayed the fields with drops of water as the breeze shook the rain out of them. The heavy roofs of Cadivescovo reflected the eerie light that was coming through a break in the clouds as the watery sun appeared.

The two boats had moved well into the lake away from the town now and seemed to huddle together, with a cluster of smaller boats around them.

"Any time now," Caporelli said.

There was a group of people standing on the end of the jetty where the ferryboat came in, watching for the explosion, and a whole line of them along the esplanade. They'd be tourists, Henry knew, because Caporelli had said the locals had long since lost interest in the search for Arcuneum. They'd all be there with their heads down and their cameras focused across the steely sheet of the lake, waiting for the eruption of the water.

"There's so much clay off the mountain in the mud," Caporelli said. "This cracks it. It can't do much damage. The mud cushions the shock. Several bombs were dropped in the lake during the war. They were after Trepizano and they jettisoned them when they got into trouble so they could get back over the mountains. They never did much harm. Not even the mines. There's one still in there somewhere. They were flying them from Sicily and dropping them in the Rhine. It was an aircraft that ditched. I hope they don't set it off."

"It'd be the end of Bishop Lazzaro's barge if they do," Henry observed.

Caporelli chuckled. "They'll never touch the barge," he said with confidence. "It's under the mud, and mud protects wood.

They say when they find it they'll find Arcuneum. The fishermen used to say that the cross plucked at their nets. But no one ever believed them."

There seemed to be a lot of activity on the boats now, and Caporelli leaned forward eagerly.

"We're off," he said, and as he spoke the water erupted just off Cadivescovo, and seconds afterward they heard the thud of the explosion. The water seemed to lift upward in a bubble and fall back, and Henry could just imagine all the cameras clicking away below. He could hear shouts down there, coming up through the rinsed air toward them, and the faint beat of the brass band still plugging away in the square, and he saw the boats begin to move inshore.

But as they changed position, something happened that neither he nor Caporelli had expected—nor, judging by their behavior, anyone else on the boats or the ferry jetty or among the crowd under the chestnuts along the lakeside.

The sun, which had been trying all morning to break through, made it at last and a shaft of watery gold fell on the lake near the Punta dei Fiori, bringing the first sparkles to the water that the town had seen for days. As Henry turned to look at it, he saw the whole surface of the water toward the east heave as some vast underwater eruption forced it upward. This was no minor detonation set off by the archaeologists in the boats. This was something more, and for a moment, with Caporelli's words about the earthquake that had destroyed Arcuneum still in his ears, he thought that this was another subterranean upheaval.

As the water slowly rose in a vast shining, inverted bowl, broke apart and fell back in a shower of spray, with the sun picking up the atomized drops and turning them into rainbows, they heard the rumble of the explosion and felt the air shake around them as the shock wave beat back at the mountains.

20

"The mine," Caporelli said. "Mamma mia, they've set off the mine!"

The boats in the bay were bobbing and swaying now, their masts swinging backward and forward like pendulums as the waves that the explosion had set up flung them about like corks. From where they stood, the vast ripple looked a couple of fathoms high. It would roll right around the lake, tugging at the larches and the willows and the water lilies and the reeds at the Punta dei Fiori, and across to Trepizano on the other side, setting the spade-shaped, hoop-topped boats that were peculiar to the district rocking against the piles, and pushing the tourist *pedalos* higher up the beach toward the water-front cafés.

There was a great deal of hither and thither now on the shore and they could see a vast susurration among the tourists and sight-seers along the front. Henry took the binoculars that Caporelli held out to him and he could see that the glass had fallen out of the windows of the Wolfhof, one of the restaurants by the pier, and the Stöckli Bar near the jetty, the first place that all the passengers from the boat visited when they arrived in Cadivescovo, and that there was a waiter standing outside in a white coat and apron with a group of bandsmen from the square in their red trousers and blue jackets, staring at the damage. The water-front crowd had suddenly grown more dense, and he could see people running like ants from the shops and offices along the shore to see what had happened.

"Look!"

Caporelli pointed, and through the binoculars Henry saw fragments floating on the surface around the turbulent stretch of water where the mine had gone off.

"They've found something," he said.

"Look! Look!"

Caporelli's voice rose higher as he snatched at the binoculars.

21

But they didn't need binoculars now. Right in the middle of the patch of sunlight they saw a few more fragments of what must have been wood break surface just to the east of where the mine had gone off, and as they stared they saw something else bob up, shooting clean out of the water, as though its buoyancy had been increased by its being held securely in the depths of the lake.

It leaped up, like some great surging wild animal from the black bottom of the lake, and, as it appeared, great gouts of water leaped up with it, so that it seemed to be alive. Then it fell backward, flat on the surface with a smack that could be heard even up the mountain, righted itself and finally floated upright, bobbing gently in the water.

A sound like a sigh rose from the people along the front, then Henry saw Caporelli, who, although he was a Catholic, could hardly have been called an ardent churchgoer, crossing himself, his eyes wide and bright as he stared down at the lake. Surrounded by fragments of debris and a widening ripple that was fading fast on the calming water, a great blackened cross floated upright, majestic, catching the widening patch of sunlight that was spreading, as the clouds parted, across the surface of the lake.

"*Madonna mia!*" Caporelli said in a whisper. "It's the Cross of Lazzaro! The mine must have broken it free from the barge! The fishermen were right. It was there all the time—just where they said it was!"

2

By the time they reached the town, there were already several boats out on the water, their passengers staring at that vast black cross that floated so serenely in the new sunshine, as though they dare not approach too closely, as though they stood in awe of it and couldn't summon up enough courage to take it in tow.

"Why don't they put a rope around it?" Henry heard someone say as Caporelli stopped the car under the chestnuts on the fringe of the crowd.

The speaker was an English tourist in a flowered shirt, standing on a seat with his camera, trying to change a spool of film in the mottled shadow under the trees. "The damn thing'll sink if they don't."

He fiddled with the winder of his camera, dropping his lightmeter to the gravel in his haste, and swore in confusion as though afraid he'd be too late to get his picture. But he needn't have worried, for the cross showed no signs of sinking. It floated there serenely and magnificently upright, as though it were a symbol of the coming of the Lord.

"Blast this bloody camera," the Englishman was saying, his hands all fingers and thumbs in the urgency of the moment. He looked again at the cross, as though to make sure it hadn't been snatched away, and went on winding. "It must be fastened somehow to the bottom of the lake. An anchor or something."

The boats were edging more closely to the cross now, and Henry could see Father Anselmo, the old priest from the Church of Lazzaro di Colleno, on one of them, hanging on to a guy rope with one hand, the other hand outstretched to the cross as though he were blessing it.

"*Un miracolo! Un miracolo!*" Henry could hear the word all around him, murmured in an undertone. Women were on their knees by the lakeside, praying, and he kept seeing men crossing themselves. "*Un miracolo!*"

"A miracle be damned," Caporelli said shortly, recovered from his surprise now and seemingly unmoved by the drama. "*Anything* as buoyant as wood would always shoot to the surface like that if it were suddenly released. It's supposed to be about twenty meters deep just there."

Now that they were at shore level, Henry saw the cross wasn't as perfect as it had seemed to be through the binoculars when they were up on the mountain. Obviously there had been deterioration, and what he had thought had been sharp teak edges now had a blurred look as though erosion had taken place. But, all the same, the thousand microscopic organisms whose secretions could eat into the hardest granite and all those worms which could tunnel happily through rock like a rat through cheese had not had *much* effect on it. The ends of the cross member were roughened as though time had taken its toll, but, considering the centuries, it was in a magnificent state, floating upright like a symbol of Christianity come again to a sick world as a warning. For fifteen hundred years it had been

24

preserved under the mud until the shock wave from the mine had torn it loose.

Nobody doubted that it was anything but the symbol and badge of office of Bishop Lazzaro. The story of the drowned cleric and the lost monastery he had come to visit had been told around the shores of Lake Colleno from Trepizano to Cadivescovo and back for fifteen hundred years. Nobody had ever doubted that it was there, but nobody had ever believed it would ever be seen again.

And now, here it was, dramatically re-emerging from the darkness of fifteen centuries. Even as Henry stared at it, he half expected it to melt away.

He had never been particularly absorbed by archaeology, but he knew about Ur and Sutton Hoo and Jericho and Pompeii, and about the other lost cities that had been dug out, about the *Mahdia* wreck and Tutankhamen and the shriveled body of the Tollund man who had been dug out of the peat bogs of Denmark. But, even so, staring at the serene cross out there on the water, rising above the surface of the lake like the sword Excalibur with hardly a ripple around it now, he found it hard to believe he was looking at something which had so dramatically crossed fifteen centuries in a matter of seconds. Neither he nor anyone else in the crowd lining the shore would have been very surprised if Bishop Lazzaro himself—for all that he was known to be safely interred in the crypt of the church that was named after him and was known to be only a pile of moldering bones—had leaped to the surface of the lake alongside it, complete with his episcopal robes and bishop's crook.

The bigger of the two boats belonging to the archaeological group was approaching the cross now, edging gently through the fragments of blackened wreckage. They had been staring at the cross for some time now—ever since it had first emerged

25

half an hour before—debating, it seemed, on what to do about it.

There was a big man in a bathing costume standing on the littered deck, his feet among the hose pipes and discarded aqualungs and colored floats they used, with a heaving line in his hand.

"Alois," Caporelli said. "Alois Stettner. My brother-in-law. Or he *was*, until my wife ran off with an American artist from Florence. His family lived in the Stettnerhof for three hundred years. They sold it to me after the war to pay their debts."

Henry had met Stettner with the archaeologists the night before in the bar—a big, smiling man he'd not noticed the previous year, full of arrogant self-assurance. Caporelli clearly didn't like him very much, which wasn't surprising because it seemed he'd never had a regular job and only followed seasonal occupations that gave him enough to live on.

He had slipped over the side of the boat into the water now, with an American student from Oxford who'd told Henry his name was Frank Maggs, and they were swimming around the base of the cross. Then a girl appeared on deck, small and slender in a yellow costume, her hair long and wet on her shoulders, and Caporelli sighed as she jumped into the water alongside them.

"I wish I were an archaeologist," he said, kissing his finger tips in mock ecstasy. "The Signorina Daniells makes a good swimming companion."

The girl had been with Stettner the night before, standing with the other archaeologists, the only woman in the party. She had the room next to Henry's and he'd heard her several times moving about and singing to herself in a croaky voice. She was a dark girl with the burning look of a Ban-the-Bomb marcher, and as they'd been introduced at the bar, the first thing he'd noticed was that she might have been pretty if she hadn't insisted on wearing heavy sun spectacles all the time.

26

Like most of her generation, she favored dark clothes, mostly black—and an ugly diminutive of her name. All the archaeologists seemed to have short blunt labels like Frank or Joe or Sam, and Henry sadly put it down as a sign of age that he still called himself by his full Christian name.

Caporelli was watching the maneuvering and splashing around the cross with black nostalgic eyes.

"She looks even better in a bathing costume," he said sadly, "than she does fully clothed. I must get her to pose like that on the lawn of the Stettnerhof and use it on next season's brochure."

The cross had been moved alongside Father Anselmo's boat and the three swimmers had climbed out. Stettner was first, and he yanked the other two up with a quick heave of a muscular arm, then he grinned and slapped Maggie Daniells' behind as she reached for a towel hanging on the compressor they used to fill their aqualung bottles.

"He likes girls." Caporelli frowned. "There's a woman over at Trepizano and another up the mountain. Just below the dam. Dieter Oswino's wife. He's always up there on some business or other. She's from Innsbruck. He goes up on his scooter when the husband's away. I don't like to see young girls get into the hands of Alois."

The boat containing Father Anselmo was close alongside the cross now, and the men on board appeared to be shouting instructions to one another. There was still a marked trepidation in their manner, however, as though they felt that at the first touch the moldering wood would simply fall to dust beneath their fingers and the miracle they themselves had brought about would no longer exist.

As Father Anselmo's boat edged closer, the bigger boat drew back, as though Father Anselmo was warning it to take care. Gingerly a rope was passed around the cross, below the

27

cross member, and there was an awed gasp from the crowd, as though they expected some fresh miracle to take place.

Then, with the cross secured alongside the boat, wrapped around with canvas and old clothes to prevent it rubbing against the hard gunwhale, the bigger boat slowly drew alongside and Henry saw them maneuver the boom into position. A strop wrapped in sacking was put in place, then the hook of the boom came down to it. The winch began to turn and they could hear the thud as puffs of steam came from the smoke stack, and the cross rose higher and higher until it was clear of the water, huge and magnificent, demonstrating, it seemed, the vitality of Christ and the triviality of man—sharp against the mountains and the misty pines on the far side of the lake.

Immediately women all around them began to fall to their knees. There was a deep and immediate silence. Above it, Henry could hear someone behind him muttering quietly, and even the cameras seemed to have stopped clicking. A fat German woman in hipster trousers that showed a brown loose stomach like a punctured balloon was praying softly, her hands together in front of her face.

As the cross rose higher and hung above the water, they saw what had been keeping it upright—heavy rusty strops of iron or bronze which originally must have held it to the bow of the bishop's barge and now served as sinkers to keep the base down in the water. It was no miracle that it had floated upright. Any wooden object so weighted would have done the same.

They were lowering it now onto the stern of Father Anselmo's boat and the other boats were moving into position to help, and Stettner and the girl were in the water again, collecting the fragments of blackened wood that had come with the cross and passing them to the others on the boat.

Caporelli was staring over the water and, unbeliever though he seemed to be, he was obviously impressed. His eyes glittered as they heard the engine of Father Anselmo's boat start up. Then, as the bow came around and it swung toward the shore, he slapped Henry's shoulder.

"They're going to bring it in," he said. "They're bringing it ashore near the boat station. It's a good job there are plenty of policemen about."

The black-and-red-garbed carabinieri, who until that moment had been occupied with making inquiries about the explosion on the railway line and the plastic missing from the quarry on the Via Colleno, had begun to move through the crowd, which was breaking up as men and women started to move toward the boat station and the white-painted kiosk that acted as a ticket office. Several children broke into a run, shouting with excitement, then a man with a camera, then finally the whole colorful summer-garbed crowd of them, streaming toward the tree-shaded jetty.

Caporelli stared after them and at the police trying to retain their dignity as they struggled to break through in order to get there first.

"They'll never bring it ashore yet," he said. "There'd be thousands killed in the rush. Father Anselmo's got more sense than that. He's got a sure-as-hell miracle there on his boat and he's going to get it to his church if it kills him." He stared at the lake, where the patch of sunshine was widening, as though the cross which had emerged in its center had brought glory with it too.

"We were going to have a beer," he reminded Henry. "I'd forgotten. Come on. Let's go."

Henry had forgotten all about the beer they were going to have and the plans they'd made to drain the dam. The arrival of Bishop Lazzaro's cross had knocked everything out of his mind. And, with the rain clouds miraculously backing away, against all the expert advice of the weather forecasters on the

29

radio and the television, it suddenly didn't seem important about the dam any longer.

But Caporelli was walking across the cobbles toward the nearest bar in long strides that were un-Italian but somehow typical of him. There was no one in the bar, not even the owner. There was no one in the shop next door, either, where they sold maps and souvenirs and head scarves and Tyrolean hats. *Or* in the wood-carving shops in the Vogelweidestrasse opposite, or the wine cellars or the little shops where cuckoo clocks filled the air with the murmur of machinery. They were all outside in the increasing sunshine, staring down toward the lake, and in the end Caporelli went around the back of the counter himself and extracted two bottles of beer from the cold cupboard. By the time the proprietor arrived, they'd drunk half of it. Caporelli indicated the coins on the table and the proprietor picked them up, his mind not on the job.

"Signor Caporelli," he said, his voice breathless with wonder, "it's the Cross of Bishop Lazzaro! You must have seen! It's a miracle!"

"There are no such things as miracles, padrone," Caporelli said firmly. He lit a cigarette and began making notes on the back of an envelope, tossing comments all the time across the table to Henry as he did so.

At first Henry didn't realize what he was talking about. He was still thinking about the cross and found it hard to appreciate that Caporelli's single-mindedness did not allow him ever to forget why Henry was there.

"The dam, *Dottore,* the dam!" Caporelli gestured irritably. "We still have to convince them it needs draining, and you're the man to do it."

"I hope you're right," Henry observed.

"I am right. You have Birmingham, Aberdeen, and London Universities behind you. You're known here in Italy. You worked in Florence and in Rome. There's Wiesbaden and the

Alexandria breakwater behind you, and the Canabral rocket site, and the bridge at Pontemorvo. What you said about them has been read by engineers all over the world. Even our own. They're bound to take notice of what you say."

"I'll let you have the report as soon as I can."

Caporelli shook his head and smiled. "That would be too late," he said. "You will fly home. You will write the report and forward it to me. And I will request an interview with the civic engineer. And Mornaghini, who's so old he doesn't know what day it is, will be rather busy. He'll suggest next week. And next week, because he's Mornaghini and an ex-soldier and not used to hurrying, and has a title of some sort somewhere in the background and therefore has too many friends to lose, hasn't the courage of a mouse. He'll request a little more time to consider it. And then he'll suggest that we put it before someone else. Then the Council will consider it and pass it to the Province, and the Province to Rome. By the time anything is done the winter's rains will have arrived and the danger will be greater than ever. You must come with me yourself to see them. Let's go and have a word with him now. Not when you have seen the dam and prepared your report. *Now.*"

3

The Municipio had originally been the summer palace of the Von Benedikts, and the long, shabby corridors, with their hacked plaster and dog-eared notices, were full of officials, most of them hurrying for the door. The steps and the entrance which overlooked the lakeside and the statue of Andreas Hofer were as crowded with people as the Piazza San Marco in Venice with pigeons.

Caporelli thrust through the crowds angrily and made his way to the office of the Engineering Department. But the door was wide-open and there was no one there, only a pile of scattered papers on the floor and a telephone that rang persistently.

For some time he leaned on the counter, tapping with his fingers against the woodwork, then the telephone stopped and he turned and stamped outside into the corridor and returned leading a scared-looking girl by the arm.

"Where is the staff of *Ingegnere* Mornaghini?" he demanded.

"I don't know, *Signore*," she said. "I work in Accounts."

"Well, where is someone who *can* tell us where they all are?"

"I don't know, Signore. I expect they're all outside." She gestured, so violently that a lock of her piled hair fell down. "Signore, there's been a miracle!" she said, her voice high and excited. "The Cross of Bishop Lazzaro has appeared!"

"I know," Caporelli said. "I saw it. It came up like a jack-in-a-box."

"But, Signore, it's a manifestation!" —

"It's nothing of the sort," Caporelli snorted. "In fact, it's becoming a nuisance. Especially if everyone's outside watching them bringing it ashore. Where is Major Mornaghini? Is he outside watching them bring it ashore also?"

"I expect so, Signore."

Caporelli released the girl's arm and, giving him a scared look, she shot off like a frightened mouse.

"Watching them bring the miracle ashore!" he said bitterly.

By the time they reached the square again, the whole police force was out there, it seemed, together with ropes and crush barriers. And they were all needed. It was as though the news had sped around the lake already and people were coming in from miles around. They could see cars stopping along the fringes of the crowd and people jumping out and running to the water's edge. More were climbing on the Hoferdenkmal now and the steps of the war memorial with its top-heavy column weighted with sorrow and broken swords. There were also the black soutanes and shovel hats of several priests, and someone had backed up a great dark truck to carry the cross to the church.

Caporelli was standing on the crumbling steps of the Municipio staring at the crowd on the jetty where the archaeologists' boats now lay. Judging by the noise and the crowd down there, they had obviously landed the cross or were just about to do so. They could still see people heading there from all the streets around the Piazza della Citta, and the noise seemed to indicate that it was Bishop Lazzaro himself who had risen from the depths of the lake, not his cross.

"Did you see the size of it, man?" Caporelli said slowly. *"Madonna,* no wonder the barge capsized with a goddam thing like that attached to the bow."

Henry could see he was angry. The arrival of the cross didn't seem to have moved him in the slightest, but it didn't seem to be because he was unimpressed. It was simply that the cross was distracting everyone from what he considered a more important emergency. The cross had waited fifteen hundred years, and he felt it could well wait a little longer. He had been struggling to bring the dam to everyone's notice long enough and unsuccessfully enough to feel frustrated by any delay. There was a file in his office six inches thick with the work he had done in an effort to draw attention to that great ugly, unsafe edifice above the town.

"The dam started deteriorating the day it was first built . . ." "The stability of the dam can only be measured by a thorough overhauling . . ." "The dam has been neglected for twenty years. . . ." "The old dam is an inferior piece of work. . . ." "Techniques of dam building have so improved in recent years as to render this work as archaic as the dodo. . . ."

Henry had seen all the comments in the file, most of them in Caporelli's vitriolic sarcasm, but some of them the sober efforts of working engineers and designers, men whose books Henry had read as a student, men whose structures he'd examined as an expert.

Caporelli was frowning at the mass of people under the chestnuts and the acacias by the edge of the lake. "You can't go home now," he said to Henry. "With this miracle on us no one will ever have time for reports. Doubtless they've got Major Mornaghini down there advising them how to erect the cross in the church and what sort of lighting to use. You've got to give your report to him and to the mayor in person. *This is going to occupy their attention for the rest of the summer.*"

Henry looked at him and he shrugged. "The newspapers'll be here soon," he said. "They'll know already. Tomorrow—or even tonight—they'll be swarming around the place like vultures, their faces full of sanctity and their mouths full of soft words, and their minds thinking of their circulations. This'll bring the tourists here in thousands, and Cadivescovo lives on tourists these day. Big business, the Chamber of Commerce, they'll all be in on the act, and every goddam archaeologist in Europe will want to see it as well, especially as I expect they'll now find the rest of Arcuneum. Doubtless the Church will arrive in droves, too, and there'll be talk of sanctifying Bishop Lazzaro." He glanced at Henry. "You've got to force your way through *that* lot, Doctor Cappell, and make your voice heard above the tumult."

They were still standing there when they saw Father Anselmo go hurrying past, clutching his soutane out of the way of his flickering rusty boots, and following him, Father Gianpiero, one of his curates, holding on his shovel hat with one hand, both of them tense and urgent.

"Off to report a miracle," Caporelli said shortly. "Tomorrow there'll be a bishop here to make a report, and then all that talk of sanctification will start again. They've been at it for years without success. I don't see how they can refuse now. If this isn't a sign, nothing is. The place will be full of cardinals from the Vatican Library before long, all making inquiries and writing reports."

The Stettnerhof was full of people when they returned and the atmosphere had changed abruptly to one of blazing excitement. Everyone could see money in the arrival of the cross.

The previous night when Henry had sat in the bar to drink his coffee there'd been nothing but tension and anxiety in the

35

air. The papers had been full of the blown bridge near Bolzano and the political arguments that had arisen from it, and everyone was on edge at the knowledge that more explosives had been stolen from the quarry on the Trepizano road. There'd been photographs in the newspapers of startled-looking quarry officials pointing fingers at the open door of the explosive store, and close-ups of the note that had been left behind by the thieves—*Dankerschön, Andreas Hofer*—in German, like all the other notes that had been found on damaged hydroelectrical installations and railway bridges and in station luggage rooms where suitcase bombs had gone off.

Police had been stopping students in the streets and searching their pockets, and hatred—one against another, Italians against Austrians, Northerners against Southerners, everyone against the Montanari—had been in everybody's eyes. The Sudtyrol Volkspartei, the minority group in the Dolomites, had been the center of every controversy, the object of accusation and the subject of pride at the same time. There had been an edginess that showed in the muttered conversations and stiff greetings between acquaintances in the bar, and the sudden explosive arguments that kept breaking out, and the abrupt silence, thick enough to cut with a knife, that had fallen over the room at the appearance in the hall of a couple of policemen on a routine checkup.

And all the time, throughout the evening, Henry had been aware of a strange alertness in the air, and it wasn't until Caporelli, his face drawn and strained like the rest, had explained that he had understood. Everybody had been listening, sitting with their ears cocked, waiting for the crash of an explosion. Explosives stolen by the Montanari *always* meant explosions and trouble, somewhere, for someone, and they'd all been waiting for the bang and the clatter of tiles and broken glass and wondering where it was going to be. But now, with the arrival of the cross, the sullen resentment against the ter-

36

rorists—even from people with the German names that had brought on angry arguments with the hard-core Italians in the town—had given way to infectious effervescence.

Alois Stettner, a noisy, handsome man with gold teeth and heavy German jewelry, was shouting across the room to a crony and waving a beer stein. Caporelli gave him a bitter look.

"During the summer he is a guide or a skin diver," he said. "And during the winter he is a ski instructor at Cortina. Everybody is a ski instructor around here. Dittli, the waiter. Franco, the porter. Even the girl who washes up is a ski instructor. She's so goddamn strong she breaks all the plates."

He gestured angrily, with his hand flat along the table, sending the ash tray spinning to the floor. He looked up slowly at Henry sitting stiffly at the other side and smiled apologetically.

"I forget," he said. "I feel. Here." He thumped his chest. "Things I don't like bite me. Perhaps *you* never feel bitten?"

Henry shook his head, and Caporelli signaled for the porter to clear away the mess and sat still, with a chastened look on his face, as though he felt Henry disapproved of his violence, until all the cigarette ends and matches had disappeared into the dustpan.

As the porter moved away, the door of the telephone booth beyond the bar opened and Maggie Daniells appeared. She came across to where Caporelli was sitting with Henry, her hair still damp from swimming, and Stettner immediately left the counter and stood alongside her, one arm loosely around her waist in a posture that seemed to indicate possession. Henry wondered what there was between them. The skin diving Stettner was doing for the archaeologists didn't seem enough to give him this proprietorial air or explain the warm, intimate look the girl flashed at him.

The glance wasn't lost on Caporelli, and Henry saw his eyes flicker, then the girl was beaming at them, her face radiant.

"You saw it, I suppose?" she said, stuffing away notebooks and pencil into the heavy sling bag she wore on her shoulder. "You saw what happened? I've never seen anything more dramatic in my life."

"A miracle," Caporelli said dryly as he signaled for drinks for them all.

"Professor Dei Monti says we'll find Arcuneum now for certain," she went on. "We've already sent off to Siebe Gorman and Normalair for more gear. We've been looking in the wrong place all these weeks."

"I could have told you that when you started," Caporelli said quietly.

She glanced at him quickly, then removed her spectacles to have another look, as though she suspected he was being sarcastic. She smiled and managed to look quite beautiful.

"But if you had, Signor Caporelli," she said eagerly, "just think how much we'd have missed! We'd have found Arcuneum straight away and then this would never have happened. Lazzaro would never have sent his sign. You know"—she put her hand on Caporelli's arm—"I not have been the slightest bit surprised if Lazzaro himself had pushed the lid of his tomb up and come to give us a hand." She laughed, unable to hold back her excitement. "The press have been wonderful. Most considerate about everything.

"Of course—" she leaned across the table—"we've not seen any of them since it happened. Every telephone in the town's red hot by now, I imagine. I had to come all the way up the hill here to get one. I've been in touch with Utoio, the professor of archaeology at Milan. He's Director of the Society for the Protection of Historical Monuments in Trentino and the expert on Lazzaro. He comes from Trepizano himself. He'll tell us just how genuine the cross is, though I haven't the slightest doubt it *is* genuine."

She seemed to notice Henry for the first time. "What about

38

you, Dr. Chappell?" she asked. "How're you getting on with your dam?"

"We're not," Henry said. "Everybody's watching you people and they've no time to listen to what *we* want to do."

"What *do* you want to do?"

"When I've finished, I expect we'll want to drain the dam."

She stared at him, and he noticed for the first time that her eyes were bigger than he'd thought and he wondered again why she always wore those monstrous spectacles.

"Well," she said, "that shouldn't be difficult, should it?"

"No, but we have to get permission because we have to remove a gate in the stopper wall and that would result in mud being dumped on the beach by the Punta dei Fiori."

He caught a quick glimpse of Caporelli's eyes flashing him a warning and realized that she was staring at him with a shocked look on her face.

"It would do *what*, Dr. Chappell?" she said, and her voice, which had been warm and friendly before, was suddenly chilly and cautious.

Henry glanced at Caporelli, but it was too late to retract.

"It would dump a certain amount of mud and silt in the lake by the Punta dei Fiori," he said again. "And that would interfere with the holiday facilities over there."

"But why would draining the dam affect the beach at the Punta dei Fiori? The stream comes down through the town and into the lake by the boat station."

Stettner shook his head. "No," he said with a smile. "No, Maggie, it doesn't. That's an *artificial* stream. That was cut by the Von Benedikts. The real stream flowed around the back of La Fortezza and through the Val Caloroso and out by the Punta dei Fiori."

She stared around at them for a moment in silence. "But that would mean that this mud and silt you're talking about would be deposited over the remains of Arcuneum," she said.

"There wouldn't be enough to worry about," Henry pointed out. "It might put another inch or two or top of what's there already. No more."

"But you can't do that," she said angrily. "Not now! Not now we've established that's where Arcuneum must be. That's where the cross came up. That's were Bishop Lazzaro's barge must be. That's where the remains of the city must be situated. You can't direct silt and mud over that."

"We might have to," Henry said.

"Dr. Chappell," she said stiffly, "I know I haven't your authority, or even your learning, and I probably ought not to talk to you like this, but even *you* must be aware of what this will mean to us."

Her manner annoyed him. "I'm perfectly aware," he said.

"It'll mean that after years of searching, after a whole wasted summer diving in the wrong place, you're proposing to cover up what we've uncovered."

"An inch or so, no more. It will all have been dispersed by the time it reaches the lake."

For a moment there was silence, so heavy it was embarrassing. She was staring with flushed cheeks and hot eyes at Henry, who was trying hard and not very successfully to look unconcerned. Caporelli was lighting a long German cigar, his gaze on their faces, a faint flicker of amusement in his eyes, as though he were thoroughly enjoying himself.

Then she drew a deep breath.

"No," she said explosively. "I won't have your mud over Arcuneum, Dr. Chappell. It'll ruin everything we're doing."

"You'll hardly notice it," Henry pointed out.

"I don't believe it."

"It will darken the water," Stettner put in. "We'd never be able to see to work. The visibility's already bad. The Rolleimarines wouldn't photograph."

"It'll settle," Henry said.

"Dr. Chappell, that's a silly thing to say." Maggie Daniells' eyes flashed, the big spectacles forgotten as she waved them in her hand. "It'll take weeks for that much mud to settle. We couldn't do a thing."

"There's always next year."

"We can't wait until next year."

"You might have to."

She stood up angrily. "Over my dead body," she snapped. "I've just been in touch with Professor Utoio, of Milan. I've asked him to bring with him anybody he thinks necessary. He's promised to bring Dr. Wertz of Berne and he's getting in touch with Dr. Martini of Bordeaux. They'll be coming. Martini's an underwater expert himself, and he won't want to wait until all your precious mud's settled."

Henry had also risen to his feet now. "I don't give a damn about Dr. Wertz, of Berne, he said quietly. "*Or* Professor Pooh Bah of Milan, *or* your precious underwater expert from Bordeaux. I came here, Miss Daniells, to give an opinion on the safety of that dam up there"—he gestured quickly—"and I think it's dangerous and should be drained before the winter rains start."

"Then you'd better find some other way of draining it, Dr. Chappell, because you're not going to drain it over Arcuneum. We're on the brink of a discovery that could rate with Jericho or Tutankhamen's tomb, and you and your beastly dam are not going to interfere with it." She clapped her spectacles on her nose and glared at Henry. "There are people behind me with authority and I'll invoke every one of them, the press included. Neither I nor the people who are coming here to advise us are going to have a whole summer's work spoiled just because *you* want to fool around with a dam that ought to have been pulled down years ago."

She gave them one last glare through the ugly spectacles,

41

then swung around on her heel and stalked off, followed by Stettner.

Caporelli watched her, with an admiring smile on his face.

"You know, Dr. Cappell," he said slowly, "if that young lady didn't wear those spectacles and such awful clothes, she'd be a remarkably attractive young female."

4

By next morning it seemed as though the whole world of press and television had descended on Cadivescovo. Every single newspaper in the Stettnerhof, hung on hooks in neat rolls in German fashion, seemed to have Bishop Lazzaro's name plastered across the front. *Lazzaro,* they all screamed. *Lazzaro!* As though he were a cross between a saint and some sort of patriot like the original Andreas Hofer. They'd all forgotten the previous day's blazing headlines about the blown railway line and the tension that had sprung from the stolen explosives and the possibility of new outrages. In all of them, except the Sudtyrol Volkspartei paper, *Dolomiten,* the organ of the German-speaking minority, Lazzaro had elbowed politics off the front page, and even in *Dolomiten,* where everything was slanted to draw attention to the claims of the South Tyroleans, Lazzaro had not been allowed to go unnoticed. They had given him his German name, Lazarus, and claimed he was a Viennese friar who had traveled south and joined the Church of Rome.

It had all been on the previous night's television, with somewhat hysterical interviews with Father Anselmo and scrappy newsreel shots of them hauling the cross from the water. In all of them they had seen Dei Monti, the Italian professor in charge of the Underwater Exploration Group, peering through his pebble glasses at the camera, surrounded by his archaeologists, all obviously pleased with themselves, and always in the background Alois Stettner or Maggie Daniells, looking to Henry far more attractive than she ought without her spectacles.

There was also an interview with Dei Monti in which he had stated categorically that they were satisfied that they had been searching in the wrong place and that they now confidently expected to produce results, and another one from Maggie Daniells, who stated—ominously, it seemed to Henry—that nothing would be allowed to stand in the way of success—nothing.

Henry was down to breakfast early. The lawns outside the Stettnerhof were still wet with dew, and the mist to the east gleamed reddish in the first light of the sun. He was surprised to see a police car in the courtyard outside with a bored man in uniform yawning at the wheel and more uniforms in Caporelli's office.

Caporelli was in the hall, his shoulders hunched and gloomy.

"Alois," he said shortly.

"What's he done?" Henry asked.

"Nothing. Just the usual. The police are asking about those explosives that were stolen."

Abruptly all the tension that had lain over the valley came back, insinuating itself into Henry's consciousness through the thoughts of the dam which had been occupying his mind through washing, shaving, and dressing; all the police questioning and all the delays and all the suspicion that hung about the corners of the town. Caporelli was obviously annoyed at the presence of the police in his hotel, and worried, too, by the deeper implications behind the visit.

"Why are they interested in Alois?" Henry asked.

Caporelli frowned. "He's a member of the Volkspartei," he said. "So was his father. He takes part in the student demonstrations."

"He's a bit old for that sort of thing, isn't he?"

Caporelli shrugged. "He's a bit old for a lot of things," he observed. "But he doesn't like to admit it. He's past his best as a climber even, you know. That's why he joins the students. Because he's got a name—Alois Stettner, the best guide in the Catena di Saga. The first man up La Spiga. The explorer of La Fortezza. They all look up to him." He gestured. "They're the only ones who do now. They're the sort who think Andreas Hofer is a hero."

"Who is he? Anybody know?"

Caporelli made a sweeping movement with his hand. "The original was shot by Napoleon. This one just wrecks bridges and hydroelectric installations. He's made the lake a bear garden with the police he attracts and the notes he sends to Rome."

"Does *nobody* know who he is?"

"He's got friends. They've got a headquarters somewhere around. One thing is certain"—Caporelli flashed his hand palm down across his chest—"he's no hotel proprietor! He's ruining the tourist trade. We have more trouble in this valley from the students than anywhere else, and more plastic bombs. They dress like Austrians and behave like Sicilians, and no tourist wants to get blown up in somebody else's quarrel. It's all so goddam stupid! Like schoolboys or the Black Hand Gang."

He seemed depressed and bitter, which was unusual for Caporelli.

"It is always the schoolboys who cause the trouble," he went

45

on. "Boys who don't even remember the Austrians. I wish it were over and done with, but it never will be, because the Dolomites are Italian and now they'll always be Italian. Without them it would be like England without the Channel, France without the Vosges. They are Italy's natural northern frontier."

He paused and went on slowly. "They forget, these bomb throwers," he said, "how long Italy was occupied by the Austrians. In those days, when Austrian bands played in the square the population used to go home."

"And Stettner?" Henry asked. "Is he in with the Montanari?"

Caporelli shook his head. "Alois is just a show-off," he said contemptuously. "He just likes admiration, and this is a way of getting an audience. Besides"—he gestured—"he likes girls, young girls."

"Like Maggie Daniells?"

Caporelli looked worried. "It is not my business what people do in my hotel," he said shortly.

"What about you? Which side are you on?"

Caporelli looked up, his eyes narrow, then he gave a quick smile. "I was in the Partisans," he said. "I have had enough of fighting. Nowadays I only want to live in peace." He shrugged. "They are no more Austrian here than you are, anyway. They are just mountain people. They fought the Italians and Hapsburgs both at the same time. They talk the same language as they do in Swiss Engadine, and the war in the Dolomites in 1917 was almost a civil war because both sides took their men from the same valleys. It's a problem that'll never be solved."

The door of the office opened as Caporelli finished speaking and the policemen came out. Inside Henry could see Stettner lighting a cigarette.

"This is Inspector Castelrossi," Caporelli said, introducing a small, square-built man with sad black eyes like a spaniel. "What have you found this time, Inspector?"

Castelrossi shrugged. "You should tell your brother-in-law," he said, "to hold his tongue more. I'm always being sent to talk to him and I always know it will come to nothing. One of these days I shall take him down to the Questura and lock him up for a spell, just to teach him to keep his mouth shut."

"And the explosives? No sign of them?"

"Did you expect there would be?"

Caporelli matched Castelrossi's shrug with one of his own. "I thought maybe—"

"They are holding a boy in Trepizano," Castelrossi said wearily. "He jumped off a train they were searching. They found a case in the lavatory containing wire for detonating explosive charges. There's also a boy called Von Franck. A German. He was arrested in Trepiazze. Son of an S.S. colonel. He had a map on him—a dangerous map. And there's a man called Wasescha. There are a lot of questions we would like to ask *him*."

He moved toward the door and Caporelli called after him.

"I thought maybe there would be a miracle," he said. "There's been one already. There might be another."

Castelrossi halted with the door open. "We can do without miracles," he said flatly. "The Bishop's demanding protection for the cross now in case the Montanari decide to show an interest in it. And there's a service today over the spot where Lazzaro was drowned. That'll mean two dozen policemen to keep the crowds back and another dozen on point duty. We've more to do than control traffic."

After breakfast Henry took the key of the Fiat van Caporelli had offered him and drove around to the Orphanage of St. Francis higher up the hill. Although it still clung to the valleys, the mist had broken and he could see the pinnacles of the Catena di Saga, cream, yellow, gray, and cold purple, craggy and serrated, a stark scoop of bare rock and scree with savage crests and steeples clawing the sky.

The orphanage was a strange mixture of utilitarianism and beauty. It still bore the look of old Von Benedikt's sawmills, but here and there, in little corners, shrines had been placed with a loving care that helped to take away the harshness of the crumbling old building. The place seemed all brown wainscoting with black crucifixes and paintings of the Virgin and St. Francis, and sad-eyed little doll-like figures under the words, *Ave Maria,* and musty rooms smelling of washed stone floors, varnished wood, and airless passages.

Sister Ursula was in the corridor by the schoolroom, standing among dripping tables bearing drab zinc bowls full of gray water. She appeared to be making certain that several of the older children had cleaned out their ears. She looked up with a smile as Henry entered and shooed the children away. She was not good-looking and wore spectacles that made her eyes look bigger than they were, and her skin was rough and not very attractive. But she was obviously intelligent and practical, and is was clear that the children adored her. Caporelli had said in his cynical way that it was because she had the gift of keeping goal while they played football without any loss of dignity, but it was obvious her compassion was unemotional and her character was dominated by a clear mind and an immense love for her charges.

"I was just preparing some of my little ones," she said, almost as though they were her own offspring. "They've been asked if they'd like to help in washing the things they're finding in the lake, and they must be clean—at least to start off with. They've been bringing things up since dawn. The Signorina Daniells was here. They will be paid, of course. Not much, but it will be pocket money and they'll feel these things belong to them, not merely to a vast organization centered on Rome."

As she finished speaking, there was a sudden outburst of noise in one of the rooms alongside and the stamp of boots and boys' voices that lifted Sister Ursula's head. Then there was a flash of a white wimple through the glass door and another nun appeared. She was small and fat and she was obviously agitated.

"Sister Ursula," she said breathlessly above the din. "Come quickly! Come quickly!"

Sister Ursula looked around, unmoved. "What is it, Sister Agata?" she asked. "I thought we had all our excitement *yesterday*."

Sister Agata flapped her hands. "Giovanni's fighting again," she said. "With Ercole Battista this time."

Sister Ursula turned to Henry. "Excuse me," she said in her soft voice, still completely unruffled.

Two minutes later the noise in the room had stopped and Sister Ursula reappeared, followed by two boys, one of them tall and slender, with dark, burning eyes, the other thickset and sturdy, a surly expression on his face.

"I want you to apologize to each other and shake hands," she commanded them. "And then, please, get yourselves ready."

The short, thickset boy muttered something and stuck out his hand. The taller boy ignored it, averting his eyes.

"Giovanni!" Sister Ursula's voice hardened.

His eyes flashed and he gestured quickly. "Sister Ursula, I didn't hit him," he said. "At least, not until he said what he did say."

Sister Ursula pursed her lips. "That will be attended to later," she said. "For the moment we must have peace. We have a job to do. Now shake hands."

Again the thickset boy stuck out his hand. Again Giovanni ignored it. Sister Ursula sighed.

"He must be punished," Sister Agata shrilled.

"Sister Agata"—Sister Ursula's voice was quiet, but it was very firm—"Giovanni's *my* charge. I'll deal with him."

Sister Agata stuck her nose in the air and disappeared, and Sister Ursula turned to the thickset boy.

"You may go, Ercole," she said. "I will punish you both later."

Ercole bobbed his head and vanished, and Sister Ursula looked at Henry and turned to Giovanni. He was obviously distressed and she spoke gently to him.

"Tell me, Giovanni," she said. "Tell me what happened."

The boy's eyes filled with tears. "He spoke of my father and mother," he pointed out bitterly. "He said that although he was an orphan, at least he had a father *once*."

Sister Ursula frowned. "I see. It was very stupid of him and he will be punished. But Ercole *is* stupid and can only be corrected by physical punishment. I expect more from you, Giovanni."

"More, Sister?"

"When Our Lord Jesus Christ told us to turn the other cheek, he didn't mean we should stand still and offer ourselves to further blows. He meant simply that we should have the strength of character to ignore wounding remarks. He was humble, yet He was strong. He was often insulted, yet He was never violent, because violence only breeds more violence, Giovanni. An intelligent person has the strength to see this. You have your cross to bear, Giovanni, but so has Ercole. He has his stupidity. He will never understand things. So I would like you to be friendly with him."

For a while the boy considered, then he nodded. "Very well, Sister. For you."

"No, Giovanni. Not for me, for you."

"Very well, Sister."

"Now, for the time being, please help to clean up here."

As the boy turned away, she moved toward Henry and

smiled. "Sometimes it is very difficult," she said apologetically. "They have such sad histories. But we must teach them to bear the responsibility their parents failed to show to them. I'm sorry to have been so long. It must be very tedious to listen to a foreign language."

"I speak Italian, Sister," Henry explained. "Very well. I studied in Florence for a while."

He turned her attention to the dam, and she paused, thinking.

"It was Giovanni who first noticed it," she said with a little smile. *"This* Giovanni. He is slightly older than the others, you see, and intense for his years. He never knew his parents and has always been rather difficult. Perhaps because he is more intelligent. He is always fighting, though I think I have now almost won him over."

She called the boy across from where he was straightening the bowls.

"Tell the Signor Dottore what you saw up the mountain, Giovanni," she said.

He stared at her and then at Henry, then he drew a deep breath.

"There was more water than last year," he said in a rush. "It was quite clear there was more water. It was coming through the wall."

"There has always been water coming through the wall," Sister Ursula went on gently, waving him away. "We have been going up there for picnics for ages, and always there was water. But this time there was more than usual."

"I see. Go on, Sister."

She smiled. "I knew the dam was in need of repair. So did everyone, of course. Every time it rains the older boys run in to me and shout, 'Sister, the dam has given way.' It is a great joke, just as it is with the men in the bars in the town."

She managed another smile. "I was daydreaming," she said.

51

"I'd been watching the people on the lake and thinking that if we had all the money they were spending to find the past, and all the money that was being spent to destroy the past by the Montanari with their bombs, we might be a little better off in the future. New blankets. New books for the schoolroom." She indicated the rows of chamber pots on little shelves along the corridor. "Lavatories," she said. "So that the younger children would not have to use these.

"I went up with Giovanni to look," she went on. "I like to take notice of Giovanni in case he feels like breaking out again. He did so once and ran away. He got as far as Trepizano before we found him, and I feel I must help him. It is a home he needs, not an orphanage—someone to make him feel he belongs, something we can never give him, however hard we try." She paused, then seemed to realize she was daydreaming again and pulled herself sharply back to the subject of the dam. "You could see the cracks," she continued. "The trickles had become streams, and the river below was broader than I'd ever seen it before. I felt it was my duty to tell someone. I decided on Signor Caporelli. He's a good man and a good friend of ours. He was once an engineer himself and has always been concerned about the dam. Besides, everybody else has always seemed to be too occupied with politics, I'm afraid, to have much time for us."

She sighed, then she gave a sad smile. "It would be so satisfying to see an end to all the hatred we have here," she said. "So satisfying to know we could move out of our four walls, certain of the safety of the children."

In her words Henry saw how deeply the fear of the Montanari had bitten into the life of the valley. It was never obvious on the bright surface that the tourists saw and he hadn't properly seen it himself, but underneath it had penetrated into everything, even into the activities of a few nuns and the parentless children they cared for.

"There would be so much more money and so much more happiness," Sister Ursula ended, "and we all know how much love is needed in this world of ours. These children aren't concerned with whether they're Austrian or Italian, and neither are we. We take them all in, no matter which part of the mountains they come from."

The rain seemed to have cleared as Henry set off for the dam. Outside the Church of Lazzaro di Colleno the newspapermen and television technicians were standing in groups, talking with Father Anselmo among the peasant women with net shopping bags. By the fountain a couple of girls were slapping at their washing, watched by a fat Franciscan friar in brown dusty habit and sandals and a gloomy-looking policeman reading a newspaper strongly marked in the corners with hammers and sickles. In the bay the two archaeologists' boats were busy and Henry could see the waiting youngsters on one boat, their feet among the piles of gear. Stettner was in the water alongside, draped with aqualung gear and oxygen bottles, his wet shoulders gleaming in the sunshine, and Maggie Daniells, on her knees on the deck in the yellow swimming costume, was talking to him over the side. As he watched, Stettner heaved himself up the ladder with a powerful lunge, without waiting for her to take the heavy cylinders off his back, then he climbed over the bulwarks, slipped the buckles and wriggled out of the straps, and Henry heard the thud as the lead weights fell to the deck.

He sat in the van, staring at them for a while, his mind full of questions about them both, then he started the engine again and drove up the mountain. The sun had dried away the rain and the road was covered with limestone grit in a gray film that had been scattered on the grass and the trees like the dust from a cement works by the big Lancia buses of the Societa Automobilistica Dolomiti.

He turned off the main road toward the dam, past a woman trudging downhill with a bundle of twigs piled high on her back, and there were millions of gentians among the grass, and buttercups in the crevices, and massed clumps of the dwarf hydrangea they called the alpenrose among the cushions of moss and soldanella between the rocks.

It was a brilliant day now and the clouds had quite disappeared except for a little mist drifting along the crags with a hint of an afternoon storm. The meadows gave way to the dazzling white scree and then to the outer bastions of the Catena di Saga that sparkled against the deep blue of the sky. He could see the saw-toothed ridge plainly and in front of it, like the spike it was named after, La Spiga. Away on the right rose La Fortezza, the Fortress, a series of spires like battlements out of a fairy tale, and farther to the east more proud pinnacles above the Val Caloroso, grave and silent, yellow-white, venerable iron walls that had braved centuries of time. Below him a peasant cart moved on the winding road that swept in vast curves to join the highway along the broad valley of the Adige, the link between the German and Italian peoples since the days of the Romans, the road that had brought the conquering Visigoths and Vandals down to the Lombardy plains with their leagues of maize and corn and vineyards.

Up at the dam there was an immense silence. The trees below looked like dark cotton wool through the nearer acacias and wild laburnum, and along the skyline the firs stood up around the jagged tooth of La Spiga like bristles on the back of a giant hand. He could see the rock strata lined with firs, too, showing where the land had heaved thousands of years before to produce the mountains and the bottomless lakes of Switzerland and Italy. Even now, centuries later, the land seemed to slide down to the dark green water.

He left the Fiat by the dam and examined the gates of the stopper wall, which were situated in small tunnels that led to what had once been an artificial spillway. But the spillway was choked with rubbish and the gates looked old and solid. There were the remains of a fire in one of the tunnels, as though some climber had been using the place for a shelter, and he noticed to his surprise that the embers were still warm.

As he left the tunnel, he saw a man standing just below him among the rocks—a small dark man with a beard and piercing eyes.

"*Grüss Gott*," Henry said in the ancient salutation of the mountains, but as he tried to talk to him in German, the man turned and was off among the crags and had vanished within seconds. It was eerie and unnerving. The man had been small and stunted, and the way he had vanished as soon as Henry had spoken had made him seem like one of the mountain trolls from *Peer Gynt*. It was obvious the fire was his, and Henry wondered briefly if he were one of the Montanari the police were so diligently seeking.

It worried him a little, but the quarrel had nothing to do with him, and he started to climb to the main wall of the dam, where some youngster called up for the army had daubed in tar the year of his birth—*Evviva 1940*—in a sarcastic farewell to civilian life. Trudging up the rocks at the side, he reached the top of the wall, where the dusty road that ran across had subsided in parts. There were cracks that had been crudely patched with concrete, and in the little stone huts that had been built up there the great iron wheels intended to lift the gates in the spillways were rusted solid. He guessed that those on the stopper wall were just the same. As Caporelli had suggested, it would have needed a charge of explosive to move them.

He sat for some time on a rock alongside the old fortress-like barrier, examining the plans he'd brought. The original dam had been reinforced with an outer wall of stone which was a good twenty feet thick at the base and tapered to four feet at the top, and there was a layer of slate inside to hold the

55

earth filling in place. There were five discharge pipes extending through the rock culvert at the base of the dam, but there was obviously so much rubbish behind them the water coming through was a mere trickle.

The dam was leaking in a dozen places, and the water seemed to be eating into the outer wall and so into the earth it was designed to protect. There appeared to be danger in the absence of a discharge pipe to take the water out of the dam for repairs and in the poor method which had been used on the last occasion anyone had bothered to repair it. This had left a large leak which seemed to be cutting into the new embankment and, as the water couldn't be lowered, Henry couldn't see any means of reaching the point of the leaks. The only alternative seemed to be, as Caporelli had suggested, to drain it somehow through the stopper wall.

According to the reports, the sluice gates had not been opened for years. It was no wonder the wall was rotten. There had been little planning behind it. It had been erected in the last corrupt days of the old Austrian Empire by men who had known little of the stresses and strains of such vast undertakings as this, men who had grown up in the nineteenth century's atmosphere of brash overconfidence, men of importance who had been less skillful than they had thought they were. They had believed the dam impregnable and, judging by the dimensions and the engineering standards of the time, they had probably had considerable justification for their beliefs. But the years had had their effect on the dam. It had been an inferior piece of work to begin with, and it had been neglected for generations. The old original wall of earth had been well rammed down, but though the earth in the new one had been chosen for its clayey quality, it had never been anything else but merely dumped in place between the containing walls. And the carelessness of the construction had allowed it to be lower in the middle instead of higher, and the stone core, which was supposed to extend twenty feet above the normal water line was, in fact, only a matter for speculation. Henry could find no real details about it or any clear reference to it ever having been built.

He did his job carefully, collecting earth and rock samples, and walked slowly back along the wall and down the bank of rock, inspecting the choked-up sluices and examining the jammed and useless gates. There was a farmer there, a sharp-eyed, long-jawed man in thick clothes and clodhopper shoes stumbling behind an ox that struggled with a plow in the rocky soil. He lived below the vast artificial lake on a few cows and goats and pigs and a square of turned earth. Henry tried to talk to him, but he spoke in German and his strange mountain accent made him difficult to understand. It was clear, however, that *he* didn't think much of the dam either.

He invited Henry in and they crossed a yard full of barking dogs and strutting chickens to the house which was a curious mixture of carved galleries and the white-walled grace of the Italians to the south. There was a large dark room with a wood fire burning at one end, gray with ash, and a stone-flagged floor, and walls hung with copper pitchers, salamis and ham, and tallow for greasing boots and a vast calendar with a gaudy picture of St. Stephen's in Vienna.

The farmer said his name was Dieter Oswino and he offered Henry a drink of *grappa*. His wife brought the bottle in, and Henry saw she was a buxom woman with a plump, handsome figure laced into the Austrian embroidered bodice and white blouse. She had cold, dramatic eyes and spoke stiff, unrelenting German, and he suddenly realized he was looking at one of Stettner's mistresses. She was just the sort who would appeal to him—handsome, intelligent, and animal like himself, with none of the independence or practiced humility of the peasant —and he wondered how they solved the problem of Dieter Oswino.

When he left, he drove down the mountain back to the main road where the nerveless drivers of the S.A.D. buses swung their vehicles around the tight corners and over the bridges that crossed the artificial cutting that led the stream from the dam through the town. For a while he sat in the Fiat staring at the rubbish that choked the gulley and examining the rest of the documents that Caporelli had given him. He'd been painstaking and had gathered information from the town archives, the library, and the Trepizano and Bolzano newspapers. Henry studied them with a frown, then he slowly closed the folder and started up the van.

When he got back to the Stettnerhof, Stettner was in the bar, drinking beer, his head close to that of the waiter. They were talking in German and broke apart as he entered, and Stettner sat staring around him, his eyes cold, as though he resented the fact that the place no longer belonged to his family.

After a while he moved up to make room for Henry and offered him a cigarette. Henry didn't like him very much, but it was difficult not to respond to his rough charm.

"It should all have been mine," he said, indicating the carved woodwork on the walls. "My ancestors made all this. They were all wood carvers. They learned their trade at the State School." He grinned. "But that's life, isn't it, Herr Doktor? They built it; the politicians and the soldiers destroy it, and I come here just to eat my meals. Because I used to live here, because my ancestors carved all these walls, I am allowed to have my meals for nothing, even with a carafe of wine thrown in. Because I bring tourists here to dance and drink, you understand. It is the way of the resort. You kiss my backside and I'll kiss yours."

He smiled and went on cheerfully: "I don't live here, of course. My brother-in-law guards his pretty little tourists like a hen with its chickens. I have a bad reputation, you see." He gestured with a big hand and smiled, showing his gold teeth.

"I have a room in the town," he explained. "But it doesn't get used a lot. You understand, I am always out at night, perhaps with climbers or tourists or swimmers, who are pleased to buy Alois Stettner a glass of wine because they've heard of him. As for sleeping"—he chuckled—"there are plenty of girls who're pleased to share their beds with me." He sighed, mocking himself. "There are so many, Herr Doktor," he said in a pained voice, his eyes merry. "They are so demanding. *E morte!* It's death. I have a reputation for virility, you see."

He stubbed out the cigarette he was smoking and was silent for a while. When he went on, he seemed to be choosing his words carefully and speaking slowly, as though he wished to open a new and controversial line of conversation.

"They have not yet found the explosives that were stolen," he said. "The police came to see me this morning."

"I saw them."

Stettner paused, his eyes thoughtful, then he laughed. "I don't believe in politics," he said, "but they know I am an Austrian, you see, and prefer to be called Austrian. They think, even, I might know who Andreas Hofer is and who has got the explosives, because I know everybody in the mountains. Because I am a member of the Volkspartei, you understand, and have taken part in the parades in Bolzano."

"Although you're not a student?"

Stettner shrugged his big shoulders. "If I were a babe in arms," he said, "it wouldn't alter the fact that I was born an Austrian."

"Here?"

"This is Austria," Stettner said firmly. "We were given to Italy by your Lloyd George and Clemenceau and Woodrow Wilson." He sounded unexpectedly bitter and his voice was harsh as he continued. "All the German place names in the valley were changed and the use of the German language was forbidden. Lawyers had to plead in Italian. Schoolboys—me,

59

I was one—we had to learn our lessons in Italian. Nobody ever passed their examinations, of course, and all the government jobs went to Mussolini's men. It still never made us Italian, though, and when they said religious instruction had to be in Italian, two hundred and twenty-seven priests announced their intention of disobeying."

"For a man who doesn't believe in politics," Henry pointed out, "you know your facts."

Stettner shrugged. "I grew up with them," he said. "They're engraved on the hearts of everybody who lives here."

He suddenly seemed to think that perhaps he had talked too much, because he began to smile again. "Except mine," he said. "It doesn't affect me. I just like young people. Especially young girls—and particularly in summer when they wear thin clothes and you can feel the flesh underneath. This is why I have not married, you see. Why do I want a wife? I get plenty of girls."

He was goading Henry deliberately, and Henry found it difficult to accept his irresponsibility like Caporelli. He seemed to be far too intelligent a man to be merely a fool.

Stettner was gesturing to the waiter now and, as he brought him rolls and coffee, he slapped the boy on the shoulder.

"This is Dittli," he said. "Hjalmar Dittli. He is from Bolzano University. He lives in Trepizano and works here during the holidays. He, too, is Austrian and a member of the Volkspartei, aren't you, Hjalmar?"

The boy nodded, a faint, embarrassed smile flickering across his weak mouth as though he disliked Stettner discussing his politics.

"The police came to see him, too," Stettner went on. "Also about the explosives. They're afraid it'll be used to blow up the Questura, you see, and, being Italian, that doesn't appeal to them at all."

He hooted with laughter. "I see Rome is already claiming

60

Lazarus," he went on, using the German name of the drowned bishop. "I thought they would."

"I don't care who claims him," Henry said sharply. "I just wish he'd stay in his grave and not get in my hair."

"You haven't a chance, Herr Doktor," Stettner said with a grin. "It isn't only the archaeologists you'll have to contend with."

Henry looked up sharply.

"I saw Father Anselmo with the Bishop of Trepizano last night. They must have considered it urgent to bring *him* around to this side of the lake as fast as that. You haven't just Dei Monti to worry about. You've got the whole Church of Rome against you. They'll want to take the cross to St. Peter's. You see."

"Because this is Trentino," Dittli joined in bitterly. "Because here it might be damaged." He turned to Stettner. "Alois, we must resist it to the limit. It belongs to *us*. It belongs in this valley." He leaned toward Henry. "This man they call Bishop Lazzaro," he said angrily, "was actually a German friar, Herr Doktor."

Stettner indicated the waiter and winked. "He's a believer," he said. "A good party member. Hjalmar, what do *you* think of the Cross of Lazarus?"

The boy's eyes lit up. "It is a sign that Arzen should be free." He gestured fiercely. "I expect they'll find Arcuneum now, Herr Doktor. They've been searching for it ever since I was a child. My father says they were searching when *he* was a child. And now that it's found, everything in it will go to Rome instead of to Vienna."

"After fifteen centuries," Henry was tiring of the argument, "I wouldn't have thought it mattered."

"The Volkspartei will support Vienna all the same. This is Austrian soil."

"It's been Italian for forty years."

61

"Alsace was German for forty years," Dittli said quickly, as though it were an argument he'd used often. "But it never ceased to be anything but French and the people who lived there never ceased to be Frenchmen. We aren't Italians and never will be. Who ever heard of an Italian hotel called the Stettnerhof? You can change the name of Die Sägekette to the Catena di Saga and Die Eisenspitze to La Spiga, but you can't tell a man whose name's been Dittli for years that it's suddenly something else. You can't stamp his forehead with the word 'Italia' and make him an Italian.

"I just hope," he ended, "that whatever they bring up from the lake is stamped all over with the German language. I hope *nothing* stops them uncovering Arcuneum."

"Something will," Henry said.

"What can, Herr Doktor?"

"Mud. From the dam. It's got to be drained."

"It won't affect Arcuneum."

"It'll be drained *over* Arcuneum." Henry felt faintly defiant as he spoke, but he was beginning to feel that he ought to establish his position firmly and at once.

Dittli was staring at him, his eyes narrowed.

"What do you mean?" he demanded.

"The dam must be drained before it collapses and washes Cadivescovo away. It's unsafe."

Dittli's face was shocked. "You can't drain it over Arcuneum. It would bring down God knows what sort of rubbish. There might be damage done. It might spoil our hopes of proving the nationality of Father Lazarus."

"I'm neither Austrian nor Italian," Henry pointed out. "I'm merely an engineer, and as I see it the dam should be drained—now—not tomorrow, now. A heavy downpour could set every mountain stream up there draining into it. It could rise twenty feet in no time, because there are no sluices that work. Another twenty feet would be a disaster."

"It can't be drained," Dittli said slowly. "All my life I've believed that Lazarus was an Austrian. His name will be all over everything they bring up."

Stettner waved the boy aside and grinned at Henry. "There," he said. "That's what it means to *believe*. Frightening, isn't it? You've got quite a lot of opposition, haven't you, Herr Doktor? Rome and big business and the Sudtyrol Volkspartei all together. We shall be against you, you see. Every one of us. Patriots, one and all."

5

When Henry told Caporelli of his conversation with Stettner, the Italian seemed unwilling to discuss it at length. He was an odd character in many ways, normally affable and pleasure-loving, but occasionally withdrawn as though there were some secretive spring of caution within him that had a tendency to damp down his enthusiasms at times, a mountain wariness that he had picked up during his years with the Partisans. His indifference had a flattening effect, and Henry tried to brush off what Stettner had said as unimportant.

"It's as well they have no friends," he said.

Caporelli's reaction this time was surprising. His head came up at once and his voice became brusque. "You think not?" he asked. He jerked his head toward the door. "Come with me," he went on. "Tonight we'll take our *apéritifs* in another bar. *Avanti! Andiamo!*"

He drove the Alfa Romeo up through the narrow streets to the top of the town toward a little inn on the edge of the meadows, without any apparent concern either for their own or anyone else's safety. He made no attempt at conversation and was in a strange, quiet mood as they took their seats and ordered *apéritifs*.

The Edelweiss Bar was like hundreds of others of its kind in the mountains of Germany and Austria and Trentino. It obviously catered less for tourists than for locals, and the walls were of unstained wood and the plain wooden tables were bare of cloths.

The custom seemed to be comprised of students and the air was filled with smoke and the buzz of their conversation. In one corner was a separate group, who all seemed to wear Tyrolean clothes, leather shorts or green-lapeled gray jackets with horn buttons, and they all seemed to know each other, a fact which first drew Henry's attention to them. All the youths wore arrogant expressions and seemed entirely to ignore the girls with them in the eagerness of their conversation. Among them were one or two strikingly handsome youths with blond hair who clearly came from the north and an occasional taller youth who seemed to be regarded by the others as a leader. There was something about them that seemed strangely and strikingly familiar to Henry, and with a shock he realized he was looking on a new image of the Hitler Youth who had been brought up before the war to be the backbone of a perfect nation. The realization struck him like a physical blow and he thought at once of massed formations and long red banners and the volleys of *Sieg Heils*. The group even had that typical Nazi air of being in possession of some instinctive, drilled-in mystique that they kept safely hidden at the backs of their brains.

"Good God," he said involuntarily.

"You notice?" Caporelli asked. "You have seen?"

"By God, I *have* seen!"

Caporelli jerked his head toward the group of youngsters.

"Those are Alois' friends," he said. "These are the friends they haven't got."

"They're not what I think they are, surely?"

Caporelli shrugged. "Why not? That sort of thing takes a long time to die, and what else is *any* nationalistic organization? These are just the children who don't understand, the types who think it clever to be rude to their elders, the types who see the fun in the jokes on lavatory walls. But the others have not entirely disappeared and a lot of them see their chance in the Volkspartei and the Montanari. Give them the chance and they would put me across a rack because I don't think the same as they do."

"But, surely, they'll never come back?"

Caporelli shook his head. "I think not," he said. "Not really. We are all too wary. But they exist, eh? They are an added complication in Trentino. They supply some of the motivating power behind the irredentism, some of the iron if you like." He leaned forward, his face full of disgust. "Dr. Cappell, is *this* why I lived in the mountains through those dreadful winters, is this why your young men fought at Tobruk and Alamein, and why soldiers died at Stalingrad and Normandy and along the Rhine?"

Henry felt a tense sensation of anxiety. "Where do *they* come into it?" he asked.

"The old frontier satisfied no one. Neither did the new one. When Mussolini collapsed, the price he paid for Hitler's aid was a promise to return Northern Italy to Austria." He jerked his hand toward the students. "*They* know that. That's what they want."

"And is Alois a pro-Nazi?"

Caporelli shrugged. "There are the would-be Nazis these days in any political movement in Europe," he said. "*And* the genuine patriots, and the ambitious and the restless, and the fools like Alois. I dare swear that one tenth of the Montanari—

66

or the Berg-gewöhner, as I suppose they'd prefer to be called—
are active members. Another tenth are interested, and a third
tenth would be if they could be assured of success."

"I can't believe it."

Caporelli's expression was one of faint contempt. "That's
the mistake a lot of nations are making," he said. "Only in-
fantile minds fail to take *this* seriously. It is an error to think
of the Germans merely as unemotional militarists. They are far
more passion-torn than any Latin. Only a German could cry
into his beer over a song about true love or exile from home,
and only a German could see a valley like this as a symbol of
patriotism." He paused, then went on slowly. "The Montanari
claim to be German. Or Austrian, if you like." He shrugged.
"What's the difference?"

It was a frightening experience and Henry shuddered.
Caporelli seemed to have lost interest now that he had brought
it to Henry's attention. He finished his drink and rose to go.

"I thought you would like to see," he said. "Whatever the
Volkspartei are, the Montanari are different. Don't under-
estimate them. I don't."

Henry followed him to the door. "How far does Alois go
along with—with"—he gestured helplessly—"With this?" he
ended.

Caporelli humped his shoulders. "He doesn't realize what
he's mixed up in," he said contemptuously. "All the Stettners
were fools. How else could they lose the house they built and
lived in for three hundred years?"

The incident left a nasty taste in Henry's mouth. It was as
though it was part of a recurring nightmare, as though he'd
turned over a stone and found something repulsive beneath.
It stayed with him all the way back to the Stettnerhof and, in
an attempt to force it to the back of his mind, he busied himself with Caporelli's file on the dam. He was so absorbed in

67

making notes from it over dinner that he didn't notice Maggie Daniells sit down opposite him. Then, as he turned a sheet of paper, he became aware of movement at the other side of the big oak table and looked up.

She was dressed as usual, in black ski pants and black jersey, her hair over her face, her eyes heavily made up, and those ugly black spectacles on her nose. She had a large-scale chart of the Cadivescovo area of the lake and had been outlining in red the position of the walls they'd found already.

She nodded to Henry and smiled immediately, and she seemed to be trying to think up some way to start a conversation, because she opened her mouth, paused, then shut it again and blushed.

Henry put down the file and took off his glasses. "If you've got something to tell me," he said helpfully, "I'm quite prepared to listen."

She gave a little relieved laugh, "Yes," she said. "I thought you would be."

"What's it about? The Cross?"

She nodded. "Yes, I suppose so. And Arcuneum. We've found more walls—one of them a beauty, fifty feet long."

Henry raised his eyebrows but carefully avoided comment.

"Made of hand-carved blocks," she went on. "And two more running at right angles. She looked up as though she hoped to find him interested. "The cement's visible," she said eagerly. "We think we're right on the site of the monastery. With a little luck we ought to find some sign of Lazzaro's barge soon. The *National Geographic*'s been fishing. They're wanting pictures and a story. They're going to pay well too. It'll help with the cameras we're hiring and the high-speed film we'll need."

Henry put down his spectacles and smiled. "I suspect," he said, "that it's about more than this that you want to talk. I can't imagine you thought *I'd* really be interested in your walls. Not in view of what I'm wanting to do to them."

She smiled back at him. "No," she admitted. "I didn't. It was something else. As a matter of fact, Professor Dei Monti's coming to see you tonight. I told him you wouldn't mind. I hope you don't."

Henry's eyebrows rose. "No," he said cautiously. "I don't."

She looked grateful. "Thank you. I thought I'd better warn you. Sometimes, you see, he's a bit hot-tempered." She hesitated and went on slowly. "To tell you the truth, I've been wondering all day if we couldn't work together somehow. I should have thought we could."

Henry pushed Caporelli's file aside. "Look," he said. "I've nothing against Arcuneum *or* your group. Nothing in the world. I know you've got a job to do and you're trying to do it. Unfortunately, so have I. And *I'm* being paid, so I've got to do it properly. I was called here to advise on that dam. I inspected it today."

"So I heard."

"My advice will have to be that it must be drained at once. And the only safe way to drain it is by removing a gate in the stopper wall and emptying it down the bed of the old stream."

"Can't you do it by the present route?" she asked patiently.

"The sluice gates are too heavy and they're jammed with rubbish. It'd be a major engineering job. The other way, it could be done within a matter of a few hours."

Her friendliness vanished as she began to get angry. Her voice grew cold and stiff. "I can see we're not going to get anywhere."

Henry tried not to show his annoyance. "There just isn't any alternative." He paused, feeling his voice was harsher than he'd intended. "Would you like some more coffee?"

"No, I wouldn't. I think you're just being stubborn, Dr. Chappell. It's typical of the science side. You never have any time for anything else but your damned figures."

Henry shrugged. "Our damned figures have more than once

69

stopped you woolly-headed lot bringing everything down on your heads with your digging," he said.

She got up in a hurry, knocking over her cup as she did so, and she began to dab at the spilled coffee with her napkin.

"I didn't expect to get any sympathy from you really," she said. "But I thought I'd try."

She seemed furious and all she was able to do with the napkin was transfer the coffee from one part of the tablecloth to another.

Henry handed her his own napkin without a word.

"Thank you," she said. "I just thought we might be able to help each other, but I can see I'm wasting my time."

She suddenly seemed to realize she was getting nowhere with the spilled coffee, and she slammed the saturated napkin down and, picking up her papers, stalked out to the hall.

When Dei Monti came, he was hostile from the start. Henry talked to him in the lounge, but he'd obviously been briefed against him by Maggie Daniells. He was a short-tempered man in spite of his mild appearance, and they bristled around each other like a couple of fighting cocks looking for an opening. It started quietly enough, but Dei Monti clearly expected to be able to convince Henry that nothing was so important as the unearthing of Arcuneum and seemed surprised when he didn't succeed.

"How can you fail to see what damage you might do?" he finally exploded. "We are unearthing the past and you are proposing to stop us."

"I'm not interested in the past," Henry pointed out. "I'm an engineer and more interested in the future. And I rate people's lives more highly than a few old ruins that'll be stuck in some museum and never be looked at by anybody except stuffy schoolteachers and bored schoolgirls."

He realized he'd overstepped the mark with his comment, but he knew he couldn't back down.

Dei Monti stared at him, shocked for a moment, as though he were a monster.

"Very well then," he said with icy patience. "When *will* the dam fall?"

"I don't know when the dam will fall."

"Why not?"

"Because I don't know when the Tower of Pisa will collapse or when the waves from the police launches will wash away the foundations of Venice. But they will, one day, unless something's done just the same."

Dei Monti stepped back, his eyes narrow behind the pebble glasses. "You're stupid, stubborn, and soulless," he breathed.

They didn't get very far after that and Dei Monti stormed out, with the drink Henry had offered him still on the table, untouched.

The argument sent Henry to bed in a bad temper and full of an increased determination not to give way. He was an engineer who'd been called in to give advice and in all honesty he couldn't back away from the decision he'd made. The dam was dangerous and should be drained—at whatever cost.

Caporelli was waiting for him as soon as he arrived downstairs next morning and insisted on dragging him along as soon as possible to see Mornaghini, the engineer.

"I've fixed an appointment," he said. "He doesn't know yet what it's about, but he soon will."

He listened carefully to what Henry had to say, nodding all the time, his face grave, and his eyes flashed as he told him about the strange bearded man he'd found near the sluice gates. The incident had almost slipped from Henry's mind, but Caporelli seemed to think it was important.

"Wasescha," he said at once. "Carlo Wasescha. Small farmer from Madonna del Piano. Troublemaker. Ex-Nazi. The police want him, if you remember. He's believed to be one of the Montanari. He was seen near the quarry when the explosives were stolen. He's never been home since, because the police are watching his farm."

"What was he doing up there?"

"Certainly not planning to blow the gates off for us," Caporelli said dryly. "Using the tunnel, I suppose, as a shelter. They've got a hide-out up there somewhere."

"Are you going to tell the police?"

"I suppose so. It won't do much good, though. He was born there and they'll never catch him in a thousand years."

Inspector Castelrossi was in his office in the Questura, a narrow-gutted building smelling of stale smoke and stale wine in the twisted streets behind the Municipio, gloomily staring at maps and papers, his face dark in the shadows from the shuttered windows.

"Wasescha undoubtedly," he said. "Somewhere up there they hide their weapons. I wish we could find them. I'd like to tell you you'd done us a service because we know he belongs to the Montanari." He shrugged. "But unfortunately we shall never catch him. I shall send a patrol up to the dam, of course, but I don't expect them to find much."

He sighed. "We must have interrogated everyone in the town below the age of twenty-five," he said. "But we still get nowhere, and they are still questioning the student who jumped from the train." His brows came down and a worried look came into his eyes. "Unfortunately," he ended, "the boy, Von Franck, managed to commit suicide this morning. In his cell at Trepizano. He hanged himself with his own bed sheets."

Caporelli's face darkened. "More trouble," he growled. "They'll make speeches at the funeral."

Castelrossi shrugged. "He was guilty," he said. "The map we found on him had things marked with circles. The Bolzano railway was one. This police station was another."

He seemed low in spirits and there was an atmosphere of

defeat and failure about the office, in spite of the maps on the walls and the constant arrival of messengers with telegrams.

Caporelli was frowning as they left. "They arrest a few students," he said bitterly. "They will eventually find 'Hofer,' too, I suppose. But it will never stop." He looked up and saw Henry's eyes on him. "Because simple justice is subordinated to military strategy and economic factors," he explained, "and because every decision's bedeviled by a hundred complexities. The fact that Trentino remained Austrian after Italy became a nation was an affront to the patriots who'd fought for her. They'll never give it back now." He lit a cigarette slowly, then looked up and smiled, as though he were trying to push his unquiet thoughts to the back of his mind. "Let's get back to things we understand," he suggested. "Dams."

The Mayor was waiting for them in his office in the Municipio, sitting like a plump spider below the huge eagle of Colleno and a picture of Dante Alighieri. He was a small, slight man with restless eyes like sloes, who showed them to their seats and even produced a bottle of vermouth. He seemed to want to talk politics and appeared anxious they should hear his views on the inevitable subject of the Sudtyrol Volkspartei and the Montanari. Caporelli let him go on for some time, allowing him to discourse on what he clearly thought was the ingratitude of the Austrian minority, then he brought up the subject of the dam abruptly, as though he'd grown tired of talk.

The Mayor's face fell at once. "The dam?" he said. "Yes, of course. That's been a source of trouble for years. It's like the sword of Damocles hanging over our heads."

"It won't hang much longer," Caporelli said bluntly. "It'll start to fall soon unless it's shored up."

"It's as bad as that?"

"It's dangerous," Henry put in. "I've examined it. It's impossible to estimate how disastrous a breach could be. If there *were* one, it would wipe out the town."

"Yes. Of course." The Mayor rubbed his face with his hands and thought for a while, clearly not understanding the implications of Henry's words.

"And is the dam full?" he asked at least.

"Not yet," Henry said. "As a matter of fact, it's down at the moment because there's been no rain for a few days and it's leaking. But with heavy rainful it rises around the shores at the rate of one meter per hour. The feeders can pour in twelve million liters in the same period of time, and the gratings are clogged with branches and debris from the mountain."

"*Eh, gia!* Of course! I understand." The Mayor spoke slowly, as though he were trying to play for time. "We must have the engineer in here."

They waited in silence while he sent for Mornaghini, and the old engineer listened carefully to them, his lined aristocratic face grave, his head nodding from time to time as Caporelli talked.

"I've heard of Dr. Chappell, of course," he announced. "I've read his articles on the Alexandria breakwater and the Pontemorvo bridge, and he's by no means unknown to us in Italy. He must let us have a report on the dam at once so we can act."

"A report will take too long," Caporelli announced curtly.

Mornaghini looked up. "We can't possibly act *without* a report," he said sharply. "How can we discuss it when we don't know the facts?"

"We do know the facts," Caporelli exploded. "Dr. Cappell's just given them to you. We should drain the dam at once. That's the most important of them."

Mornaghini still seemed uncertain. "I happen to know that the sluice gates are immovable," he said. "It would cost a great deal of money. And, besides, the bed of the stream has been filled up for years. There'd be flooding in the town."

"We could remove a gate in the stopper wall on the east side," Caporelli said gently. "They're lighter and smaller, and the water wouldn't go near the town."

"Yes, of course," Mornaghini said. "That's true. But we should need authority from the province."

"We can get it. We've *got* to get it. Another set of thunderstorms like last week's and the dam might decide to drain itself. And there *will* be more storms. It's already too warm. We've had no spring this year."

Mornaghini rubbed his nose and adjusted his glasses. "There's just one point," he said. "I've had Professor Dei Monti in to see me this morning. Together with a young lady who seems to be a press representative for his Universities Underwater Group."

Henry said nothing. He knew what was coming.

"I've met them all before, of course," Mornaghini said to the Mayor. "As you'll remember, Counselor, we entertained them to drinks when they first arrived. In my office. It seems the professor has also heard of this project to drain the dam through the stopper wall. They are absolutely against any such thing. Particularly since the appearance of the Cross of Bishop Lazzaro."

The Mayor looked a little puzzled and Mornaghini hurried to explain.

"The cross," he said patiently. "The Cross of Lazzaro. If we drain the dam through the stopper wall, the water will follow the old stream bed through the Val Caloroso and will run into the lake at the Punta dei Fiori. And that's where we now know Arcuneum stands."

The Mayor looked startled. "But if Arcuneum *is* discovered," he said quickly, "it could well become another Pompeii! A

75

wall and a few pumps could make a lot of difference. It's not very deep there and it wouldn't be difficult."

"We already have more ruins in Italy than we need!" Caporelli exploded. "Without finding any more."

The Mayor looked away, as though he hadn't even heard. "Oh no," he said to Mornaghini. "We can't possibly drain the dam into the Punta dei Fiori. We must do it some other way."

"What other way?" Henry asked. "There isn't another way."

"Can't we dig a spillway around the end of the *main* wall?" Mornaghini asked.

"Through rock? That's what it is. I was up there yesterday. It would cost a fortune. There's only one way to do it."

Mornaghini rubbed his nose vigorously. "We *must* find another way," he said firmly. "We simply must. We can't chance covering Arcuneum again now. Father Anselmo also came with Professor Dei Monti," he added.

"I have an appointment this afternoon with the Bishop of Trepizano. Father Anselmo arranged it."

"What does *he* want?" Caporelli said sharply.

"It seems that the Church is completely behind the professor too. It's thought quite possible there might well be sacred relics in Arcuneum."

Caporelli's face was dark with rage as they went outside again, and he was literally spitting with fury.

"Dwarfs," he said. "Gnomes! Intellectual, overreligious gnomes!"

His raging dislike of Mornaghini was infectious. "The Church is behind it all," he said, "and we'll get nowhere with the Church in on it. And half the universities of Europe, too, I suppose, and every goddam archaeologist who ever grubbed about in sand for a set of old bones. Even the television and the press people will be against it."

76

"*And* the Sudtyrol Volkspartei," Henry pointed out. "If Lazzaro's going to be a saint, they're determined he'll be an Austrian saint."

"*And* the hoteliers and the travel agencies and the bus operators," Caporelli said, going on with a sour pleasure at the growing list. "My friends! My associates! Cadivescovo will be the new Lourdes. A wall, he said, and a set of pumps. To preserve the ancient burial ground of a man who died so long ago we don't know whether he was good, bad, or indifferent. All we know of him is that he must have been goddam crazy to cross the lake on a stormy night with a cross *that* size attached to the bow of his barge. *De mortuis nil nisi bunkum,* as you say."

He smiled unexpectedly. "Dr. Cappell, old friend," he went on, "you and I have quite a fight on our hands. Archaeology, education, radio, television, the press, the hotel trade, the travel trade, and now even the Church. The Bishop of Trepizano wouldn't have come here just now for any other reason. "He looked slyly at Henry. *"Après nous le déluge,* eh? A pity we don't have less prayers and more practicality, a few less saints and a little more sense."

6

As they left the Town Hall, Caporelli touched Henry's arm and they stopped on the steps.

A small procession had just emerged from one of the side streets near the Municipio and was heading across the pearl-gray wooden cobbles toward the Church of Lazzaro di Colleno. They were all youths, most of them around twenty, and they moved solemnly across the square carrying a large wreath bearing the single word: *Lazarus*.

"Alois' friends," Caporelli said grimly. "Volkspartei members. Students, every one of them."

"What are they up to?"

"Out to embarrass someone, I expect. See the colors on the ribbon on the wreath? Red and white—Austrian."

The procession had halted outside the door of the church now, in the shadow of the great beam carrying the carved words, *Gebet Gott Was Gottes Ist,* Give to God What Belongs to God. Father Anselmo had appeared in the entrance with

Father Gianpiero behind him, and they were carrying on a fierce argument with the leading students.

"They're wanting to put it at the foot of the cross," Caporelli explained. "To establish the fact that Lazzaro belonged to the Volkspartei, I suppose. It's like this all the time here now. We're always waiting for an explosion—as though everything were on a hair trigger."

He gestured toward the youngsters crowding around the door of the church, their faces stiff with unrelenting idealism. "It's been like it for months," he said. "They're all in it, the patriots, the fools, and the people you saw yesterday. All wanting different ends from the same beginning. It's like hearing the thunder in the mountains and waiting for the next flash of lightning to strike and wondering where it'll be."

"I'd have thought the cross might have united everybody a bit," Henry said.

Caporelli's mouth twisted cynically. "Don't fool yourself, old friend," he advised. "Christ's cross never united the Jews in Jerusalem."

Henry glanced at the church, impressed by the anxiety in Caporelli's voice.

The argument had already grown fiercer and the voices louder, and a policeman who had just turned the corner from the Questura began to run. He took up his position at the side of Father Anselmo and began to gesture with his hand away from the church.

For a while it looked as though the students might still try to push past, but the policeman unfastened the flap of his pistol holster and the students drew back, turned, and marched toward the statue of Andreas Hofer, where they silently laid the wreath down. Several of them knelt for a moment, praying.

"Melodrama," Caporelli said bitterly. "Melodrama. Politics is always melodrama."

After a while the students drifted away, watched by the

79

anxious eyes of the locals and the curious glances of the tourists who had drifted up from the lakeside to see what was going on. There were twice as many sight-seers about the town as there had been when Henry had first arrived. They were coming from Trepizano by road and water, and there were others from Trento and Bolzano and Milan and Venice, to say nothing of cities farther to the south such as Florence and Rome. They were obviously presenting quite a problem for the police.

When the officials at the Questura had organized their road-blocks, they'd been out merely to unearth "Andreas Hofer" and his Montanari. The police couldn't cope with the flood of traffic that had started with the arrival of the cross and now were standing about in groups, still officially on duty, but all of them with a helpless look of frustration on their faces.

The feeling of resentment against the cross that Castelrossi had shown was clear in their expression. They weren't interested in religious revivals, and the crowds who were flocking into the town only served to confuse them in their search for "Hofer" and the missing explosives. There were so many people coming and going in and out of Cadivescovo it was impossible to stop and search them all, and it was difficult to tell who was merely a curious sight-seer from Trepizano and who was an enemy, anxious to take advantage of the fact that the police had their hands tied. Their roadblocks had already had to be moved further out of the town because of the interference with the crowds, and half their number were now engaged in traffic duties on the Via Colleno or around the boat station.

Caporelli watched the jostling people and the slow-moving cars directed by the disgusted police, then he threw away his cigarette.

"Let's go and see the miracle," he suggested bitterly.

Inside the church the cross was lying flat on a tilted dais. It rested majestically on a red velvet cloth, unadorned in any other way, except for a few wreaths that had been placed at the foot. There were crimson ropes around to keep off the sight-seers and a queue had formed and was shuffling past—tourists, foreigners and Italians alike. Father Anselmo, or his curate, Father Gianpiero, had shown a great deal of stagecraft in the presentation of the spectacle because they'd fixed up a spotlight so that there was a bright beam picking out the cross, just as it had first been seen in the lake—gaunt, black, and dramatic.

Henry and Caporelli joined the queue and stood staring at the cross—Caporelli with a bitter fascination, almost as though he were confronting an enemy. It lay on its tilted dais with the dark bands of crudely fashioned metal on the base looking like the roots of some giant tooth. It was obvious on closer inspection that it had suffered more from its long immersion than it had seemed at first. Parts of it were decayed and, in spite of the care with which they had handled it, there were tiny splintered fragments, which had crumpled from it as they had laid it down reverently on its red plinth.

There was a notice alongside, hurriedly printed in Indian ink by Father Gianpiero, stating all that was known about it together with the information that it was hoped eventually to erect it either in the church or in the cathedral at Trepizano. There was also a large offertory box nearby, with a notice to the effect that it was for the restoration of the cross, and there was a steady chink of small coins.

In the queue people were crossing themselves as they passed and, further back, in the shadows, women wearing black shawls were kneeling with their faces to where the bright spot of light fell on the red velvet, fingering their rosaries, their lips moving in prayer. Still farther back the television technicians had erected an extending ladder and had mounted a camera to film the queue and the cross, and newspaper photographers, muttering in reverently low tones, were exploding flash bulbs from all angles.

As Henry watched, a group of young men approached, knelt quickly and crossed themselves, huddling together in a bunch. When they rose, they had left a broad strip of white ribbon lying across the corner of the red velvet.

Caporelli sighed. "They never give up," he said sadly.

"What's happened?"

"The colors," Caporelli whispered. "Red and white! The colors of Austria! It's all happening in reverse now. It's not so long since the ballerinas of La Scala had their dresses designed in red, white, and green and people threw them bouquets in the Austrian colors just for the pleasure of seeing them decline to pick them up."

Someone snatched away the white ribbon and there was a little angry pushing going on in the shadows by the church door, where a policeman had intercepted the young men. At the entrance to the sacristy Henry could see Father Anselmo and Father Gianpiero watching anxiously and just behind them the crimson of the Bishop of Trepizano. Beyond him, further inside, there was a man in a black soutane edged with red who was writing rapidly in a notebook.

"From the Vatican Library," Caporelli murmured. "Getting it all down for posterity."

In the afternoon they noticed that the Wolfhof Restaurant near the lake had changed its name. From being the *Ristorante del Lago* it had suddenly become the *Ristorante del Santuario*.

"I've seen three *Ristorantes della Croce*," Caporelli said with a grin, "and one which rejoices in the name of *Ristorante della Croce di San Lazzaro di Cadivescovo*. That's a mouthful if you want to take your wife out to dine. To say nothing of the fact that they're jumping the gun a bit and sanctifying him before the Church's made up its mind. Every wood carver in the district's at it carving crosses, and they've even sent to Berne and Brienz in Switzerland for more. They can't make them fast enough."

Henry laughed at his cynicism.

"The next step's a floating chapel anchored out there in the lake," Caporelli went on. "I've already heard that there's been a suggestion that they borrow an old boat for Father Anselmo to do up."

He saw the look on Henry's face and his smile disappeared. "I was born in Naples," he explained, "and in Naples it seemed to me that we always had too many churches and not enough homes, too many fine ornaments and not enough funds."

He gestured. "Soon it will be the same here. We shall not be able to move for relics."

Out on the gray water of the lake there was a cluster of boats in the direction of the Punta dei Fiori, and they could see cars all along the edge of the beach. Already a few of the more enterprising painters from Madonna del Piano were offering dramatic daubs marked "Emergence of the Cross" among the tourists, and they had their wares propped against the back of the former Customs House that Dei Monti had taken over for his equipment.

Sister Ursula was standing among the crowd with an apron around her middle, a group of her orphans squatting about her feet over bowls on a canvas sheet, all of them rubbing with their fingers to clean the mud off salvaged objects.

"Let's go and see what they've found," Caporelli suggested.

As they stopped the car on the old mole the biggest of the boats was drawing alongside. Professor Dei Monti stepped ashore, followed by Maggie Daniells and two young men. They were met by two other men standing by a big French Citroën, and they all shook hands warmly. There seemed to be excitement in the air.

The sun had come through the clouds and there were several young men working on the deck of the boat among the aqualung equipment. There seemed to be a number of dark-green objects on the deck and the winch was already going, lifting them ashore, the exhaust thudding away in the still air. Maggie Daniells broke away from the group on the mole and approached them.

She stopped as she passed, and the look in her eyes as she stared at Henry was one of triumph.

"I don't think you'll ever drain your dam this way now, Dr. Chappell," she said, her voice high with excitement. "Not now. We've definitely established that Arcuneum is under the water there. We've done a series of exploratory dives and we've found the remains of more walls that link up with the ruined fort up there." Her arm gestured toward the hill. "And we've brought up several fragments of timber—obviously from Lazzaro's barge."

Henry was conscious of a flattening of his spirit. "I'm very pleased for you," he said sincerely. "But I'm very sorry for Cadivescovo. God knows what will happen this winter now."

She didn't seem to hear him. She was excited and eager as she indicated the men by the boat. "That's Utoio from Milan," she said. "And Wertz from Berne. Martini's expected later in the day. They're very excited by what we've found." She turned away, then she stopped and looked back. "I'm sorry," she said with an impulsiveness that made her seem very young. "Honestly, I wouldn't want to interfere with your plans, but we just couldn't let you get away with it, could we?"

By evening the exploration group had laid all their finds on the quay, watched by small boys and tourists and the policemen they'd managed to wheedle out of Inspector Castelrossi to act as a guard. Their discoveries, black from their long

84

immersion and crusted with the minute life of the lake, lay on the sheet of roped-off tarpaulin.

Sister Ursula's orphans worked behind the ropes, all of them looking pleased with themselves. There was the neck of a thick pottery jar and what was clearly the head of a column, together with a few torn fragments of aluminum that looked oddly out of place and were obviously from the ditched aircraft which had carried the mine that had started the search. Most of the objects were unidentified by notices, but Maggie Daniells, returned from her telephoning and skipping around the edge of the crowd with her notebook, seemed only too anxious to point out to the pressmen who had appeared just what everything was.

"Timbers," she was saying. "From Bishop Lazzaro's barge. We think we might even be able to reconstruct it in time." She knelt, the dark hair falling across her face as she fingered the small objects on the tarpaulin. "Clench nails and lead— from an anchor. They can only mean one thing. This is where Lazzaro's barge sank and this is where Arcuneum stood. This was the place he was visiting when he was drowned."

She straightened up. "We've found walls and mosaic," she went on. "And we firmly believe they are part of Arcuneum. It was certainly established here by the Greeks and fell to the Barbarians in the sixth century. It was rebuilt, of course, over there"—she indicated the town with a sweep of her arm—"and became known as Arcono and later as Cadivescovo or Arzen. We've already identified four circular pits as grain cellars and we hope to get an echo sounder and put more buoys down"— the reporters were writing quickly, then she looked up and caught sight of Henry—"if we're not prevented," she ended.

One of the reporters looked up from his notebook. "Prevented?" he said. "What is there to prevent you?"

"There are interests," she said, "that would like to destroy Arcuneum before it's been properly explored."

"Who'd want to do that? What are these interests? Political?"

"No."

"You've not had threats from the Montanari?"

"Not about Arcuneum."

"You can speak openly. We're not afraid to publish."

She gave the reporter a sudden scared look, as though she
were becoming too deeply involved, and began to back away,
raising her hands in front of her.

"No, no," she said. "It's not political."

"Religious?"

"No, no. I can't say. Not at this stage."

She almost broke into a run to board the boat.

The next morning *Corriere di Colleno* carried a headline:
ATTEMPT TO DESTROY ARCUNEUM. SABOTAGE AT SITE OF
NEWLY DISCOVERED TOWN.

"Sabotage," Henry said. "That's the end!"

Caporelli shrugged it off and almost dragged Henry from
his breakfast.

"To see the Bishop," he said. "To see if he can call the
dogs off."

Trepizano seemed to huddle beneath the limestone cliffs of
Monte Cano that towered behind it as a background of spires
and fortifications. Although it had been Austrian until 1919,
it was Italian in character and had been for centuries. And
at the moment it seemed to be full of police.

There was a barrier just outside the town gate, with two
police cars parked across the road so that there was room for
only one vehicle at a time to pass, and the inevitable policemen
standing in the gap, a flash of red and white and black against
the gray crumbling walls of the town.

"*I documenti, per favore!*"

They waved Caporelli to a stop and insisted on inspecting their papers. They seemed to know Caporelli well, but they only spoke to him in monosyllables, their faces frozen and uninformative as they worked. Nearby another group of policemen were searching a small van, dragging sacks out of the back and dumping them in the roadway while the owner stood mutely alongside, his face full of disgust.

Caporelli climbed out of the car and unlocked the boot, and they removed the spare wheel and the jack and examined every corner of it.

"You'll find no plastic in there," Caporelli told them.

They ignored him and worked silently, examining his brief case and looking under the seats. Then they placed everything back and waved them on.

Caporelli clicked his heels in a mock military salute and bowed before climbing back into the car. The policeman stared at him expressionlessly. He grinned at Henry and started the engine and they moved slowly through the great arched stone gate into Trepizano, watched by the policemen who seemed to be waiting in every doorway and every alley end.

It was a narrow, antique town of curiously spacious piazzas where water welled sluggishly from the mouths of bronze dolphins into the shallow basins of fountains, of basilicas and tall shuttered buildings and churches where shadows were brought before their time by the great rock pylons of Monte Cano behind the city. Although its streets had Italian names and houses optimistically painted in the Italian style with non-existent balustrades and windows and even statuary, there were still Tyrolean names on the shops and Austrian squares, and here and there Tyrolean ironwork signs and the Gothic-lettered signboards and steeper roofs of a more snowy northland. There were plenty of white stockings and leather shorts about, too, and a red granite church with an openwork spire standing in defiance of the Renaissance-style buildings of Mussolini's day.

Across the lake the mountains glittered in the sunshine, and they could see the saw-toothed edge of the Catena di Saga.

Henry had been in Trepizano only once before, for a few minutes on his way from the Bolzano train to the bus to Cadivescovo, and it had been full of students then, on their way from the university to their homes. The police had been vetting them on the station as he'd passed through because there'd been riots with the ending of the term at the university and massed students had staged a sit-down protest in the center of the Martin Knoller Strasse, and there had been a few blows exchanged with the police.

As the train had drawn into the station, there'd been groups of hard-eyed, excited boys standing in groups with cardboard notices—*Freedom for the Tyrol* and *The Tyrol Was Never Italian*—and just behind them, so there'd be no trouble, groups of frozen-faced policemen. There had been a lot of shouting and a few South Tyrol slogans yelled at the unmoved police, and everybody had been edgy because they all knew that "Hofer's" Montanari were largely students. When Henry had deposited his cases in the left-luggage office to find some food, they'd made him open them before they'd accept them, and the waiter in the bar where he'd gone for a sandwich had obviously been ready to suspect him because the Italian he spoke had a northern intonation.

The Bishop's Palace was a spacious building looking out onto gardens full of oleanders and palms, and the Bishop's secretary, a grave-faced cleric in black, escorted them down to a room overlooking the lake. The palace was silent and cool, but the Bishop was a busy man, obsessed by the new fame that had sprung on him overnight. He was young, with a pale face, and he reveled in his titles and saw in the rising of Lazzaro's cross and the unearthing, after centuries, of the site of Lazzaro's monastery the symbols of his own career. The diocese of Trepizano was no sinecure. It was too far from Rome, and he was a Florentine and wanted to move further back into the main thoroughfare of events. He had already seen that the Cross of Lazzaro might well be the vehicle that could carry him there.

"Dr. Chappell," he said, "we ask only for a little time. Next season it will be different. By the end of the summer all that is of real value might well be found."

"By next summer, my lord, it might well be too late," Henry pointed out.

The Bishop spread his hands and sat back in his chair, fingering his episcopal ring. "Even you, Dottore, though I assume you are not of our faith, must see how important these discoveries are to us—and to the Church generally. We are unearthing a civilization."

"I see all of this, my lord." Henry tried not to feel frustrated. "But I'm an engineer, and it seems to me that the safety of Cadivescovo is of far greater importance than the discovery of a few relics."

He realized immediately that in his blundering way he had said the wrong thing. The Bishop's face grew stern.

"A few relics?" he said coldly. "Dottore, we are unearthing the very beginnings of Christianity in the areas out of the influence of Rome. In the discovery of Arcuneum we are witnessing the very spread of Christ's word in the hinterland beyond the reach of the Church. *I* would not call them a few relics."

"My Lord Bishop!" Caporelli interrupted as he saw Henry floundering. "Surely you have the safety of Cadivescovo at heart?"

The Bishop frowned, as though he regarded the words as a criticism. "But, of course. Who would dare to suggest that I haven't?"

"Perhaps the Lord Bishop would be prepared then to go with us and see the dam for himself?"

"I'm more than prepared to do that," the Bishop said. "If

you'd care to submit a report to my secretary, I'll give it my earnest and immediate attention."

Caporelli fidgeted and sighed, but the Bishop didn't seem to notice.

He was staring at Henry and gesturing with his ringed hand. "I have on my hands what amounts to a minor miracle," he was saying. "There has been a movement on foot for years for the sanctification of Bishop Lazzaro. Inevitably Rome is interested. Inevitably it will be investigated by the Congregation of Rites. Inevitably I shall be called upon to supply information. Inevitably the rising of the cross will be considered. There is a great deal to be done in the collation of evidence."

He managed a smile. "As I'm sure you've been told more than once," he went on, "this is a neglected district. We haven't sufficient funds for our churches. We haven't the population to support them. We haven't many of the things we ought to have. And among these things we haven't got is a saint."

He allowed himself to smile further, but behind the smile his eyes were serious and, as he went on, Henry suddenly began to see him in a different light, troubled like Caporelli and Sister Ursula by "Hofer's" Montanari, uncertain how to act and eager for peace, yet aware of his own "foreign-ness" in a district where the family spirit was narrow and hostility to anything or anyone from south of Verona was marked and active.

"We could do with a saint, Doctor," he concluded sadly. "This is an unhappy district with a great deal of political bitterness. There are men and women here who feel they don't belong to us, and a saint might unite us all."

Caporelli nodded and for a moment he was at one with the Bishop, the dispute about the dam forgotten in the emergency the terrorists had brought about. The Bishop caught the movement and smiled at him, then he turned to Henry again and went on slowly. "You see, Dr. Chappell," he said, "a saint is

important to us, and because of that, every relic we can unearth is important too."

Caporelli was subdued as they brought the interview to an
end, and he bowed his head slightly as the Bishop rose and
lifted his hand in a blessing.

"Good day to you," he said. *"Benedicat te Omnipotens
Deus."*

"Claptrap," Caporelli said when they were outside. "Eccle-
siastical claptrap. But he's right, of course. In Italy a saint is
always useful. Especially a new one."

When they got back, the Stettnerhof was full of young men
from the archaeological group, who had obviously just finished
work for the day.

"A gold altar vase today, Doc," Frank Maggs called out to
Henry as he passed the entrance to the bar. "More pottery, a
lead anchor, and a statuette."

"Up the saboteurs!" The voice came from the back of the
group, and there was a burst of laughter that made Henry go
red.

He felt he needed a drink badly, but, unable to face the
crowd in the bar, he went through to the dark little wood-and-
cushioned lounge at the other side. Maggie Daniells was in
there, writing up the notes from her book onto fresh sheets
of paper, and Stettner was hanging around her, his hand on
her shoulder, looking at photographs which were spread on
the table in front of her.

"The Sudtyrol Volkspartei is completely behind your group,"
he was saying earnestly as Henry entered. "We will back you
to the hilt against any attempt to sabotage your work."

Henry stood in the entrance watching them, and they both
became aware of him at the same time and looked up.

"Coffee," Henry said bluntly as Dittli appeared.

He sat down and picked up the newspaper, then he became

aware of Maggie still watching him, and he threw the paper down again.

"Please," he begged. "Please don't say again that you're sorry."

There was silence for a while, then she spoke softly. "But I am," she said. "Truly I am."

"We went to see the Bishop of Trepizano today," Henry went on. "You'll be happy to know he's completely on your side. Together with the Mayor, the town bureau of information, the *Commissione di Turismo* and, I'm sure, the railways, the press, and the television authority. Doubtless, also, all the people of the town itself. I expect they'd much rather stuff their pockets full of the money the tourists will bring than make certain their children will be alive next year."

"It's a materialistic world, Herr Doktor," Stettner commented.

"Unfortunately."

"I'm doing my best to hurry things," Maggie said apologetically.

"Thank you."

"I'm trying to be helpful," she went on more sharply. "I'm fully aware that you feel we're being simply obstructive. But we're not. We simply want to do the work we came here for and for which we raised funds—not easily either, I might add. This afternoon we came across what can only have been a crude vase from an altar. It's been identified as being of gold. It's not fine metal and probably won't be very beautiful even when it's cleaned, but it *is* gold and it's evidence that we're on the site of some sacred building."

"I hope it's still there next year," Henry said.

Dittli appeared just then with Henry's coffee, and they sat in silence as he placed it on the table. As he disappeared, Stettner passed the photographs that littered the table top across to Henry. There was a jeer in the gesture.

92

"Have you seen today's treasures, Herr Doktor?" he asked as he strolled out.

The pictures seemed to be of rocklike objects, covered with weed and shell-like growth.

"Ten years from now," Henry said, staring at them, "there'll be hotels all around the Punta dei Fiori and probably a grotto with underwater lifts to let the tourists see the remains, and booths of pieties and pictures of the saint's tomb all along the front. It's what happened in Apulia. Because Padre Pio had the stigmata, the whole district grew prosperous and there are Vespas in the outhouses now instead of donkeys. They had police to control the crowds, when I was there, and you could even touch his hand if you shoved hard enough. But there were still people starving not far away, and the money that comes into Italy for the relief of poverty and the opening up of Calabria and Sicily still finds its way into the pockets of people who don't need it."

"It isn't my fault that Italy's what it is," she said angrily. "I don't run the Church of Rome either, but I'm quite sure there are enough intelligent people in it who want it different."

"There are none around here," Henry said bitterly. "Your confounded relics are still more important than my dam."

7

For some time it had seemed to Henry that the tension in the town had been slackening a little. The missing explosives had been pushed clean out of the news by Lazzaro's great cross, and like everyone else Henry had tended to forget them in the excitement around the church.

The town had always been as full of police, however, as it had of tourists and newspapermen, a great many of them sent over from Trepizano to reinforce the local men. But so many had been occupied with the crowds who wished to see the cross and the relics that were being brought up from the bottom of the lake that nobody had seemed to notice that there were also others still occupied in searching for the missing explosives.

When Henry stopped to think about it, he realized that the air of tension about the place had not really vanished at all but had merely been obscured by the excitement generated by the arrival of the cross. There were still groups of policemen on the corners, and there were still always two or three with a car or a group of motorcyclists on the road to Trepizano, or on the ferry station, examining passports and looking into suitcases and boxes and car boots. They were always there but politely inconspicious.

It was a warm evening, the sun glowing among the crags above the town, the rocks bright pink in the last of the light. It had been a hot afternoon, but with the lowering of the sun, the veil of heat had lifted and the sky looked calm enough for Henry to have doubts about his insistence on the dam being drained. They seemed at last to be in for a period of fine weather which would take away all the urgency.

There was a lot of singing in the bar, because the hotel was full of excited tourists and the bottles of Lacrimae Vescovi were coming over the counter in dozens. The party had started sedately enough with an accordionist, but the younger element had congregated at the bar, preferring the jukebox and the records of Elvis Presley, and in the end the accordionist gave up trying and began to enjoy himself on brandy.

"He takes his teeth out in summer and goes around the cafés in Trepizano," Stettner was telling Maggie Daniells. "He looks so decrepit he makes a fortune from the visitors."

The noise was increasing as the bottles of wine crowded the tables, then suddenly the accordionist came to life again and started to sing. One by one the others joined in, standing around him, their voices blending together, young and strong, their faces glowing with good health. Then young Maggs borrowed a guitar and the archaeologists began to sing all the outrageously partisan songs they could think of—"*La Bandiera Rossa,*" "*La Strada del Bosco,*" and the infuriating "*Zu Mantua im Banden,*" which Stettner had obviously taught them, the choruses interspersed with gusts of laughter. Stettner was enjoying the singing and was well to the front with Maggie Daniells, waving a wineglass and shouting the words at the top of his voice, his face flushed, his shirt open—deliberately,

Henry decided, so that it was possible to see the hair on his chest. He had his arm around Maggie's waist and his hand well up under her breast, and he had a salacious look on his face as he beamed at her.

"The police were around the boats this afternoon, Herr Doktor," he told Henry. "They insisted on examining our store of explosives. They insisted that they should be kept locked up and the key deposited at the Questura every evening. Maggie's taken over the responsibility. She likes to take over responsibilities. "He dropped his voice and put his mouth close to Henry's ear. "Some even for me." He gave Henry a sly look and went on cheerfully. "It seems sensible, I suppose, or my friends of the Montanari might decide to steal them."

He seemed to be enjoying himself and went on without any encouragement from Henry. "They're always shooting at the sentries in the mountains, you understand, always taking away the fishplates from the railway and jamming the points. They urinate into the petrol tanks of police lorries, a thing which does no good to a petrol engine, and leave notes outside explosives stores. It's a pity they don't tell me more. I might be able to help the police." he shrugged, mocking himself. "But I am just Alois Stettner, the climber," he said. "That's all. They just like me around to give tone to their hysterical little meetings. They don't tell me what they're going to do. They know I like life too much. They're afraid I might talk if I were pressed too hard."

They were still singing downstairs when Henry went to bed, and he was brooding over Caporelli's reports when the explosion brought him back to life at once. It wasn't very loud—and was muffled as though it were some distance away—but he knew at once what it was. They'd been waiting for it for days.

He sat up abruptly, and in the stillness that followed he heard an ass bray and the sweet notes of a nightingale, then the night seemed to break apart into a thousand noisy fragments. There was shouting in the street outside and the singing in the bar stopped as everybody flooded out under the trees. The telephone bell jarred insistently in the hall.

He got out of bed and dressed, and he was just pulling on his jacket when a couple of police cars went past, horns wailing stridently up and down. He jumped to the window, scattering Caporelli's papers, and as he flung it open he saw the flashing lights vanishing around the corner by the Church of Lazzaro di Colleno.

When he reached the hall, the roadway seemed to be full of gesticulating people. Caporelli was standing by the door, staring upward toward the mountains over the little valley that lay between the Stettnerhof and the town.

"The railway again," he said as he saw Henry. "I just heard. They killed a policeman. Sergeant Guidotti. I know him well." His face looked bitter. "It'll stop all the traffic," he went on. "They'll search every train and every car and every bus. Everything will be held up. Mail. Telephone calls. Everything."

There was a lot of chattering around them and some drunk in the bar made a halfhearted attempt to sing "The Red Flag." But the gaiety had gone and there was no longer any joy to be found in hearing political songs or speeches, however much in fun.

Someone shut the singer up abruptly and an argument started, bursting immediately into loud voices. Tension was suddenly there again, taut as a wound-up spring, and Caporelli went inside, his eyes blazing, and Henry heard him talking angrily. The argument stopped and he reappeared, his face wooden.

After a while Maggie Daniells came down the stairs. She looked bright-eyed and interested like the rest of the archaeological group, seeing only the excitement in the explosion, uninvolved, untouched, and without the narrow-eyed alertness of the townspeople.

97

"Is it the same as last time, Signor Caporelli?" she asked.

Caporelli nodded, and her eagerness vanished abruptly before his grimness. "It's *always* the same as last time," he said. "Tomorrow there'll be a picture in the paper of a note left by someone signing himself 'Andreas Hofer' and there'll be requests by the police for people to come forward and identify the writing. And a few crackpots'll say it's their mother-in-law or the neighbor they don't like, and that's all. They'll get nowhere."

A police lorry went past, half a dozen men huddled in the back, and as it vanished, Stettner appeared around the bushes from the garden. He crossed to Maggie immediately and gently put his arm around her with his hand under her breast in that familiar way of his that irritated Henry so much.

"Bang," he said, and she jumped and turned around, laughing up into his face and trying to indicate Caporelli who was glaring at them, his eyes glittering and angry.

"They're at it again," Stettner said, ignoring her. "Proving what we Austrians have always said—that Italy's just a geographical expression. Bang, bang, bang. Always someone. If it's not at the quarry, then it's the terrorists. And if it's not the terrorists, then it's you people trying to blow the bottom out of the lake."

She gestured again, quickly, warning him of Caporelli's mood, but he laughed and cocked a thumb. "Somebody left a wreath on the Hoferdenkmal," he said. "The statue to Andreas Hofer. Decorated in black and yellow, the old colors of Austria. Nobody saw who did it. It just appeared. They've impounded it in the Questura for the experts who'll come from Rome. Let's go and have a drink."

Maggie glanced at Caporelli again, but Stettner caught the glance and shook his head, pulling a face at Caporelli's grimness. "Not here," he said softly, his voice barely audible. "The Stöckli Bar down by the boat station. We might see something.

Besides," he added, "it's darker there and there's an orchestra. Much more fun."

By the following morning the press and television people who had satiated their followers with the cross and vanished had all returned to Cadivescovo, but the direction of the excitement had changed now, and the effervescent buoyancy that had come with the cross had disappeared again and given way once more to the sullen edginess that had been in the town before, waiting in the corners among the brooding groups of men like a starving dog, never obvious, but always definitely there.

Pictures of the dead sergeant appeared in the newspapers, a smiling, handsome mustached man who looked like Gregory Peck, and of his weeping wife being helped into the Questura, alongside shots of the twisted rails and the hole torn out of the railway embankment by the explosion.

Caporelli was in a gloomy mood because he'd been staring at the blaring headlines all day, his eyes narrow and speculative, his manner irritable. He'd been drinking brandy steadily and pushing glasses of it at Henry, too, whenever he'd appeared.

Apparently Sergeant Guidotti had not been the only man involved in the explosion. A student by the name of Stalder had been gravely injured at the same time and was now in hospital at Trepizano, blinded and burned and not expected to live. Abruptly all the gaiety that had come to Cadivescovo had departed again and voices were kept to undertones as though their owners were afraid to express their opinions out loud. It had its effect on the bar that evening, because, with nobody laughing, nobody was drinking either, just a silent group of farmers in a corner playing cards and eating sausage with their beer.

Caporelli sat with Henry, his heavy face set, his eyes on the moving shadows outside where the horse chestnuts wavered in the breeze that was getting up. The sun had vanished during the afternoon and the sky had filled with cloud, so that only momentary gleams of starlight came through the fitful breaks in the black banks that hugged the crests of the mountains.

Caporelli swallowed his brandy and picked up the bottle, signaling to Henry to empty his glass. His mind was obviously busy and he seemed indifferent to the silence in the bar.

"Dr. Cappell," he began after a while.

Henry sighed. "Chappell," he said.

Caporelli looked up, startled, then grinned unexpectedly. "Sure," he said. "Dr. Shappell—"

"Look, Signor Caporelli," Henry suggested. "Call me Henry."

Caporelli laughed. "I was wondering when you were going to suggest it," he said. "O.K., Aynree. Call me Ettore."

He fiddled with the bottle and filled the glasses, then stared at his brandy, his eyes far away. "Did I ever tell you about my father, Aynree?" he said. "He was a doctor. He lived in Cava Catanzaro, south of Naples. He died there as he lived— a poor man. The Fascisti sent him there because he didn't think the way they did. That's what they used to do with thinkers and Communists and Socialists before the war. Send them to Calabria and tell them to get on with it. No wages. Nothing. It was worse than prison. They lived only on what the peasants gave them out of gratitude. That's all. But they didn't destroy my father. Never."

He looked fierce as he spoke. "He was always in trouble, Aynree. He was always standing up for his new people. There was a drain in Cava Catanzaro. Not a deep one, but a very smelly one. It was cracked. My father decided it was fouling all the water and causing epidemics. He fought for months to get the authorities in Rome to build a new one. But they never did. In the end he stole some explosives from a quarry nearby

100

and with another man he lifted the manhole one night and dropped them down. I can remember the bang to this day."

He grinned at Henry. "They had to build a new drain after that," he said.

"Pity they can't do the same with the dam," Henry commented.

Caporelli placed his glass down carefully and looked up. "*I* could blow that gate out of the stopper wall," he said slowly. "I could do it easily. I could blow a hundred-lire note off a gravestone without damaging the marble. I did it in the Partisans. All I need is the material."

Henry stared at him. "Ettore," he said slowly, "I think you're drunk."

"Yes." Caporelli rolled his eyes. "I guess I am."

Henry had a headache the next morning from all the brandy. The papers had screaming headlines a foot deep. The trains to Bolzano had all had to be rerouted and there was an express denial from the Volkspartei to say they were in no way responsible for the explosion. But, at the same time, there'd been an outbreak of fighting in Trepizano and several men who'd boasted that they belonged to the Volkspartei had been arrested. The inside pages were devoted to the private life of the dead Sergeant Guidotti and contained pictures of the parents of the blinded student who was fighting for his life in the Trepizano hospital.

The Piazza della Citta was full of police vans and lorries again, and from his window Henry could see them standing by the boat station where the eight-o'clock boat to Trepizano was waiting, examining the papers of everyone who wished to go aboard. The whole town seemed to be squeezed into a narrower confine, as though the roadblocks outside were expressly designed to hold its inhabitants within easy reach for questioning. There was also a police car just down the road from the hotel, waiting near the lane that ran up toward the mountains.

"In case anyone tries to escape that way," Dittli told Henry as he brought his coffee.

Henry was feeling depressed, partly because of the brandy and partly because of the tension in the town. He was sipping his coffee on the veranda, trying not to lean too far forward because of his head, when Maggie Daniells joined him.

"Enjoy yourself with Stettner?" he asked.

She blushed and he went on in a disinterested tone. "I suppose he's good-looking," he said. "In an animal sort of way. Pity he's got so many gold teeth."

"They go in for them here," she pointed out coldly.

"He'd look better without them, all the same."

She looked angry and Henry had the sense to stop baiting her. "How's the archaeology?" he asked.

"We've found more ornaments," she said, faintly hostile. "It's a treasure-trove down there. There's a lot more to come."

Henry moved uneasily. "Does all this—well, these politics— do they interfere at all?"

She shrugged. "It's virtually impossible to make a telephone call," she said. "There's a constant delay. Every time we wish to verify something, we're held up 'somewhere.' "

"The price of making a rare archaeological discovery in an area torn by political strife," he commented.

"That boy in the hospital's dying," she pointed out, her eyes unexpectedly anxious, so that he knew that she, too, was suffering from the tenseness in the town.

"Perhaps it's his own fault," Henry said realistically. "After all, Sergeant Guidotti's *dead*. It wasn't anything to do with *him*. Or his wife and children."

"But the boy's blind!" She was being feminine and unreasonable. "He's only eighteen."

Henry shrugged. "I'm going home soon," he said. "It'll be

102

nice to get back to England where there's nothing to worry about but my income tax."

"It's so stodgy in England." She sounded very young as she spoke.

"How long is it since you were there?"

"Four months."

"Perhaps you've forgotten what it's like."

"No, I haven't. I can remember everything. The weather. The narrowness. The Establishment. All the things I hate."

Henry felt very old. He could remember saying the same things himself ten years before, and it was like staring at his own reflection in a mirror. He hadn't realized what a gulf there was between the twenties and the thirties.

"What will you do when your job here's finished?" he asked. "It can't last forever."

"There'll always be another," she said. "They've found some wall pictures in a cave in Germany."

"And you'll go there?"

"Of course."

For a moment they seemed to be thrown together in spite of their differences, as though, like all the other outsiders in the town, they formed an island of exclusion among all the shifting tides of feeling.

"Doesn't it all sometimes seem a little endless—as though you're pressing ahead all the time without ever getting anywhere?"

She looked at him as though he were ancient, as though he belonged to some period in time that had existed long before her comprehension, and he wondered if it had always been like this with young people—if *he*'d been like it himself ten years before. Some time something would make her grow into a woman, jolting her into adulthood with misery, pain, and wretchedness, but until then she'd be impatient with people

103

like himself, a little intolerant and always faintly patronizing.

"Dr. Chappell," she said cheerfully, "you're an awful square, aren't you?"

"Yes." Henry managed a smile. "I suppose I am."

She laughed at his expression and he thought how pretty she was. "You should get with it," she said. "You don't know what you're missing."

Caporelli appeared as she picked up her coat and the sling bag she wore. He stared after her as she disappeared, his eyes sad and nostalgic.

"What a pity I was born so long ago," he said.

He sat down alongside Henry and signaled to Dittli to bring him a coffee.

As the waiter went away again, he looked at Henry for a long time in silence.

"Aynree," he said at last, "perhaps I wasn't so drunk last night after all."

Henry sat up abruptly, wondering what was coming, and Caporelli gestured vaguely.

"You remember," he pointed out, "I said someone ought to blow the gate in the stopper wall. There are worse things than flooding the valley and getting a bit of silt over a relic or two."

Henry eyed him cautiously. "What are you getting at?" he demanded.

"My father blew up a sewer. Why shouldn't I blow up a dam?"

"You couldn't."

"I could blow the hair off your chest without scorching the skin. I've blown bridges and trains and motorcars. I haven't forgotten how to do it. Sometimes I think I'd like to do it again—just for the sheer joy of destruction."

His eyes gleamed and Henry eyed him carefully. "You couldn't get the explosive," he said. "They'll keep too careful

104

an account of it. Especially now. If they find you trying to get hold of any, they'll think you're 'Andreas Hofer.' "

Caporelli paused for a long time, and Henry could see young Dittli trying to hear what they said.

"They have no problems from terrorists and dynamiters in Florence," Caporelli pointed out quietly. "I have a cousin who's a quarry manager down there. A little fiddling with the books and what we want won't be missed. What do you say?"

Henry stared at him. "Signor Caporelli—Ettore," he said, "last night I thought you were drunk. I think now you're mad."

Caporelli leaned forward eagerly. "They'll think it's 'Andreas Hofer,' " he urged. "Everything that's been blown up around here for the last eight months has been 'Andreas Hofer.' You've seen how it is in the town. They'll think this was too. We'll leave a note to say so."

"No!" Henry stood up. "Look, Signor Caporelli, I'm a consultant engineer, not an anarchist. I'm not going to have anything to do with it. I'll put in a report. I'll give you advice. I'll even try to persuade people to your view. But if you want to blow the blasted thing up, blow it yourself. Don't include me."

As he stormed out of the room, he saw Caporelli watching him from the table. Dittli was staring from behind the bar, one hand on the handle of the coffee machine. Then Caporelli gave him a glance and followed Henry.

"Why not?" he said, as he caught up with him in the hall. "Don't you feel the rightness of it? Here." He placed a hand on his heart and gazed earnestly at Henry.

There was an urgency in his expression that reminded Henry of the scene in the Edelweiss Bar and the stiff faces of the thrustful young men with their wreath outside the church, the fanatic faces of patriotism gone mad, and he found himself backing away instinctively. Caporelli was too intelligent to suffer from any of the apocalyptic visions of the Montanari,

105

but there was somehow the same tense eagerness about him now as he stared at Henry.

"No," Henry said shortly. "No, I don't."

"Aynree—!"

"No!" Henry's face went red with anger. "I've done what I came to do and now I think I'd better go—tomorrow—before you get me too involved for comfort."

8

Henry was sitting in the hall waiting for information on the trains from Trepizano when Caporelli appeared next morning. His face was gloomy and his shoulders were hunched as he crossed to the veranda and stared out at the weather, his eyes searching and anxious. The sun had gone and the lake's surface was stirred by the wind into little ripples. The clouds were rising up the mountain opposite in great gray swirls like a charge of cavalry and, although the valley was bright, to the east the sky was dark and La Fortezza was shut out and thunderheads were building up at the other side of the lake.

As Caporelli turned back into the Stettnerhof, Henry indicated his baggage standing by the door, labeled and ready for departure.

"I'm off," he said.

"So!" Caporelli seemed indifferent. He shrugged, a small, hopeless shrug, different from the one he reserved for customers who complained about the food, then he gestured at the sky.

"Have you seen the forecast?" he said heavily.

"I don't need to. I'm leaving."

Caporelli didn't seem to hear him this time even. "Rain," he said. "Rain. All rain. There's a storm coming."

"I don't need a forecast to see that."

"I have a friend in Bolzano," Caporelli went on. "He works in the weather bureau. They've traced it. It started in Switzerland—where *all* the bad weather starts—and it's moving east. It's now broken into two fronts, one heading north toward Vienna, the other south toward Italy. There'll be severe local thunderstorms for the next few days."

"What time's the train?" Henry prompted.

Caporelli shrugged again and turned at last to look at him.

"The line is still blocked," he said, a suggestion of triumph in his voice, as though he'd been holding the information back deliberately until it was most likely to shock and annoy. "There'll be no trains through Trepizano until tomorrow. In any case, there are such queues waiting for the boats, you'd never get there in time. It's the police," he explained. "They're examining everyone."

"I've got a British passport," Henry pointed out.

Caporelli's shoulders lifted and there was a hint of amusement in his eyes. "That won't hurry them. They're being very thorough. It's causing them great distress at the Church of Lazzaro di Colleno. The crowds are falling off and the offertory box doesn't rattle as much as it did."

He managed to smile at last, as though he considered anything a joke that could wreck the sanctification of Bishop Lazzaro.

"They've just let it out how Sergeant Guidotti was killed," he went on, the smile fading. "It seems there was a fight and they both got blown up. The boy's from Bolzano. He's not

108

likely to live. They've had young Dittli in for questioning. It seems they knew each other."

"Have they kept him?"

"No. They let him go. But I'll have to get rid of him as soon as I can get a replacement. It looks so goddam bad. Fortunately it's his day off, so nobody noticed."

"What about Stettner?"

"Oh, him, too, of course. They always ask *him*. But he'd just left here and was drinking in the Stöckli Bar with Elena Oswino at the time. Oswino was in Trepizano for the night. It's students, of course. Not even students from this area, I expect. From the North Tyrol. People who aren't even affected by the frontier." Caporelli picked up Henry's bags and signaled for the porter. "I think you'd better stay another couple of nights till it's all blown over."

Henry sighed. There was something about Caporelli that swept people off their feet.

"Just another few days," he was suggesting. "Enjoy yourself."

"Here? Enjoy myself?"

Caporelli grinned. "There are no bombs in the Stettnerhof," he pointed out. "Have a holiday. Till all this has finished and things are normal again. On me. I don't mind." He looked quizzically at Henry, and Henry nodded.

"Till the end of the week," he agreed. "No longer."

Caporelli smiled and slapped his shoulder. "O.K., Aynree. End of the week."

Henry watched silently as the cases were sent back upstairs, curiously unmoved by the change of plans. There was something that held him in Cadivescovo against his wishes—a sense of impending drama. All the time he'd been packing he hadn't really been anxious to go because, somehow, he knew there was more to come.

He rose slowly and lit a cigarette, his mind oddly empty,

109

like a man waiting for a sentence to be passed on him, then, as he had decided to stay, he suggested that they might as well go up the mountain and take another look at the dam from above before the storm broke against the ramparts of the mountains. He was surprised when Caporelli raised his hands in negation.

"Not me." He smiled. "I'm away on business today. Urgent business."

"I thought the dam was urgent."

"It is. It is." Caporelli had a bland, secretive look on his face, and Henry found himself wondering what he was up to. "But so is my business. I'll tell you about it when I return. I'll arrange for Alois to go with you. He's free this morning. There's no diving."

"I'm not so sure I want Alois," Henry observed slowly.

Caporelli grinned. "To go beyond the dam you do," he said. "You'll get lost otherwise. He knows the mountains like the back of his hand, and you don't *have* to talk to him." He slapped Henry's shoulder and laughed. "He won't try anything on. No swastika badges or salutes. You'll be quite safe. I'll leave a message for him."

Stettner turned up about an hour later, on a scooter, wearing a heavy jersey and *kletteschühe*. He grinned at Henry and waved, and they climbed into Caporelli's van.

"Better than a scooter," Stettner said. "Especially when it rains. And it *will* rain. Soon."

He indicated the dark masses of clouds in the east. "There," he said. "That means rain."

He was in good form and, for once, seemed not to be goading Henry. He was an entertaining rogue and, in spite of the fact that Henry didn't trust him and didn't like him and couldn't get out of his mind the memory of the hard-faced

110

young boys in the little inn above the town, he kept him laughing at the outrageous stories of the tourists he dealt with.

"They are obsessed with lavatories." He grinned. "You can hear them all the time. 'It's all right, Ada—' " He imitated a woman's voice. " '—there's a seat on this one.' I hear them in every café where I stop for a beer. They don't know I speak English, so they talk freely. It is a very good job being a courier. I show them the goats and tell them they are chamois, and I have a standard joke for when the bus is coming down the mountain. I tell them that if they are frightened they must shut their eyes—like the driver. It makes them laugh and hides the fact that I am charging them ten dollars for a five-dollar trip."

As they climbed higher it was possible to see the whole length of Lake Colleno. With the approaching rain, the air was crystal-clear and devoid of mist, and Henry could see Trepizano like a brown and white speckled carpet below the slopes of Monte Cano at the other side.

"I love the mountains," Stettner said, and for once there was no suggestion of laughter in his voice. "They are clean and smell good and the air's like wine. And what is more, they are *mine*. They are something we can't have taken from us and sent to Rome. We can't even share them with anyone else, because you have to live here just to understand them."

He pointed out La Spiga, now clear of cloud. "Die Eisenspitze," he said, using its German name. "I climbed that last year. And I was paid to do it, too, by a group of Americans who wanted to go back to Chicago and say they'd been up a mountain. All they've got are plains, you see. It is very easy. You should try it."

He insisted on calling at Oswino's farm as they passed and the dramatic blond woman with the cold eyes gave them a *grappa*. Oswino came in while they talked and nodded to Stettner, almost as though he knew what went on between him and his wife and was powerless to stop it. When they left, Stettner stood with Frau Oswino, talking in low secretive tones in German, while Henry started the van, then they drove up the narrowing road toward the dam.

The dam looked safe and calm, without a ripple on the green surface of the water. Even the wall looked safe, with the level well away from the summit, and Henry began to wonder again if he'd made too much of his fears.

"It'll last a thousand years," Stettner said confidently. Henry shrugged, somehow unconvinced again in the face of his certainty.

"Not if you have rain like you had last week," he said. "You can see the crack there. Every time the water runs through that it pulls away the earth. Just a little at a time, but it goes, and the greater the pressure, the faster the water flows and the faster it tears away the earth."

Stettner grinned at him. "I think you worry too much, Herr Doktor," he said. "Here in Austria we never worry. We never worried even when we were great and powerful, because we always lost our wars, and we knew we weren't expected to win. Then when we lost the Empire, we didn't worry because we hadn't anything to worry about, anyway. A man without money never worries about losing it. I don't. It's only the wealthy who worry. Not worrying is as typical of Austria as the waltz."

They walked back toward the van and Stettner offered Henry his flask. It contained brandy, too raw for Henry's taste, but it was an indication of Stettner's good humor and his willingness to be friendly.

"Higher up," he said, "you can see the currents in the water. The way it flows, the way it builds up. You can see the depth. Over there by the stopper wall it's deepest of all. That's why the stopper wall was built there, of course. So it could be emptied, if necessary."

112

Henry smiled. "Only now it can't, or it would cover Arcuneum with mud."

Stettner laughed and slapped his shoulder. "Or it would cover Arcuneum with mud," he agreed. "And then we should not have our Saint Lazzaro, and the Church would lose face and the television would lose its pictures and the newspapers their stories, and the big businessmen their money, and the restaurateurs their customers, and the sight-seers their sights, and Cadivescovo its ephemeral notoriety, and Alois Stettner his tourists. No?"

Henry laughed again. "Yes," he said.

"Would you *like* to go higher?" Stettner asked. "So you can look down on the dam. There is no bulge in the wall. The curve is perfect. You can see it from the side of Die Festung. Come and have a look. It's an easy climb. You don't need special shoes."

"O.K."

"Besides"—Stettner winked—"we're safe up there from the ministrations of the police. They've brought a couple of lorryloads over from Trepizano and the eight-o'clock boat was full of them. There'll be none up here."

He was wrong, however, because farther up the winding track they were stopped by a couple of uniformed men with rifles who stepped out from among the rocks, materializing from nowhere.

Henry showed his passport and indicated the dam, and Stettner explained their business. They seemed satisfied and didn't ask Stettner *his* business, merely nodding at him as though he were an old friend.

"A customer, Alois?" one of them asked, not realizing how well Henry spoke Italian. "Will he pay all right?"

Stettner laughed and they moved off again.

"They are so stupid, these Italians," he said contemptuously. "From the South, most of them."

Following his directions, Henry drove up the rocky road until they stopped by the wooden refuge hut at the foot of La Fortezza, a low, weathered building with rocks on the roof to hold the heavy tiles down in the winter winds and with a gaunt iron crucifix outside, stark against the sky. They parked the car at the bottom of a bank of dazzling white scree where the meadows finished. At the top was the cliff face. It looked terrifying to Henry as they scrambled across the maze of tumbled rock and up the slope.

Below them the woods fell away from the fringe of dwarf pine and the scraggy rock-hugging shrubs under the mountain which rose, cliff on fantastic cliff, ridge on massive ridge, tower on tremendous tower, until the sharp curving wedge of the summit pierced the sky like a pyramid of granite and limestone, layer on layer of precipices, crags, ledges, rocks, and cornices, all of them bare of growth, even the moss gone from the wind-swept faces.

It was ghostly up there, and terrible in the silence away from the streams. There was no sound, not a tree, not a blade of grass. The translucent bastions of rock seemed to sparkle in the weak sun against the sky, as unreal as a stage setting, with the approaching storm dragging itself to shreds among the polished limestone pinnacles.

"*Wunderschön*," Stettner breathed. "Incomparable."

They could see the country spread out like a map below them now. The town was visible again over the curves of the meadows, close-set houses with low pantiled roofs and stuccoed walls, and the campaniles of Madonna del Piano and Trepiazze and the old *castello* gleaming on its crag above the lake like a toy. In the clear air, with the rain waiting in the valleys across the lake, it was indescribably beautiful.

"Our land," Stettner said, his voice full of proprietorial pride. "Our town. We have more elegance and artistry in our streets than half the villages of Switzerland with their careful

114

commercialism. We avoid all the arrogance of Prussia and all the instability of Italy."

It was a surprising note to strike because, although Henry had heard him holding forth on the problems of the district, he had never suspected he felt at all deeply about the country itself, and again he had the odd feeling he'd had once before that Stettner was not the buffoon everyone thought he was and that Caporelli was wrong to dismiss him as nothing but a boaster.

At the top of the scree they stopped and stood there for a while as Stettner pointed out the landmarks, and the rocks covered with bilberry growth, and the pine clumps and the streams and the ranks of trees below the Catena di Saga with its red ochre summits and tall ghostly peaks and pale towers, like a squadron of men-o'-war in line abreast.

"They were made to be climbed," he said, a tense pride in his voice. "They've never been glaciated and the rock's not smooth."

It was as they started up the rock face that Henry noticed the two men below them. They weren't far away and it was quite possible to recognize young Dittli, the waiter. They'd been hidden by the slope, but now, as he began to climb, they'd become visible over the rocks. They were in a small valley, young Dittli with a scooter, the other man on foot and with a rucksack.

"That's Dittli," Henry said. "The waiter from the hotel."

Stettner's face had changed and the happiness had gone out of it, to be replaced at first by anger and then by the intent remote look of a soldier at the alert.

And there was a strange glassy-eyed withdrawnness about him suddenly that made Henry involuntarily think of those stiff faces he'd seen under the square steel helmets before the war, a distant, farseeing, ambitious look that was mixed with secrecy and camouflage and the backstairs freemasonry of the

115

political idealist prepared to go to any limit to achieve his ends.

"Yes," he said abruptly. "Come. Let's go."

He set off ahead of Henry, making more of the climb than Henry had expected an experienced mountaineer to do, so that dislodged boulders started rolling and rattling down the slope.

"Come," he shouted, so that the words echoed among the crags. "Hurry!"

At the sound Henry saw Dittli's head turn, the movement abrupt and sudden, his face white against the light, and in that clear air he could see the startled surprise on his face. The other man was squarely built, short, and dark with a black beard.

Dittli stared for a second, then he seemed to half slap, half push the other man's shoulder, and they broke apart. Henry saw the bearded man break into a run, his head down, among the rocks, next he heard the sound of Dittli's scooter starting and he, too, vanished, down the rocky track toward Oswino's farm, trailing a puff of white exhaust smoke. They looked like a couple of criminals.

"That's the man I saw up here the other day," Henry said. "Carlo Wasescha. The police are looking for him."

"They'll never find him," Stettner said flatly. "Carlo was born in a shepherd's hut at the foot of the Catena di Saga. He knows the mountains better than he knows his own face."

"I wonder what young Dittli was up to?"

Stettner's face had shut down. "Day off," he said abruptly. "He's free to do as he pleases."

"They seemed surprised. They disappeared smartly enough when they saw us. As though they were up to something."

"Yes."

Stettner obviously had no intention of volunteering any information and Henry couldn't help wondering if young Dittli, with his ardent patriotism, was one of the sort who frequented the Edelweiss Bar and if Stettner knew about it. With his pale face and weak mouth, young Dittli didn't look tough enough to belong to any subversive organization, but you could never judge a man by his looks, especially where ideals were concerned, and a pasty face was no indication of the tortuous mind that might lie behind it.

Stettner appeared to be waiting for him, his eyes empty and discouraging, and there was a certain amount of defiance about the way Henry persisted in his questioning.

"Won't the police catch them?"

Stettner's laugh was sneering. "Romans? Neapolitan slum boys in uniform? No man brought up here from Italy could catch a mountain man. Dittli will get back safely."

"What about the scooter?"

"There are plenty of places I know about to hide it. I expect he knows them too. He'll walk down. There are plenty of ways down that the police don't know about. Dittli will know them. All mountain men know them."

Suddenly the air seemed as cold as Stettner's new mood, then a ragged-winged crow circling near the spires of rock gave a raucous croak that sounded like a warning, and Henry had a sudden uneasy wish to be back by the lakeside.

The saw-toothed edges of La Fortezza were above him now, scraping at the sky, craggy and serrated, stark in a great scoop of bare rock, the savage crests and steeples on every side, and as he looked back he could see the whole shape of the dam, clear and well-defined, like a great pear, with the bulge the curve of the ancient wall. There was a distinct sag where he knew the weak saddle to be in the center, but it didn't look as bad as he'd expected. Down by the stopper wall that projected like a pimple on the side of the pear the water was darker, and up toward the stalk of the pear it was darker again because of the shadow thrown by the mountains on either side. The feeder streams, small and narrow, ran like silver ribbons down the mountainsides, and Oswino's farm, just below the wall, looked like part of a huge model.

117

Stettner was standing on a ledge just alongside Henry's shoulder, indicating he should join him.

"Come," he said. "Come up."

His face was still grim and every last vestige of laughter had gone from his eyes. Henry stayed where he was.

"What was Dittli doing up here?" he said, looking up. "I didn't know he was a climber."

"He's not."

"It's a funny place to go riding on a scooter. He looked as though he was making a plot to blow up the Questura."

Stettner managed a smile at last, but it was forced and unnatural. "Perhaps he was," he said.

"You get a good view of the dam from here," Henry pointed out.

"Much better higher up."

Henry stared upward, not sure whether he had the head to climb further.

"I think this will do me," he said

"Much better higher up," Stettner insisted. "There's an easy route."

"Perhaps for you. Not for me."

Stettner reached down and put his hand on Henry's shoulder, his fingers gripping it hard, trying to force his will on him. "You don't know what you're missing," he said.

The grip tightened as he tried to pull Henry after him, but there was something now in his manner that worried Henry and he wrenched his shoulder away.

"No, thanks," he said. "I'll leave it at this."

"You are afraid, I suppose?" Stettner's goading manner had returned, and his smile had changed to one of unpleasantness.

"If you like. I'm no climber."

"You are easily afraid, Englishman."

He was deliberately taunting Henry now, trying to shame him into going higher.

118

"No, thanks."

"You are typical of your country. You back out when the going is rough. You have no guts."

His eyes were hot and his whole manner had become insulting and rude, and Henry had a curious sensation of expectancy that was compounded of fear, excitement, and uncertainty.

Good God, he thought, he wants to kill me. The startled realization hit him hard, and in the same flash of intuition he realized that somehow it was because he had seen Dittli and the little bearded man with the rucksack, and he remembered again the Edelweiss Bar and all those arrogant faces he'd seen. There hadn't been one of them with an atom of kindness in them. There hadn't been one without this same lost, desperate, fanatic gleam in their eyes that Stettner had.

He shivered, aware of coldness and a sickening sense of being caught up in something he could only vaguely understand.

"I'll go down," he said. "I'll wait for you by the van."

As he set off back down the crags, he realized how right he'd been to go no farther. He was already conscious of a swimming in his head and a weakness around his loins, and he knew he could never have stood on the crag where Stettner had stood and looked down below him as Stettner had.

They were just above the slope of the scree when something —a movement of light perhaps—made Henry look up and, from the corner of his eye, he caught the swift shadow of a falling boulder. Flattening himself against the face of the cliff, he saw it pass over him and bounce on the stub of rock where he'd been standing. Small splinters of stone flew off and arced down the valley, as the boulder bounced again, striking sparks, and went rattling down the scree, finally rolling out into the meadow at the bottom and coming to a stop in the long grass.

Henry looked up and saw Stettner grin at him, but it wasn't

a natural grin, and Henry climbed down the last thirty feet of cliff face so fast that at the bottom he missed his footing, slipped, and fell onto the scree slope.

He rolled down it, turning and twisting, unable to stop himself, and fetched up against a rock halfway down, unhurt, but with a torn trouser knee. Stettner was following him, jumping down the lower crags like a gazelle, completely confident of his footing. Henry stood up and made his way to the bottom of the slope and waited for him there.

"You went down in beautiful style, Englishman," Stettner said as he jumped off the last rock. "As though you were frightened out of your wits."

"I was," Henry admitted.

"Accident," Stettner said shortly. "Loose boulder. You loosened it with your foot. I caught it with mine."

"It would have killed me if I hadn't seen it."

Stettner shrugged. "One of the chances of the game," he said.

"It's not a game I like playing."

Neither of them spoke on the way down the mountain, and Henry was glad to get away from the area of bleak gray crags to the point where the houses started. It had been altogether too silent and still up there. Down below there were people, and his instinct was to get among them. He was bolting like a frightened animal out of its element and faced with a stronger enemy secure in his.

9

Cadivescovo was like a disturbed anthill when they reached the lakeside. People were standing in the square in groups and there seemed more police about than normal, watching from the arcades and the steps of the Municipio.

"The police sergeant's funeral," Stettner explained in a cold, diffident way. "They have to make sure he is put to his rest in a manner befitting an Italian hero. They like their monuments to be rhetorical and their interments to be dramatic."

His manner was sarcastic and sneering still, and Henry was glad to pay him the money they'd agreed on for his services and watch him disappear into the Stöckli Bar near the boat station.

The funeral had not long since passed through the square and it had left a wake of excitement behind it. The crowd moved awkwardly, reluctant to go home, resentful against the police and against each other, their eyes full of suspicion. And Caporelli had been right about the boats. Nobody was leaving in a hurry. The queues seemed to be miles long—tourists trying to get away and more tourists trying to land, with the black, red, and white figures of the *carabinieri* checking papers and passports and every item of luggage, even the women's handbags.

They were everywhere, outside every shop and at every alley end, watching the faces that passed them, their eyes on the bulges in men's pockets, their fingers picking briefly at paper parcels, caps over their eyes and blank-faced as men with masks. The only people who were undisturbed by them were the archaeologists down at the mole.

But even there were two or three policemen, however, watching on Dei Monti's instructions, but the diving had not stopped and, during the afternoon, when the wind dropped and the sun appeared again, Henry went to watch them at work.

Sister Ursula was there, an apron around her waist, supervising the half-dozen orphans sitting in front of cheap plastic bowls, their hands in the water, their fingers working the mud from the crusted objects that lay alongside them. She recognized Henry and smiled.

"We are enjoying our break from routine," she said. "Especially Giovanni. He is an intelligent boy and needs something intelligent to do, and this is perfect."

She watched the tall, intense-looking youngster for a moment, then she shook her head.

"I sometimes wish life were not so serious for him," she said. "I think even the political situation worries him. Doesn't it, Giovanni?"

The boy nodded and went on with his work, his arms up to the elbows in muddy water.

"He is afraid," Sister Ursula went on, "that there'll be some move to take all this to Rome." She gestured at the articles laid out on the tarpaulin. "I suspect he's heard some of my revolutionary talk."

Henry's eyebrows rose. "Revolutionary talk? From you?"

She smiled her sweet smile at him. "I've been saying that all these things belong here in Cadivescovo and shouldn't be taken to some museum away from the mountains where they'd be meaningless. The professor promised that and I know he's right. Here in Cadivescovo people could see them in their proper surroundings, where they were found."

"Sister"—Henry gestured behind him impulsively—"if you felt that that old dam up there were dangerous and had to be drained and that the only place it could be drained was into the Punta dei Fiori, where it would deposit mud over the ruins they've unearthed, what would you feel?"

She considered for a moment, then smiled. "I suspect, Doctor, that you've already asked that of the Bishop and been told that your dam comes a bad second. Is that correct?"

Henry nodded and she laughed.

"But, Sister—"

Her face became grave as she interrupted him. "Nothing has any value when set against human life and happiness," she said gently. "Not even the Church. I'm sure the Bishop would say the same."

Henry was pondering her words when Maggie Daniells appeared. She was in a bathing costume under blue cotton trousers, and after their bitter quarrels it seemed odd to see her put her arm on Giovanni's shoulder and the smile she gave him—warm and devoid of shyness. Her manner with Sister Ursula was friendly and close, too, as though they'd talked a lot together as they'd worked.

Then she changed to brisk, uninvolved efficiency as she showed him the things they had brought up from the bottom of the lake. They were lying on the tarpaulin, watched all the time by one of Sister Ursula's children, who sat on a box like a sentinel.

"All in the last few days," she said, willing enough to talk, but wary in case one of their quarrels broke out. "We'll have to get pressure hoses on it as soon as we can. We might uncover more." She moved the small encrusted objects on the tarpaulin with enthusiastic jerks of her hand.

"These are our special discoveries," she said. "Giovanni takes care of these. He's twice as quick as the others, and he knows all about them." She gave a little sigh. "He's far too intelligent to end up as a laborer on the railway, which is where Sister Ursula says he *will* end up unless something's done for him." She pointed to a small funnel-necked vase and spoke to the boy. "What's this, Giovanni?" she asked.

He grinned and it was the first time Henry had seen anything more on his face than his normal sad smile. "It's a tear phial, Signorina," he said quickly. Privileged mourners wept into them at burials and left them on the graves so that the dead would know how much they were missed."

Maggie laughed. "Well done, Giovanni. You ought to be doing my job."

He grinned at her. "I've been listening, Signorina."

She smiled at him, then bent and turned over a heavy bronze bowl, half cleaned already of the encrusting growth on it, and indicated the marks along the side. It meant nothing to Henry, but she seemed to think it was valuable.

"Priceless," she said warmly. "This has been the greatest thing that has happened to archaeology for years. We hope to find bracelets, coins, and ornaments, and even, perhaps, fragments of armor." She pointed to a large narrow-necked vessel. "For oil," she said. "They probably carried them aboard for cooking—or even for anointing. It's heavy. We turn them upside down and fill them from the compressed air cylinder, then they float to the surface on their own. It's just one of the tricks."

She picked up what looked like a small stone cross lying on

124

a box near where Giovanni was sitting. The boy's eyes followed her as she spoke.

"An altar cross," she said. "We think it's pure gold. When we've cleaned it, it will be beyond price. Isn't that so, Giovanni?"

"*Sì*, Signorina. Beyond price."

She put the cross down carefully and smiled at him again.

"Giovanni never takes his eyes off them," she said. "He thinks the Montanari might try to steal something and use it for political purposes. As a symbol, I suppose. Like the Scottish Nationalists taking the Stone of Scone from Westminster Abbey. There's already been a threat to move the great cross from the church."

Henry smiled. "They'd need a platoon of strong men and a truck," he said.

"The threat's been made, all the same. Professor Dei Monti received a note."

"I expect the newspapers did too."

She seemed to resent the cynicism in his words and she was cool toward him again.

"Professor Dei Monti takes it seriously," she said. "We've had someone on guard in the church and at the Customs House every night ever since. He says if there's the slightest danger, he'll take all this"—she gestured around her at the tarpaulin—"to Rome."

Henry pulled a wry face. "A pity he had to say so," he said.

"What do you mean?"

"He'll only make it worse by threatening to take it all away."

The rain they'd been expecting all day came that evening. There was a brief susurration of the trees as the wind started, then a sudden flash of lightning picked out the white buildings

125

in the growing darkness and silhouetted the mountains. A shutter slammed and the leaves of the palms around the hotel started rattling. The lights on the opposite shore of the lake were blotted out abruptly and the ripples became manes that broke into whitecapped wavelets as the wind rose. The dust started to whirl and there was a sudden roar as the air rushed through the leaves of the warped horse chestnuts. Young Dittli, who'd been arguing fiercely in undertones at the bar with Stettner—as though he were defending himself against an attack, it seemed to Henry—ran outside to bring in the umbrellas from the garden as the gilt wrought-iron sign started to whip back and forth on the wall. Then the lightning began to move along the valley and more dried leaves whirled along the road, followed by little wind devils of dust. The gray clouds reached down out of the pale evening sky in long fingers toward the mountains, the dust devils flew up suddenly in a blinding storm, the air turned liquid, and the rain began to come in great drops as big as half crowns that fell with a flat splash on the road, bursting like small bombs into shrapnel fragments of water. With it came the hail, as big as peas, bouncing two or three feet high and rattling on the glass above the veranda, falling with a special violence so that the earth seemed to quiver like a drumskin.

The Stettnerhof was full of people when the storm came and no one one seemed to want to move away, and singing started in the bar for the first time since the explosion. No one had wanted to sing since then and everyone had sat around in quiet groups—even the archaeologists, who were normally a noisy lot —but now they were all in the bar, and young Dittli, a little pale and subdued, was struggling to keep them all supplied with drinks.

Stettner was sitting at a table with Maggie, drinking beer, but not laughing like the others. Once or twice cheerful shouts were flung across at Henry—things like "Up the Saboteurs!" and

126

"The dam's gone!"—then the accordionist got going, a little drunk as usual, and the singing started. Stettner, who was wearing knee breeches and the black flowered waistcoat of the locality, did a Tryolean dance with another man, with a lot of knee slapping and shouting, but though everybody cheered, his expression didn't soften. Not long afterward they pushed the tables back and Henry plucked up courage to ask Maggie Daniells to dance.

She danced well, but she seemed to have it in her mind that he might be trying to influence her toward his views on the dam in some way. They talked about Lazzaro's barge, but neither of them with much enthusiasm, then Stettner tapped his shoulder and excused him. His face was hard and unfriendly.

"Why don't you go home, Englishman?" he whispered. His eyes were burning with enmity and his heavy features were masked with arrogance and a stiff expression of contempt.

As he returned to his table, Henry saw he was holding Maggie very close, whispering into her ear, but she was frowning and shaking her head, her face troubled.

Then the accordionist vanished to the bar and someone started the jukebox going. A plummy voice began to wail "How can ah fergit?" in English, and behind it there was a chorus of what sounded like a lot of mad ferrets yelping "Fergit, fergit, fergit," and Henry saw that Maggie had escaped from Stettner and was dancing with Frank Maggs.

There was a lot of noise and smoke and, in spite of the rain, it was very warm. Maggie seemed to be busy, and in the end Henry decided to go to bed. As he crossed the hall he met Caporelli at the foot of the stairs. He looked tired, as though he'd been driving all day, but he seemed excited and triumphant.

"What weather!" he said, shaking the water off his coat. "It was like driving through a lake. But it was worth it. It was well worth it."

"Worth it? Why?"

127

Caporelli's eyes flickered sideways and his whole manner shrieked out loud of some guilty secret. "I've got it," he said.

"Got what?"

Caporelli paused as young Dittli came past with a tray of drinks.

"In here," he said, indicating his office.

He shut the door carefully behind them and spoke softly. "I've been to Florence," he said. "I saw my cousin. It wasn't difficult to adjust the books. It's in the boot of the car."

"What is, for God's sake?" Henry said, though he knew all the time what Caporelli was getting at.

"Plastic, Aynree. Pentolite."

Henry turned at once and headed for the door, but Caporelli stepped in front of him and put his back against it.

"Look, Ettore," Henry said patiently. "I'm having nothing to do with it!"

"But it's there. In the trunk of the car! In the garage. Also locked. It's perfectly safe. It's in the center of a crate of tinned fruit. I left it there till tomorrow when I can unload it and get it into the safe."

"Look," Henry said, lowering his voice to match Caporelli's. "What the hell are you going to do with it?"

"You know what I am going to do. There's no danger. I've done it before—during the war. It means a lot of climbing, of course, to get up to the stopper wall, but that's nothing. You can do the lifting. I will give the orders."

He gave Henry a flashing smile, but it only had the effect of unnerving him further. "You must be mad," he said. "The mountains are full of police. I saw two only today. It's only three days since they blew the railway track. If they find you with that damned stuff, they'll shoot you. They'd never believe you."

The rain rattled against the window and they heard the bang of thunder. Caporelli gestured fiercely, his smile gone.

"Listen," he said. "I told you there would be storms. Well, here they are. Right on schedule. With the exception of last week, we've had this on and off all spring and what we've had of summer. The mountains have been absorbing moisture all the time. The snow has all melted from the tops. It's rained constantly and it's getting worse. The feeders will be like millraces tonight. Have you seen the stream through the town? I have. I stopped to look. It's like a torrent. It's washed away some of the bank farther down, and they tell me the footbridge's gone at Madonna del Piano."

"That's your affair," Henry insisted furiously. "Not mine. I don't live in Cadivescovo."

Caporelli looked at him quietly, willing him to listen. "Perhaps you should," he said. "Then you would know about the Brenner railroad, and the alpine mountain clubs and the Volksbund that fostered German feeling for a century. You would know how Trentino was an Austrian wedge thrust into your homeland and you would have watched German language and education and trade increase and watched them raise a statue to Von der Vogelweide because you had one of Dante. You would have seen Lake Garda become Gardasee and Lake Colleno become Collenosee. You would know *all* these things."

His manner stopped Henry's anger for a moment, then he brushed it aside again. "It's not my affair," he said. "God knows, I've heard enough of both sides now to know what it's all about—first you, then Stettner, then you again, then Dittli. I saw him up the mountain today. There's something between him and Stettner."

"Boy friends, perhaps." Caporelli grinned. "Dittli is a little odd, I suppose. A *feminella* perhaps."

"Come off it, Ettore," Henry said angrily. "You know it's not that."

"No." Caporelli's grin vanished. "I joke, of course. But why

129

should there be something between them, except their interest in the Volkspartei."

"I saw young Dittli with Wasescha and I nearly got myself brained by a rock that Alois kicked down."

Caporelli grinned again. "He has no love for you, my friend. He's noticed how the Signorina Daniells looks at you."

"Looks at me? How *does* she look at me?"

Caporelli kissed his finger tips.

"I've never seen her," Henry said.

"This is because you are blinded with anger that we are not allowed to empty our dam over her discoveries."

"I don't give a damn about her discoveries," Henry snapped. "I've told you. It's no business of mine. And neither is this. I've got a desk full of work waiting at home for me. You must sort it out yourself."

"You are backing out, Aynree?"

"I've never been in. I'm not responsible for the dam. Only for giving my opinion, that's all. And I've done that."

"It's up to you to see that your opinion's implemented by action. There's no other way. You saw for yourself. We can do it two nights from now. I'll need tomorrow to collect the rest of the equipment."

With his Italian love of the dramatic, Caporelli was looking like a criminal again, his eyes moving sideways all the time so that Henry felt that everyone who crossed the hall could read his thoughts through the glass partition. Dittli passed again with a tray of empty glasses, and Henry wished to God Caporelli would shut up. But he continued to press him, his back against the door, gesturing with his hands.

"No," Henry said furiously. "I said no and I mean no."

"But, Aynree, we are ready."

"No. I'm leaving, after all. And don't tell me this time that the police are going to stop me, because they're not. Not even if I have to hire a car to take me to Trepizano."

Henry could see Caporelli watching him with sad eyes as he left the office, and he went up to his room feeling as if he'd a ton weight on his shoulders.

His mind was far too full of things to sleep and, long after he'd turned the light out, he switched it on again and tried to read, propped up in bed below the thoughtful brown wood Christ on the Crucifix above his head.

The singing downstairs had stopped at last and the hotel seemed to be silent. Then he heard Maggie Daniells enter the room next door and start moving about, and he guessed that everybody was just coming to bed. He heard drawers being opened and shut and wondered if she'd had enough of Stettner at last and was thinking of leaving too.

It was disturbing listening to her because she interested him more than he liked to admit to himself, and just then, if he could have trusted her to keep it to herself, he'd have been glad to unload what was on his mind. She wasn't worldly-wise and sometimes he had a feeling that her sense of purpose was all a pose, but she was intelligent and warmhearted and somehow he felt she'd have understood.

He picked up the book he'd been reading and was just drowsing over it when he sat up abruptly, thinking he'd heard someone cry out. He felt cold in the damp air of the storm and got down under the sheets, imagining he'd been dreaming, but then he heard the cry again.

"Go away, you fool!"

It was quite plain this time, in Maggie Daniells' voice from the room next door, tense and sharp.

He heard the low rumble of a man's voice and then the girl's voice once more. "Go away. Please go away."

Henry sat up on one elbow, then there was a thud and a short low scream, and he found himself out of bed and reaching for his dressing gown.

131

As he tied the cord, he stopped dead again. What the devil was it to do with him, he thought. The girl could have whom she liked in her room. It was her affair.

There was another thud and another short scream that was broken off abruptly as though a hand had been placed over her mouth, and, interested or not, Henry found himself in the corridor and jerking the handle of her door.

There was an immediate dead silence beyond, then he heard Maggie's voice. "Come in. Please come in."

"Open the damn door then."

There was a muttering from the other side, then the key clicked in the lock and the door opened, and Henry found himself facing a smiling Stettner. He looked a little flushed and bright-eyed, as though he'd been drinking, and he stared arrogantly at Henry, the gold on his teeth gleaming in the light from the corridor.

All the old well-worn phrases ran through Henry's head—"What are you doing in this lady's room?"—but they sounded like something out of a bad film, and in the end he did nothing but stand there, feeling foolish, as though he'd broken into something that didn't concern him. Then he saw Maggie behind Stettner and he felt almost as though he ought to throw back his head and say, "Unhand her, villain!" It was a classic situation and Henry had a feeling he ought to play it the classic way. There was even thunder and rain lashing at the windows outside.

For a long time there was silence in the room, then Henry glanced at Maggie again and saw her eyes were big and frightened.

"Please don't go," she said quickly, and he looked at Stettner, unable for the life of him to think of anything to say that didn't sound melodramatic.

"No, don't go." Stettner grinned with another flash of gold

teeth. "*I'm* going. Favors which were welcome before seem to have turned sour all of a sudden."

"You'd better shove off." Henry found his voice at last.

"What would you do if I didn't, little Englishman?"

Henry measured himself against Stettner. He was bigger than Henry was, stronger and undoubtedly fitter, but if it came to a passage of arms, he saw he couldn't back out and ever look Maggie in the face again.

Before he could reply, Stettner raised his hand. Henry thought he was going to hit him and ducked instinctively, but he merely dropped the hand on Henry's shoulder, and Henry straightened his head, flushing and feeling foolish.

"She's yours, my friend," Stettner said gaily. "There are others far more willing and far more exciting. I've been wasting my time."

His fingers tightened on Henry's shoulder, strong and hard, and Henry knew he'd done it just to show how powerful he was. Then he was gone, striding down the corridor toward the stairs.

Henry stared after him for a second, then he became aware for the first time of the draft around his legs. The double windows were open and the rain was spotting the floor.

"Is that the way he came?" he asked.

Maggie nodded.

"He likes drama," Henry commented. "Or is it romance?"

As they moved to close the windows, Stettner was just crossing the courtyard through the rain. The lightning flashed and they saw his huddled figure disappearing into the shadows. Henry turned and saw that Maggie had put on a dressing gown of yellow nylon that suited her dark hair and showed slightly less of the disturbing brown skin beneath.

"I didn't ask him to come here," she said shortly.

"No, I don't suppose so." Although Henry hadn't intended it, it sounded as though he didn't believe her.

133

"Truly I didn't."

"Of course not."

She glanced round and indicated her bag on the floor, its contents spilled out in a heap.

"He dropped that," she pointed out. "I think he had it in his hand."

"Perhaps he was short of cash," Henry said. "Though I wouldn't have thought that even Alois would have descended to that."

Again it seemed to indicate that he didn't believe her, and they were stiff and awkward with each other, both of them faintly embarrassed by the situation. Henry turned toward the door, suddenly wishing he could get back to his own room, but panic flared unexpectedly in her eyes.

"Don't go," she begged. "He might come back."

"I shouldn't think so."

"All the same—just for a moment."

Henry hesitated, and it was her turn to be uncomfortable.

"Of course, if it's a nuisance—"

"It isn't a nuisance."

She didn't seem to believe him and she suddenly grew angry. "You can go if you wish," she said. "I'll be all right. I'm sure you don't want to stay."

She looked up at him and he saw to his surprise that there were tears in her eyes. "Why do we spend all the time quarreling?" she asked.

"I've no quarrel with you," Henry pointed out quietly, trying to sound as friendly as he could. "Quite the contrary, in fact."

She looked happier. "I suppose I ought to offer you a drink or something," she said. She managed a smile. "This is an odd situation, isn't it, asking a man into your room at this time of the night for a drink."

She was fiddling with the dark glasses and seemed about to put them on.

134

"No," Henry said impulsively. "Don't!"

She looked up, startled, then she seemed embarrassed and suddenly very young. "It saves having to look at people," she explained quietly. "I find them useful sometimes to hide behind."

She picked up her bag and began to replace the contents. "Why are you so insistent about the dam?" she asked unexpectedly, her back to him.

She seemed to be trying to push aside their habitual antagonism, and he answered gently with another question, "Why are you so insistent about Arcuneum?"

"Because that's what I believe."

"That's my answer too."

She looked serious. "Is it *really* unsafe?"

"You asked me that once before, but you didn't believe me when I said it was."

She gazed up at him, her eyes frank and friendly. "Perhaps I ought to look at it," she said impulsively.

"Would you like to?"

"You came to look at *my* work," she pointed out. "I ought in all fairness to have a look at yours." She paused, smiling. "I can't guarantee to agree, though. *You* didn't. I know you didn't. *I* can't promise to, either."

"You don't have to," Henry said. "I'll take you. Tomorrow. As a matter of fact, I was leaving tomorrow, but I don't suppose another day will matter." She hesitated, and Henry was afraid for a moment that he was going too fast. "Wear stout shoes," he suggested. "There's a lot of water around up there."

She opened the door for him.

"Lock it after me," he said. *"And* the window. In case of trouble, bang on the wall. I don't know whether I'd be strong enough to hold him off if he were really determined, but I'll have a go."

Back in his own room, Henry sat on the bed, staring at him-

135

self in the mirror. He heard a car move off across the gravel of the courtyard and realized from the engine tone that it was Caporelli's Alfa Romeo, and he wondered where he was going with it. To get rid of what he'd got in the trunk, he decided, and he hoped he knew somewhere safe.

Then he forgot Caporelli because he was feeling vaguely elated and disturbed. He had the feeling of having won a major victory somehow. He'd never in his life found it easy to make contact with people. He'd always found it simpler to pronounce sentence on a hundred thousand pounds' worth of shoddy workmanship than ask a girl for a date, but now he seemed to have broken through. They'd both let their defenses down a fraction and things were a little easier.

He stood up quickly and kicked his slippers across the bedroom with a gesture of wild indifference to where they landed that was completely unlike him, and vaulted into bed.

10

Henry woke early. The sun was out again and the storm had died away, though there were still dark clouds on the Catena di Saga. He was drowsily thinking about Maggie and wondering if they could take a bottle of wine with them and some bread and sausage and make a day of it on the mountain, when he heard someone walking quickly along the corridor outside. The thump of a fist shook the door.

The door handle turned and Caporelli's face appeared. He looked drawn and sick with worry.

"Forgive me," he said. "I didn't know if you'd be here—"

"Where else would I be?"

"Alois said you'd been—" Caporelli cocked a thumb in the direction of the room next door.

Henry flushed. "That wasn't me," he said. "That was him."

Caporelli hardly seemed to hear him. He slipped inside and locked the door behind him, secretive and conspiratorial, and Henry began to wish he'd made arrangements for an early start and got himself and Maggie up the mountain before Caporelli could put in an appearance.

Then Caporelli's next words knocked all the annoyance out of him.

"It's gone," he said. "The car's gone. The box was in it."

Henry felt as though the floor had dropped away from him. He'd had no part in Caporelli's plot, but he knew he was involved, however slightly.

"Gone?" he said. "Where?"

Caporelli made a despairing gesture that was completely unlike him and beat on his forehead with a clenched fist.

"Where?" he said. "Who? Why? How? I don't know, Aynree. It's gone. That's all I know. I went this morning to check up. The garage lock had been forced. The car's gone. When I got there the doors were wide open."

Henry was sitting up in bed now. "What are you going to do?"

"What can I do? Nothing. Not yet. Suppose I report it to the police? Suppose they find it? They'd search the car with me to make sure nothing's missing. And suppose nothing is? Suppose they find what's in the box?"

Henry's mind boggled at the possibility. This would look fine in the university newspapers, he thought wildly. Senior lecturer imprisoned for trafficking in explosives. He felt himself going pale at the idea.

"Look," he said tensely. "You must be able to do something."

"Tell me what."

Henry shrugged hopelessly.

"Best to say nothing," Caporelli went on. "Probably some youngsters on their way home from the dance downstairs who knew the car was there. Though why bother to open a garage when there are dozens of cars outside the lake hotels every night I don't know."

"Do you think it was one of Hofer's people?"

Caporelli nodded, his face pale.

"God!" Henry's jaw dropped. "What'll he do with it?"

Caporelli shrugged. "We'd better wait and see what goes up," he said.

As it happened, they didn't have to wait long for information. Henry was having his breakfast when Caporelli sat down at his table.

"They've found it," he said quietly.

"The car?"

He nodded.

"Everything all right?"

Caporelli ignored the question. "It was on the lakeside," he said. "Doors open. Trunk open."

"Trunk open? It had gone?"

"Yes." Caporelli looked gray and sick and old. "The police rang. I pretended I didn't know—that I hadn't missed it. I went down and identified it. They asked me if anything was missing. I said some hotel linen and a case of tinned fruit from the boot. They didn't argue. I had to say something. People don't break open car boots except to steal something."

He lit a cigarette and indicated it with a wry smile. "About the four hundredth since I woke," he said.

Henry sipped his coffee. "What do we do now?" he asked slowly.

Caporelli's reply startled him. "Get some more," he said bluntly.

Henry put the cup down with a bang. "Count me out," he said. "I've had enough."

Caporelli leaned forward and drew on his cigarette. "It's still the only way," he said earnestly. "Those old fools at the Municipio will never give way. They have too many interests.

139

One of them runs a shop. Another runs a hotel. A third a garage. A fourth has an ambitious wife."

"Good God, man," Henry pointed out indignantly, "if you get some more, they'll probably pinch that too. I'm not here to feed Hofer's boys with plastic."

Caporelli leaned forward again eagerly. "They told me you stood up to Nasser himself over that breakwater," he said. "Because you considered it unsafe. They tell me they threatened to put you in prison because you started accusing people of corruption. You can't risk imprisonment for a belief in one country and back out for the same belief in another."

"Oh, for God's sake, leave me alone," Henry said bitterly. "Find somebody else! Get Stettner! He'll have a go at anything, so long as there's cash in it."

"He'd turn up drunk!"

Something in Henry's mind jarred suddenly and he felt he ought to remember it, but he couldn't. For a moment he struggled with it, then let it go. Caporelli was still waiting, earnest, large-eyed, like some ugly little monkey with a doe's expression.

"During the war," he said slowly, "we learned that when things went wrong, we had to start all over again, not just sit down and cry over spilled milk."

"For God's sake, man, there isn't a war on now!"

"There is between me and Mornaghini. There's my hotel. There's the valley. There's the orphanage."

"I'm not interested."

Caporelli placed both his hands on the table and stood up. "Perhaps you're afraid," he said coldly. "Perhaps what I heard of you in Egypt was wrong."

Henry looked up at him and said nothing, and he slapped his hand down on the table.

"Doesn't anything ever rouse you to rage?" he demanded furiously.

140

Henry stared at his coffee, coldly angry, but unmoved.

"No?" Caporelli went on, calm again. "Nothing?" He sighed. "God help you," he said. "I'm glad I'm not an Englishman. You can't *feel*. Here!" He patted his chest. "Because you can't be roused, you've lost an empire. You've let the world walk all over you."

He stared at his fingers for a moment, then he turned away. "You are a good engineer, Aynree," he said. "But you could be a better one if you could feel enough to act sometimes instead of just believing."

After breakfast Henry went to the garage at the back of the hotel and took out Caporelli's Fiat van. The Alfa Romeo was standing nearby with the trunk open, and Caporelli was staring into it as though he hoped the missing box would suddenly materialize from nowhere.

He looked at Henry, his face expressionless, neither friendly nor hostile.

"I thought you were going home," he said.

"I am," Henry said shortly. "I'm going up to the dam first, though, to have another look."

"Take a pickax with you and dig a little hole in the side while you're up there," Caporelli suggested bitterly. His expression softened. "Will it, perhaps, change your mind?" he asked.

"No."

While they were talking, Maggie arrived and Henry noticed that for once she was wearing a dress and had left her dark glasses behind. Caporelli noticed it, too, and as Henry clumsily opened the door of the Fiat for her, he had to fight to hold back the flush on his neck.

"To have another look at the dam, eh?" Caporelli said quietly.

"Yes."

"You won't need a pickax, though, after all." He touched

Henry's arm. "Why the opposition?" he asked, indicating Maggie.

Henry felt a little stupid. "Might convince them," he muttered, knowing perfectly well that Caporelli would never believe him.

Caporelli gave him an accusing, unfriendly look, as though he were recovering his nerve a little and considered Henry had gone over to the enemy. *"L'amore,* eh?" he said. *"Le piccole solite scappatelle*—always the little escapades. There's a good spot right under the dam face. Lots of bushes. Nobody can see."

Henry climbed into the van, blushing furiously and confused enough to scrape the gears fiercely as he set off. He was so busy apologizing he almost knocked a man down as they left the courtyard, and he realized it was Stettner. He grinned and bowed ironically, and they shot past him, both staring furiously ahead, awkward still with each other and embarrassed at being caught together.

The car shot on to the road with screeching tires, setting a man with a mule shouting angrily after them, and Maggie shifted nervously in her seat.

"Dr. Chappell," she said gently. "If you want to get us both up to the dam, I suggest you go more slowly. The road's pretty twisty."

Henry slowed down abruptly. "Sorry," he said.

The look about the mountains of ruined masonry seemed more realistic than usual. They appeared less like rock formations than the bleached skeletons of some vast animal that had long ago died, ghostly and terrible in their size and silence.

Henry deliberately stopped the van in the shadow of the great stone wall of the dam, just above Oswino's farm, feeling that there she would sense the danger more. He got out and opened the door for her, and she climbed slowly out and stared up at the gray wall that sprouted grass along the cracks and fissures.

142

Water was running down the face through the concrete patches after the rain, and the sound of it filled their ears, rushing and noisy above the sound of the wind in the trees. Awed by its size, for a while she said nothing, simply staring upward at the vast stone barrier.

"I've never been up here before," she said quietly. "I've always been too busy."

"You should come more often," Henry said, running his hand through his hair. "You get the feeling of decay better here."

"Can't it be repaired?" she asked.

"It could. At a cost. But, apart from your excavations, there's no point. It does nothing. It should be emptied and left empty. It must have started deteriorating the day it was built. They'd already spent a fortune repairing it before it was properly operative. It just grew, you see."

She stood beside him, small and silent, listening as he talked.

"It was an inferior piece of work anyway," Henry went on. "The original dam was all right, but the new one wasn't. It was too big. It's been sprouting leaks all its life and all they ever did was stop them up."

"I never realized it was like this."

Henry glanced up. "It looks like the wall of a bird's nest," he commented. "And not a very fussy bird, at that. It's been a joke for years. See that crack?" he said, indicating the water pouring from the dam. "They're all over the face of the wall. It's like a watering can. The gates are jammed with rubbish. A stone culvert underneath collapsed in 1944 and washed out part of the wall a hundred feet wide and twenty feet deep. The discharge pipes were opened to take the pressure off, but no repairs were made. Nobody had time. There was a war on and the Germans were being chased. Everybody wanted to finish the war

143

first. It was repaired with tree stumps, sand, clay, branches, anything that was at hand. And as it held, nobody bothered to put it right later. There was too much bomb damage to repair."

He offered her a cigarette and they walked slowly back to the van. Inside, she sat staring up at the wall for a while before she spoke.

"What would happen if it *were* drained?" she asked. "To the Punta dei Fiori, I mean." For once the question wasn't hostile.

"There'd be mud, of course. You know about that. And sand and gravel from lower down. But the flow could be controlled. And as you've got all the sites marked, it wouldn't make much difference, and you could use pressure hoses to wash it away."

A few heavy drops of rain fell, exploding against the windscreen of the van and on the flat surfaces of the rocks.

"I think we'd better go," Henry said. "Here it comes again."

He started the engine and began to reverse. She looked at him curiously. "How long do you think it will last?" she asked.

"I wouldn't like to bet on it lasting the winter."

"As simple as that?"

"As simple as that."

She threw her cigarette out of the window. "I shan't be able to sleep at night now." She smiled. "I shall be listening all the time for the bang."

He started the engine and they set off down the hill toward Oswino's farm. The road was steep, but the feeling that he had won her to his way of thinking at last was so strong that he enjoyed swinging the van around the corners above the drops to the meadows below.

"It would be nice to get down all in one piece, Dr. Chappell," she said, but he knew she shared his feeling of happiness and was not afraid.

They were laughing together as they passed Oswino's farm. The fact that Oswino's car was standing just by the gate registered itself on Henry's mind, but he thought nothing of it because, briefly, a little higher up, he'd seen Oswino standing in the roadway staring upward toward them, but as they turned the corner, the car shot abruptly out of the gate across their path, and what had been fun suddenly became terrifying.

With the laughter still frozen on his face, Henry fought with the wheel of the van, seeing the drop swing in front of him, rocketing across his view in a blur of trees and fields, and he felt the vehicle swing violently as he swerved to avoid Oswino. He saw the farmer's narrow face flash past him, full of concentration, as though he'd been busy and hadn't noticed them, then the fender of the van hit the fence on the edge of the road and, as he fought it to a standstill, he saw a splintered piece of timber go arcing away ahead of them and drop into the meadow below.

They jerked back in their seats and everything became quiet after the screech of tires and the roar of the engine. Henry drew a deep breath.

"I'm sorry," he said quietly. "That was very stupid of me."

"It was very stupid of *him*," Maggie said in a shaking voice. "He wasn't looking. He might have killed us."

They climbed out and walked back to where Oswino was sitting in his car, his thin face wearing a shut-down, wary expression.

"I'm sorry, Signore," he said at once. "I didn't see you. I was busy thinking. I'm always thinking these days, Herr Doktor." His voice became a whine. "I have too much on my mind. I get worried. About the dam."

Maggie's eyes met Henry's and he was almost glad for a moment that Oswino had been so careless. It seemed to bring home even more to her what he had been trying to tell her.

"Why?" she was asking. "Why are you worried about the dam?"

Oswino leaned on the wheel. "Wouldn't *you* be worried about the dam if you lived here?" he said. "Eating your breakfast every morning with the shadow of that thing across the house. Going to bed at night with the sun on it, to remind you always that it's there and that there's a lake a mile long behind it ready to drop on you." He looked at Henry earnestly. "Herr Doktor," he said, "I'd be grateful if you didn't report this. I've been in enough trouble with the police over my driving already. Living up here, you see, you get so you don't expect traffic."

Apart from a dented mudguard, there appeared to be little wrong with the van and they agreed to say nothing. Oswino asked them back to the house for a drink, but there was something about the little farmer that repelled Henry, and he refused. Full of apologies, Oswino reversed his car off the road. His wife had appeared in front of the house and he stopped the car to pick her up. As he disappeared, Maggie stood staring back at the gray wall of the dam, then she turned to Henry and gave him a wry smile.

"It seems you're not the only one who's worried," she said. "I'm sorry I was always so rude about it. I just didn't realize."

Henry said nothing and she fiddled uncomfortably with a scarf she'd brought for her hair.

"I don't know what I can do to help," she added.

"You should try getting Dei Monti up here," Henry suggested.

She smiled. "I haven't a chance. He's like a dog with a bone between his teeth. But I'll try."

Henry felt a desperate desire to tell her there and then what Caporelli had suggested, as though it were a guilt of his own he needed to share. He looked up at the lowering clouds and in a burst of confidence, feeling he could trust her, the need to get some of his secret off his chest broke out of him.

"If Caporelli had his way," he said, "the water would have been running into the Punta dei Fiori tomorrow."

146

She looked up at him quickly and he explained. "He wanted to blow a gate out of the stopper wall," he said.

She stared at him for a long time as he finished, and he couldn't tell whether it was contempt in her eyes or not.

"Would he have done it?" she asked.

"If I'd been willing to help. As it happens, though, the explosive's gone. I think some of these damn fools who're blowing up the railways have got it. I've been waiting for the police to arrive ever since. I might have to leave in a hurry. It was quite a night last night. First Stettner and then this."

"Perhaps Alois took the car," she suggested. "He went away by car. Perhaps he took the car in case we called the police."

What had been worrying Henry fell into place. He had heard a car leave, too, and he knew he'd never heard one arrive.

"Maybe he did," he said. "I expect he had some other girl friend to see. I suppose he just left it in the square where it was found, and someone came across it and broke it open and found what was in it." He paused, thinking of Dittli and the man he'd seen on the mountain. "I wouldn't put it past him to open the damned boot himself," he ended, "and sell the stuff. I expect he's got contacts with the opposition."

By the time they reached Cadivescovo again, great clouds were piling up into thunderheads, black below and building up in great breastworks of hail and rain that moved over the lake in a gray screen. The rain came again, in huge drops that splashed into the road and ran in noisy streams along the gutters. There was hail in it, too, and more dark masses were lurching up the valley at the end of the lake. The boats by the Punta dei Fiori had stopped work and now huddled against the mole. Sister Ursula had long since marched her charges back to the orphanage.

There were only a few people about in the town, hurrying along in the shelter of the walls, and the courtyard of the

Stettnerhof was like a quagmire around their ankles as they splashed from the Fiat to the door.

A group of Dei Monti's archaeologists in the bar looked up as they entered.

"Out with the opposition, Maggie?" Frank Maggs called.

Maggie blushed, and the group split up and came over to her.

"I hope you enjoyed yourself," Maggs said. "Because *we* didn't."

She looked unhappy. "It'll stop raining tomorrow," she said.

"It's not the rain I'm talking about. The cross's gone."

Maggie's hands flew to her mouth. "The altar cross?" she whispered. "The gold altar cross?"

Maggs nodded. "It was there when the kids were putting the things away last night," he said. "I saw it. They all swore it was there. But it wasn't there this morning. We searched the whole bloody Customs House."

Maggie's eyes looked frightened. "Where's it gone?" she asked.

Maggs shrugged, an expression of disgust on his face. "God knows," he said. "These bloody plasticeurs, I expect. They'll put it on a pole up the mountain and declare Tyrolean independence around it."

11

Maggie stood in silence for a moment, her hands at her throat, then she slowly turned around and went into the hall. Maggs watched her, then he swung back to the bar with a gesture of disgust.

Henry came to life and followed her, but she was already running up the stairs. He ran after her and was just in time to see her door slam. He opened it and went in.

She was sitting on the edge of the bed, a shocked look on her face, tears starting in her eyes.

"Maggie!"

She turned a horrified, beaten look toward him, and suddenly her face crumpled and she began to cry in great sobs that shook her whole frame. Henry put his arm around her and, without embarrassment, she crouched against him, sobbing.

"It's not your fault," he said.

"No, I know. It's not that. Going up the mountain made no

difference. It would have gone just the same. It's just that—well, everything's just gone wrong."

"Nothing's gone wrong."

"Yes, it has. Everything. All the way along. And now this. Dei Monti's going to insist on removing everything now—even Lazzaro's cross if he can get it."

Henry lifted her chin. "Listen," he said. "Don't let's despair too soon. Let's go and see Dei Monti first and see what he feels."

"Do you think it'll help?"

"It'll do no harm."

She nodded and Henry kissed her. He didn't think much about it and the gesture was quite natural and impulsive. For a second she sat still, staring at him as though she were surprised, then she blew her nose and got to her feet.

Dei Monti was in his hotel near the Municipio, and he was pale with rage.

"Politics!" he said. "Politics! What have politics to do with us? There were no politics when Lazzaro was drowned! Why do we have to be involved with politics?"

He'd stared bitterly at Henry as he'd followed Maggie into the room, almost as though he held him responsible for the disappearance of the altar cross. He'd confirmed its absence with a sour nod, then he'd exploded into disgust.

"We must move everything," he said. "Everything!"

"But, Professor," Maggie tried to reason with him, "we gave an understanding that we'd leave everything here. That was why everyone agreed to help us. Because we were leaving everything that we found here in Cadivescovo."

"Here?" Dei Monti seemed thunderstruck. "Here? In this bear garden? One of their damned explosions might blow the lot of us to perdition! How can I leave things here when some stupid fool might steal the lot? They've already threatened to

150

steal the cross from the church for some stupid political stunt. Erect it on the mountains and fly the Austrian colors from it, I suppose, or carry it on a float at the head of a demonstration march in Bolzano, complete with brass bands and police escort and shouted slogans and placards demanding freedom. Lazzaro's Cross of Christ!"

"Professor," Maggie begged, "we *must* leave everything here. We promised."

"If they break their promises, we break ours! Everything goes to Venice! Or even to Rome, where we can place a substantial guard over it. We'll continue our work, but everything we find will be sent away at once, accompanied by someone responsible, not a lot of orphans from a poorhouse."

"Professor, you can't!"

"Can't?" His deep black eyes flared fanatically. "Can't? Who says I can't? Of course I can! I am responsible not only to archaeology but to Christianity to see that these relics are kept safe! Every one of them! We start moving them tomorrow!"

By next morning the whole archaeological team was on the mole outside the old Customs House, dragging crates about and struggling with piles of shavings that blew about in the cool breeze. There was a great deal of shouting and angry youngsters busy with bottles of Indian ink, balls of twines, and labels. Watched by the policemen who stood guard at night over their treasures, they looked sullen and uneasy, as though some of them were in flat disagreement with Dei Monti themselves. Dei Monti moved about among the crates, stiff and unbending, gesturing with the jerkiness of uncontrolled anger, and Sister Ursula stood on one side with her children, completely ignored, as though they'd been discarded. She had her hand on Giovanni's shoulder, occasionally passing her fingers gently over his hair, and the boy kept glancing up at her, puzzled and frowning and faintly resentful, as though he were angry at having his job taken away from him. He was silent and strained-looking, as though they'd been questioning him about the missing altar cross.

Maggie was there, also, but she was standing alone like Sister Ursula, no longer a part of what was going on. She accepted Henry's offer of coffee and crossed the square with him to a small café, where a linnet in a wooden cage was liquidly lamenting its incarceration, and sat staring gloomily at her cup under the dripping oleanders.

"They don't trust me any more," she said. "I have the key to the Customs House and the explosives, and that's about the lot. And as we're not using explosives any more, and everything we've found will soon be gone, even that hasn't much point.

"The worst of it," she ended, "is that I can't feel very indignant about it." She looked unhappily at Henry. "I find I'm suddenly not on their side any more."

She fiddled with her cup, then said unexpectedly, "Why did you take me up there? All that we're doing here doesn't seem very important since I came back."

She walked slowly back to the Stettnerhof with Henry, but she was silent and indifferent to him, as though she didn't know to which side she belonged. When the archaeologists appeared at lunch time, they all ignored her except Stettner, who slipped his arm around her waist as usual. She didn't push it away, but she gave him a bitter look that caused him to take it away himself.

She made no attempt to eat with the rest of the group but sat with Henry, picking at her food in silence, neither of them saying much because Caporelli was still aloof and silent and Henry felt like an outcast too.

He had described the damage he had done to the van and had offered to pay for its repair, but Caporelli had shrugged the matter off and told him not to worry, in a tone that only served to make him feel worse about it.

"What does it matter?" he had said unconcernedly. "I already have to claim for the damage to the Alfa. What is another one between friends? The insurance company will pay."

The bar and dining room were warm, the windows blurred by the condensation from the coolness of the rain that came in thin, slanting drizzles from the north. Everybody had newspapers with blazing headlines.

It was obvious everyone in the village had heard what was going on, and there were a few surly glances in the direction of Dei Monti's group.

"These things belong to Cadivescovo," Henry heard someone say. "They're ours. They were always ours."

"Was anything *ever* ours?" Dittli said, bringing the coffee from behind the bar. "Did we ever have *anything?* My father said it started disappearing in 1919 and it's never come back."

Caporelli had appeared in the doorway and Henry saw Dittli flash him a scared glance, then Caporelli followed him behind the bar.

"Not here," he said fiercely, gesturing with the flat of his hand. "Not here, you understand? Your views are your own, but don't express them here."

"Leave him be, Ettore," one of the diners called out. "He's only saying what we all think."

"*You* can think and say what you like," Caporelli said. "You pay to come here. He doesn't. He keeps his mouth shut on his views in the public rooms—like me."

Maggie listened to the talk in silence, then she got up, leaving her coffee untouched, and said she'd like to go to her room for a while. Henry walked with her to the foot of the stairs, then, as she turned away, he saw Caporelli by the office and stopped.

"The boy in hospital." Caporelli said harshly. "The one who was blinded. He's died. That makes two. It'll mean more trouble. Someone will be bound to demonstrate. A wreath on the

Hoferdenkmal. A few arrests. More grief. More mothers weeping. More boys hurt. I wonder when this valley will be normal again."

It rained a lot during the afternoon and Henry hung around the hotel lounge in case Maggie appeared. He could hear the talk in the bar; there was obviously a lot of dissatisfaction in the town at Dei Monti's cavalier decision.

Somebody had produced a copy of *Dolomiten* and was reading from the leader article. " 'The Sudtyroler Volkspartei was not responsible for the theft,' " he was saying. " 'But it should be made clear that the party is firmly behind the motive that prompted it. Father Lazarus was a Viennese and the stolen object, like all the others, belongs in the Tyrol.' "

"They say Father Anselmo's sitting at the foot of the cross with a shotgun," Caporelli said cynically. "And Father Gianpiero at the head with another. They even say the Bishop of Trepizano has offered to take a watch, too, with the man from the Vatican Library in the sacristy to supply them with coffee. Dei Monti'll not get the cross away from Cadivescovo in a hurry."

The papers that came on the afternoon boat from Trepizano had exploded into a vast controversy embroiling not only the lakeside and Rome but two countries. There was an interview with the cardinal who'd come up from the Vatican to investigate the "miracle," and he had stated categorically that all the treasures should go to Rome, where they belonged, to be surrounded by the ancient history of the Church they represented.

He was answered by a Communist deputy from Milan who had seized the opportunity to run down the Church which was always such a stumbling block to his party at election time: " 'The treasures belong to the people—and to the people where they were discovered. Not to the princes of the Church who are already overloaded with loot.' "

154

There was also a firm and dignified statement by Dei Monti. " 'We cannot take the chance of losing more of the treasures,' he'd said. 'Our discoveries undoubtedly belong in Cadivescovo but, while there is discord there and political disagreement, there is always the chance that they may be seized for political purposes and we cannot risk that with relics which should be above regional differences.' "

And finally, briefly, but very firmly, Father Anselmo's own pronouncement: " 'The Great Cross of Bishop Lazzaro will leave the Church of Lazzaro di Colleno only over my lifeless body.' "

12

There was enough rain during the night to make Henry anxious about the dam again. The hours of darkness became a meteorological nightmare, with the wind roaring in the trees and the rain drumming on the leaves outside the windows.

He woke to the rushing sound of water as the rain continued to pelt down, obscuring the lake with what looked like a heavy fog. There was lightning coming out of the blackness at the end of the valley toward the Punta dei Fiori and the low clouds were like dirty cotton wool behind Trepizano. He was glad when Caporelli suggested they go up the mountain again to examine the dam. The coolness between them nagged at him. It was impossible to feel deeply enough about something that he would probably never see again after he left, to encourage Caporelli in his mad scheme, but at the same time he had an uneasy feeling that he might have done more than he had.

Caporelli seemed to have recovered his good humor a little, however, though there was a current of anxiety and bitterness running through everything he said, and they were distantly polite with each other.

They drove to the slopes above the top of the dam and stared across the gray sheet of water to the spires of the Catena di Saga and La Spiga just behind, blurred by the mist. All they could hear in the breeze was the music of the pines and the rush of the feeder streams roaring into the lake. The rain was still falling in an unrelieved deluge, and they could smell more of it in the rinsed air and see it in the gray-blue light. There was still plenty to come. It didn't need a meteorologist to tell Henry that. The chill damp air and the ruffled gray water stirred by the squally wind, and the clouds rolling around the base of La Spiga were more than enough.

"The water's risen," Caporelli said at once, staring along the shore where an unexpected heron was fishing disinterestedly among the rocks.

"I'm not surprised," Henry agreed. "The feeders are probably pouring in three million gallons with every hour the rain goes on."

He gestured at the streams running into the lake which had become waterfalls overnight, bursting over the crags in great foaming cascades that were atomized by the breeze into clouds of spray.

"They weren't like that last time we saw them," he said.

They climbed out of the car and examined the sluice gates again in a mood of desperate optimism, as though they half hoped that somehow, miraculously, during the night, the rusted machinery had freed itself. But they were still jammed with the rubbish of years and it would have taken an army of men to clear them, and the reddened iron was as solid as it had ever been.

On the way down they called at Dieter Oswino's farm. Oswino's wife was standing in the kitchen, underneath the calendar of St. Stephen's in Vienna. She had an old mackintosh over her shoulders like a cape, and her feet were in rubber boots. There was a sullen look of rebellion on her face.

"It's dangerous," Oswino said flatly in answer to Caporelli's questioning. There was a surly, suspicious look in his eyes and he gestured angrily with a brown knotted hand. "I called at the Municipio when I was in town yesterday. It's rising all the time. I've told them before, but nothing's ever been done. We keep getting rats around the farm from up there. They've been driven out by the flood, and I'm always having to shoot them. And the path keeps getting washed away with the water that's leaking out of it."

When they got back to Cadivescovo, Caporelli drove at once to the Municipio. Major Mornaghini was in his office, his face worried.

"I've been up there," he said defensively, retreating under Caporelli's immediate attack. "At dawn. We tried to take out the gratings, but we couldn't move them. They're not only jammed with rubbish, they're rusted solid."

"You could blow out the gate on the stopper wall," Caporelli suggested fiercely.

Mornaghini gestured quickly, nervously. "That's no good," he said. "We've been into all that and you know it won't work. We're not allowed to. I'm going to get some men up there to dig a spillway."

"You can't do it," Henry pointed out quietly. "There's too much rock. You'll never be able to take the pressure off. You'll never get deep enough."

"We must try, nevertheless."

"When?" Caporelli demanded.

Mornaghini looked hurt, his lined aristocratic face dull with the weight of the responsibility. "It will be done," he said. "I shall not forget, though I have so many other things to attend to."

"What other things?"

"Part of the Via Colleno's fallen into the lake, and there's been a landslide near Trepiazze. And I'm in constant demand by the police who wish to have this done or that done. Yesterday I was up at the railway track. They needed my advice. It meant almost a day's journey. In this weather too."

"The weather won't stop for *you,*" Caporelli said harshly. "Or the Montanari!"

"I am the authority, Signor Caporelli," Mornaghini said sharply. "Not you. *I* have to make the decisions. That's what I'm paid for, and I have to make my decisions in their order of importance. I shall be going up there again this afternoon."

"I just hope for your sake," Caporelli grated, "that the dam doesn't burst *this morning.*"

The rain seemed to go on endlessly, without the slightest relief in the downpour, and as he stared at the dripping roofs and the river of water coming down the hill below the rocky headland where the Stettnerhof stood, Henry could just imagine it higher up the mountain tearing away the soil like a powerful shovel as it rushed to its place in the dam.

The bar was full of Dei Monti's team, who stood by the windows, staring at the rain, suffering from depression and espresso stomachs.

"Goddam weather," Henry heard Maggs saying. "Does it *always* do this here?"

He had picked up a shabby tourist guide from a shelf by the counter and was staring at the spine. " 'Colleno, Lake of Beauty,' " he read out. "Oh, brother, listen to this: 'Storms on Lake Colleno are sudden and fierce, with hail and thunder and lightning and drama. But the lifting of the clouds brings unthought-of grandeur to the rock pinnacles around, which become as splendid as an army with banners.' " He glanced at the title page. " 'Stainer.' Published 1908. During the Austrian period of occupation. All the photos are here. Same as usual.

159

'Arzen mit Festung.' That's 'Cadivescovo with La Fortezza' in Austrian. *'Trepizano mit Cano.' 'Collenosee mit Sägekette.'* Like now." He touched the cup in front of him. "Coffee mit rum. Stettnerhof mit rain."

Henry listened to them, his eyes on the streaming windows and the shrouded mountains beyond. Up there the streams were filling and pouring into the dam, spreading their threatening loads in the silent dark waters behind that great gray wall that looked so strong and yet was so potentially dangerous.

Maggie didn't appear during the afternoon, and he learned she'd spent it with Dei Monti checking on the missing altar cross. Toward evening Caporelli, unable to stand it any longer as the rain lashed down, pushed Henry toward the Alfa Romeo and took him down to see Mornaghini again. Henry climbed out of the car still nagged by the feeling of having failed Caporelli but determined not to get himself involved.

Mornaghini was slumped at his desk, trying to work, but his face looked gray and haggard.

"We tried to start a spillway," he said. "But we couldn't get down as far as we wished to go. There was too much rock."

Caporelli gestured wildly at Henry who stood by the door watching them. "He told you there would be," he shouted fiercely. "He said so. I heard him. If the water flows over the top of that dam, it'll go."

"We got down a meter wide and a meter deep."

"*Madonna!*" Caporelli flung his arms up. "Pathetic. Ridiculous. Puerile. What good will that do?"

Mornaghini looked up, his eyes tragic. "We couldn't get any deeper," he said. "We tried. We couldn't hear ourselves speak. The sound of the water drowned our voices."

Caporelli sneered. "So what did you do?" he demanded.

Mornaghini's face lit up. "We've had a telephone line installed," he said. "I had the engineers go up there at once.

160

They'll be working now. From Oswino's instrument direct to my office. If there's any danger, he can telephone us. He can still use his own phone, of course," he ended irrelevantly.

Caporelli stared at him. "Ha," he snorted. "That's nice. He can still use his own phone! He can telephone all his girl friends and Alois can ring up his wife and make arrangements for a rendezvous!" He turned and thrust his face at Mornaghini and beat on his forehead. "Great God," he stormed. "What good does *that* do?"

Mornaghini pushed back in his chair to escape from the furious face. "We shall be warned," he said.

"It won't stop Cadivescovo ending up in the lake!"

Mornaghini lost his temper at Caporelli's bullying with the suddenness of a tired man who felt he had done all in his power. "Signor Caporelli," he shouted back. "I have been in touch with the Provincial Engineer at Trepizano as I promised! I can't flood the lake at the Punta dei Fiori! Not without authority! There'd be too many objections from too many sources! I've thrown the responsibility onto them!"

Caporelli whirled, his arms spread wide, his eyes blazing, and Henry suspected he was almost enjoying the drama of his appeal. "Typical," he said. "The civil service mind at work. Whirring like a broken clock to produce a result. And what have we got? Give someone else the baby. And what did the Provincial Engineer have to say?"

"He's promised to come over and look. He's asked me to send him a report at once."

Caporelli's hands came together with a loud smack just in front of Mornaghini's nose. "Of course," he said. "Of course! What did you expect? A report! More paper! Soon we shall all drown in paper. I have a file of paper on the dam fifty centimeters wide already."

Mornaghini stood up abruptly and slapped the desk. "I have no authority to act on my own," he stormed. "And the rain can't go on forever. It's June already. We are bound to get a lessening in the weather."

"How do you know? Have you had a word with God Himself?"

"There are forecasts."

"And have you read the forecasts?"

Mornaghini calmed down and smiled deprecatingly as though he found Caporelli's outbursts tiring. "We all know what these valleys can do," he said. "Tomorrow we might have brilliant sunshine lasting for weeks. That will take the strain off the dam and give us a chance to repair it. A lot can be done in a few weeks, and summer's almost here."

When he got back to the Stettnerhof, Caporelli went straight into his office to ring up some official he knew in Rome. "I might be able to do something," he said, but he didn't sound very hopeful.

As he vanished, Maggie appeared at the foot of the stairs. Her hair was wet, as though she'd been out in the rain.

"I've been to see Sister Ursula," she said. "She's very upset. Dei Monti told her he held her and the children responsible for the loss of the cross." She looked at Henry for a second, then she burst out angrily. "He'd no right to say that," she said.

"Perhaps he didn't really mean it," Henry suggested. "He's probably a bit overwrought like the rest of us."

"He'd still no right to say it," she insisted. "It was cruel and meaningless and unnecessary. Those children had no part in it. They can't be held responsible. Sister Ursula was wonderful about it, yet she knows that the children were relying on the pocket money to buy things."

She paused. "I went to see him to tell him what I thought."

"I don't suppose that did a lot of good," Henry said gently.

162

"No." She sighed. "It won't put things right for Sister Ursula and it won't give the children their jobs back. Giovanni's inconsolable. Sister Ursula said that for the first time she'd found him something that made him feel intelligent, something responsible that he needed because he *is* intelligent. Now he's sulky again. I think he feels he's been cheated and that outside the orphanage there are nothing but enemies."

"I don't think Dei Monti would take these things into consideration," Henry said. "Not just now."

She shook her head. "He said it was *my* fault, too," she whispered. "Because I was the one who suggested using the children to wash the things we brought up. I knew that was what he felt."

"He'll probably be around here tomorrow," Henry pointed out quietly, "ready to apologize for it. Give him the chance to see things clearly. He's a worried man and he's lashing out at anybody who's near."

It was all on television again during the evening. Cadivescovo seemed in the last fortnight or so to have occupied the greater part of the television news programs and an equal proportion of the columns on the front page of the newspapers.

They were all there again, all being interviewed, all looking worried and a little bewildered and tired—Dei Monti, Father Anselmo, the Mayor—some saying one thing, some another. There was a rain-washed picture of the archaeological group packing crates and a pen sketch of the missing cross by Frank Maggs. Maggie watched it with unhappy eyes, no longer a part of it, and when it had finished she insisted on going around to see Sister Ursula again.

"I must tell her what Dei Monti said," she told Henry. "I just must."

"It's still raining," Henry pointed out. "Can't I take you? I still have Caporelli's Fiat."

163

She shook her head and went off through the dripping trees, small and fragile-looking, no longer in the black clothes she'd affected, no longer wearing the dark glasses, and with her hair pinned up off her shoulders, as though she had suddenly become a normal human being again, disinterested in history or archaeology.

Henry almost bumped into Caporelli as he turned away. He seemed always to be standing behind him these days, his eyes accusing.

But this time Caporelli's face wore a shut-in expression and his mouth was tight. For once there seemed to be no hostility in his eyes.

"Aynree," he said, "come into my office. I want to tell you something."

Henry stared at him for a second, then followed. Caporelli closed the door behind him and turned the key in the lock.

"Did you get your friend in Rome?" Henry asked.

Caporelli gave a shrug, a bitter, hopeless shrug. "He wants a report," he said. "He merely wants to add to the pile of paper we have already."

"So you got nowhere?"

"No." Caporelli gestured irritatedly. "Look," he said, "haven't you noticed anything?"

Henry glanced around.

"Not here. Outside. In the bar. Dittli's left."

Henry glanced at the bar and realized the ski-instructor dish washer was there behind the counter. Even as he watched her wiping a glass, it came apart in her hands and he saw the comic look of dismay on her face.

"Well, I expect you can get someone else before long," he said.

Caporelli shrugged. "Yes," he said. "I can get some else. But do you know *why* he left?"

164

Henry stared at him, puzzled, and Caporelli gestured angrily.

"I had him in my office this afternoon," he said. "For airing his political views in the dining room. You heard him. We all know these people have political views, but nobody wants to hear them in a bar. Not from a waiter. Then I remembered he was there that night when we were talking about getting the pentolite from Florence, the night we were both on brandy. And I remembered he was in the hall when I was telling you I'd got it. I didn't say what I'd got, but he guessed all right."

Henry studied him, feeling curiously detached and thankful that he wasn't involved. "What did you do?"

"What could I do?" Caporelli said. "I couldn't hand him over to the police. Not without questions being asked. I told him he'd better take the boat to Trepizano and disappear quickly before I told Castelrossi. When he'd gone, I realized that the last boat had left already and I wondered where he'd go. So! I followed him. He went to Alois' room."

"Alois? Stettner? Has *he* got it?"

Caporelli shook his head. "I don't know," he said wearily. "He wasn't there. The door was locked. Yesterday I could have sworn he wasn't one of the Montanari. Now I'm not so sure."

"You don't think he's Hofer, for God's sake, do you?"

"I don't know. I don't know. Suddenly I know nothing and yet I know everything, all at the same time. Everything that has happened lately has happened in this valley, and Alois knows the place like the back of his hand."

"Does he know anything about explosives?"

"He did his service in the army."

There was agony in Caporelli's eyes. He was like a man with a demon on his back and no way of getting rid of it. Henry began to remember other things.

165

"The night the car disappeared," he said. "He was in Maggie's room. You remember? You thought it was me. She believed he was after her bag, to get some money. But Alois doesn't need money that badly, and she keeps the key to the old Customs House in that bag. And they store their explosives down there."

Caporelli stared, his face hardening, then he struck himself on the forehead with the heel of his hand and ruffled the papers on his desk in a distracted manner. The naked dilemma of the man was frightening. "It all hangs together," he said. "Dittli and Wasescha up the mountain. Alois' anger." He slapped the desk. "Aynree, that time when you were nearly hit by the rock, could that have been deliberate?"

"*I* think it *was* deliberate. Because I saw Wasescha. Stettner was as mad as a hornet."

Caporelli shook his head. "No, Aynree," he said. "Alois doesn't ever get that sort of mad. I think you should go home."

"Go home?"

"I thought you wanted to. If you stay here, you are going to get hurt. That was no accident with the rock."

"I never thought it was," Henry said slowly.

"You stumbled on the link between them all. You saw Dittli with Wasescha. It's only now that it begins to make sense. Nobody worried about Alois and Dittli being seen together. That was nothing, but seeing one of them with Wasescha made it dangerous. You've got yourself involved in more than we bargained for."

"Isn't there anything we can do? Can't we tell the police, for God's sake?"

"It could mean prison for me if too much comes out. And I can't go accusing people until I'm certain. I wish I knew where my box has gone, that's all. I just wish something would happen."

"Do you think something will?"

Caporelli raised his head and stared at Henry, his eyes steady. "People like those we saw in the Edelweiss don't steal pentolite to make fireworks," he said.

Maggie didn't turn up for dinner, and Henry guessed she was eating it with the children at the Orphanage of St. Francis. He knew it would please her because it would seem somehow like a penance for the unhappiness she had brought on them. He dined alone, his nerves fretted to screaming point and all his good intentions about remaining detached and uninvolved gone with the wind. Caporelli came to sit with him after a while, not eating, not even accusing any longer, and they shared a bottle of Lacrimae Vescovi, the holy wine of the valley, that he'd brought with him. He didn't say much, but his eyes still had their haunted look.

Afterward Henry borrowed an umbrella and walked alongside the lake, under the still-dripping trees, wishing it would just stop raining for a while. The lights on the mountain above Trepizano were blurred and he knew it was because the clouds were hugging the surface of the lake. He walked into the village, past the boat station, and had a drink in the Stöckli Bar, but he couldn't raise much enthusiasm, because he was suddenly as nervous as Caporelli.

The Stöckli was a small bar, paneled with wood and lit by an old-fashioned chandelier. It had once been used as a council meeting place in the days when Cadivescovo had been Arzen and Austrian, and the names of all the councilors were there on the walls, carved into the panels with the date of the first schoolroom and the first church and the first boat station. Henry recognized several of them and saw the name *Stettner* repeated several times, and somehow it seemed ominous.

He pushed his drink away eventually, not feeling like finishing it, and walked back to the lakeside. There was an odd policeman about, as usual, and Henry had an uneasy feeling that there ought to have been more of them. If they'd known what Caporelli knew and what he himself knew, and what the men who'd stolen the plastic from Caporelli's car knew, they'd have been sitting in their cars and vans outside the Questura, and there'd have been pressmen and television cameras on hand, waiting, like Henry was and Caporelli was, for the bang.

While he was standing under the trees, a man passed him carrying a brown paper parcel and heading toward the Piazza della Citta. He was in the shadows and it was difficult to see his face, but the very way he hurried made Henry turn and look around at him. As he crossed the square, he had to run from the path of a car, and Henry remembered he'd seen that run before, and with a start he realized he'd seen the man up on the mountain with Dittli. It was Wasescha, the man with the beard and the rucksack whom he'd seen on the day he'd gone climbing with Stettner, the man he'd seen by the dam when he'd first arrived.

He was still wondering what he was doing there in Cadivescovo and he had actually started across the square after him when he heard foot steps on the gravel behind him. He swung around and saw Maggie approaching at a run. He stopped and she caught up with him, panting.

For a moment he hesitated. He could still see the man with the parcel hurrying across the square, short and stocky, hugging his burden to his side.

"Maggie," he said, "that man! I've seen him before!"

She was too excited to listen. "Henry, I've something to tell you—"

Henry glanced back once more at the hurrying figure, then he decided he must have been mistaken. It couldn't have been Wasescha. Wasescha would surely never have been in the town with all the police in the district looking for him. He was obviously letting Caporelli's warning prey on his mind to the point of seeing enemies in every shadow.

"Let's have a coffee," he suggested.

"No! Not now! Not now!"

He stared at Maggie, who was gazing at him with bright, eager eyes. "What's happened?' he asked.

"We've found the altar cross! Come over here."

She drew him under the horse chestnuts again, where the barometer stood with the tourist map of the town and the lake, and the telescope that the children liked to put coins into, to see the mountains and the boats approaching from Trepizano. Henry dried one of the seats with a newspaper and they sat down. He had forgotten Wasescha now.

"Giovanni had it," she was saying, hardly able to get the words out for her excitement.

"The devil he had!"

"Yes. Sister Ursula told me. He took it for her. For Cadivescovo. He'd heard Dei Monti saying that everything ought to be moved and Sister Ursula saying it ought to stay here. You know how he is. He takes everything so deadly seriously. He thought he owed it to Cadivescovo and more particularly to Sister Ursula. She caught him with it."

"Good God!"

"Isn't it wonderful? Now they won't have to take everything away. It can all stay here in Cadivescovo."

"What about Giovanni?"

Her face fell. "They'll have to punish him, of course. Sister Ursula couldn't decide what to do. He'll not run away, though. He promised, and she knows when he promises her something he'll not break his word. He'll take his punishment all right. He was a bit hysterical when I saw him. He wasn't afraid, only upset because he'd done wrong."

"By God, he had," Henry said. "He nearly started a civil war. Does Dei Monti know?"

"Not yet. I offered to tell him, but Sister Ursula said it was her job."

"Has she gone?"

"She's gone to the police first. Because they've been up at the orphanage questioning the children. She thought she'd better take the cross to them."

Henry nodded. "What now then?"

She put her hand through his arm, naturally and without embarrassment. "I must leave the key to the Customs House," she said. "The police insist on it being signed for every day. It's the only job Dei Monti's left me. I might as well do it properly."

She smiled at him, all the misery gone from her expression. "Then I'm going to see Dei Monti," she said. "I want to get to him before Sister Ursula sees him. I want him to be kind to her."

They got to their feet and set off along the lakeside toward the Municipio and had turned into the Piazza della Citta when the roar of the bomb stopped them in their tracks. The buildings behind the Municipio were lit up by the flash that outlined the Hoferdenkmal in flaring yellow, and the crash of the explosion stopped everybody dead. For a second there was stunned silence, as though the whole town was listening, then they heard shouts and cries, and a low moaning sound as though someone were injured, and they saw the flickering of flames against the crumbling stone walls at the back of the Municipio.

"Oh, God, no!" Henry breathed.

Maggie had stopped alongside him, her face deathly white in the light of the street lamps and the shops.

"What was it?" she said.

"A bomb. Let's see where it was."

"No! Henry!" She'd never used his first name before and he stopped. "Don't! Don't go!"

"Maggie, I must! I must find out where it was. There might be someone in need of help."

"There might be another."

"I don't think so," Henry said grimly. "Look, go back to the hotel. Wait for me there. I won't stay. I promise."

She nodded, without arguing, and without really noticing whether she went or not, he entered the narrow streets of the old part of the town. Everybody was running now toward the glow of the flames, and the shouts were growing louder.

He saw a policeman staggering about without his cap, his face blackened, and blood running from a cut on his temple. A police car lay on its side with a man climbing slowly to his feet by the open door. Windows were gaping like blind eyes, and he felt glass crunch under his feet.

There was a flattened figure in black against the wall, holding a parcel, and flames were licking the woodwork where the door of the Questura had been. Policemen were running out through the flames now, their arms over their faces, shouting, all of them without their hats and some of them without their jackets, and he saw one or two people sitting in the roadway, their heads bent over their knees.

The ambulance came around the corner, the siren shrieking, almost knocking him down, and he pressed back against the wall to let it go by. There were already so many people about, bending over the sitting figures and kneeling by the flattened shape by the wall, he realized there was nothing much he could do.

He stood irresolutely for a moment, but other policemen were appearing now from an alley alongside the building, as though they were escaping from a back entrance, and he saw Inspector Castelrossi among them, hatless, shouting, and slightly unnerved like the rest of them, but clearly taking control, pushing people back against the walls and pointing.

Someone wrenched a torn awning from where it hung in tatters over the empty window of a smashed shop and threw it over the figure in black against the wall of the Questura, and others were helping the sitting figures to their feet and

171

pushing them into the ambulance. The crowd was filling the ends of the street, and Henry could hear the low murmur of outraged protest and anger rising from them in a swelling sound. It was like the baying of angry dogs.

13

Maggie was on the veranda outside the Stettnerhof when Henry returned, just sitting quietly with her hands in her lap, her eyes staring across the lake. She was silent and motionless.

Caporelli's Alfa Romeo was there, under the trees, and as Henry appeared around the back of it and sat down alongside her, she lifted her head slowly and turned to look at him.

"It was the Questura," he said. "They blew in the front. They must have planted a bomb in the doorway or something. I don't know how they did it. A parcel or a suitcase or something. There was one killed that I saw and several others injured."

"Oh, God," she said softly, as though somehow she were personally involved. "Just when I thought things were going to sort themselves out. It'll all start again now. Everything."

There was a bitterness in her voice Henry had never heard before.

"I must go and see Sister Ursula," she said. "I must tell her what's happened before she goes to see Dei Monti. It won't do much good, though. Even finding the altar cross won't help. He'll never agree to anything now."

"I'll come with you," Henry said quickly, standing up.

"No. I'll be all right."

"I'd like to," Henry said.

She gave him a crooked smile and got to her feet and they walked across the courtyard, their feet crunching on the gravel, their faces wet with the mist that had followed the rain.

There seemed to be something different about the orphanage as soon as they arrived there. Like most Italian buildings, it had always been under-illuminated, but now it seemed darker than ever, and there seemed to be a brooding stillness over the old buildings that rose in front of them out of the darkness alongside the stream and the artificial millrace Von Benedikt had built. Usually there were children about, crossing the courtyard or running in and out of the doors, but this time there were none to be seen and they could hear the mumble of voices muttering among the dark buildings.

"Hail Mary, full of grace, the Lord is with thee: blessed art thou among women and blessed is the fruit of thy womb . . ."

There was something frighteningly silent about the place that made them stop in front of the door and pause before pulling the bell.

The iron clanging made a hollow sound in the corridor inside, then they heard the bolts being drawn back.

"I'll go on my own now," Maggie said. "Please."

Henry nodded and stepped back as the door opened. The old woman who stood in the entrance, her face bleak in the yellow light of the single small bulb high up in the ceiling, was red-eyed and bowed with grief. Maggie glanced quickly at Henry and he saw her face was frightened, then the door shut behind her and she was gone.

For some time he stood in the darkness, obsessed by a feeling of guilt, knowing he ought never to have let Wasescha out of his sight in the Piazza della Citta, then he walked slowly back to the hotel, oppressed by his thoughts. Caporelli was sitting in his office when he reached the Stettnerhof, one hand on a brandy glass. He said nothing as Henry sat down opposite him, but Henry could see that he, too, was suffering from too much thinking.

After a while he lifted his head and Henry saw his face was gray and strained-looking. "Have you heard?" he said.

Henry nodded. "I was there. I was in the Piazza della Citta when it happened."

"Someone came into the bar. They told me. Was anyone hurt?"

"A few. Someone was killed. I heard there were others. It was Wasescha. I saw him just before it happened. He was carrying a parcel."

Caporelli looked up and there was a flash of life in his eyes for a moment, then he shook his head and stared at the brandy glass again.

"No," he said softly. "*I* did it. I did it."

"Don't talk like that. If anyone's to blame, then I was. I should have done something about it. I should have tried to stop him."

"Thank God you didn't, or it might have been you, Aynree."

Caporelli came to life abruptly and opened a drawer, and Henry saw there was a heavy revolver inside. Caporelli took it out and slipped it into his pocket.

"Where did you get that?"

Caporelli shrugged. "It is British," he said. "Smith and Wesson. A relic of the first war, I suspect. A lot of these were dropped to us in the mountains when the Germans were on the run. I've had it ever since. I always expected that one day some drunken Sudtyroler would come in here and do something stupid. Well, now one of them has."

175

"What are you going to do?"

"I'm going to wait for Alois. At his room. I'm going to kill him."

"Look, Mr. Caporelli—Ettore—put that back."

Caporelli gave Henry a slow smile. "Aynree," he said, "you forget. I have seen it all before. All these killings and beatings and bullyings. Sometimes the issue was political. Sometimes it was patriotic—or so they said. Sometimes it is necessary for a man to go outside the law when he is dealing with people who are outside the law themselves."

"But you're going to *kill* him."

Caporelli shrugged. "I was a partisan. I know these mountains as well as Alois. I shan't do it where he'll be found, have no fear."

"Ettore—there must be another way."

Caporelli held up one hand. "He is 'Andreas Hofer,' " he said in a heavy voice. "And he has always taken the law into his own hands. We will all be better off without him." He saw the shocked look on Henry's face. "Aynree, this area has seen more outrages than you in England ever dreamed of. Mussolini started it, and now it flows the other way. These people—and I'm not one of them—are correct to demand their rights. I would do the same. But demanding rights is different from setting up a private army before we've reached an end to talking. Killing is different. Especially this sort of senseless killing."

Henry stared at him for a moment, chilled by the unemotional logic in Caporelli's voice, then, as he got to his feet, Henry stood up also.

"I'll come with you," he said impulsively.

"Thank you, Aynree." Caporelli smiled. "I know what that means—coming from you. But no. Not you. You said so yourself. *You* are not involved in our politics. This is my affair.

176

Never yours. You could never make it yours, however hard you tried."

He patted Henry's shoulder and left the office.

As Henry followed, he heard the Alfa Romeo start, the gravel crunching under the wheels as it moved away, and he suddenly felt lost and drained of feeling and desperately in need of someone to talk to.

But the hotel seemed to be empty. The bar was devoid of customers and only the ski-instructress waitress was there, leaning on the coffee machine reading the newspaper. In the end he walked into the village. The traffic jam which had arisen after the explosion from the carelessly parked police cars that had arrived from Trepizano had been dispersed, but there were dozens of people standing about in groups still, obviously discussing the explosion. All along the front and by the boat station there were crowds of men, all smoking, some of them standing with glasses in their hands, as though they'd just come out of the Stöckli Bar.

Cars were still parked inconsiderately along the roadside and under the trees where normally the police would have moved them on, and even in this slight suggestion of the breakdown of law and order there was a chilling sense of apprehension. Voices were low and wary, and the very way the men grouped together suggested nervousness, a need to be near to other people, as though in the shadows there was danger. But there wasn't only fear. The mood was one of anger and disgust, for all that many of the men must have been Austrian by descent. No one showed any sign of pleasure or triumph, though the Italian police had never been popular. All attitudes of dislike and protest had been pushed aside by the outrage.

There wasn't much to see and Henry was just on the point of moving away when the police themselves came and began to break up the crowd. Feeling tired and beaten and on edge, Henry moved across to the Church of Lazzaro di Colleno and went in and sat down at the back in the shadows. There were several women, with black shawls over their heads kneeling in the pews, their fingers entwined, their lips moving in prayer. The bleak illuminations caught their faces and made them angular and starved-looking with the shadows they cast. The great Cross of Lazzaro still lay on its raised plinth of brilliant red, the light still shining down on it, but no one seemed interested in it any longer. All the upsurging religious revival it had started had fallen away to nothing.

Father Anselmo crossed the church and as he passed the cross he stopped and genuflected, and it seemed to Henry that he stopped longer than he need have done, staring at the cross as though he felt that somehow it had started everything that had happened, as though it were the key that had unlocked the door through which all the hate and bitterness had flooded across the town.

It lay there, like some great dramatic symbol, the light glaring down on it, and to Henry, too, it seemed to have been the beginning of everything; and suddenly, in spite of its meaning and all that it stood for, it looked strangely evil in its starkness. Until its arrival the Val Caloroso had lain silently below the Catena di Saga, not much touched by tourism, not even much touched by the political strife further to the north, in spite of the occasional explosion that had stopped some train to Venice from Bolzano. But since it had appeared so dramatically, everything had boiled up into a harsh conflict full of bitterness and emotion in which Henry was involved, too, because he was linked securely to the fringe of it by the dam.

He sat for a long time in silence, his eyes on the flash of red and black and gold, trying to sort out his thoughts, knowing that none of it was really his affair, yet oppressed suddenly with a feeling of responsibility he'd been trying all the time to avoid. When he went outside again, the rain had started once more, and the police had dispersed the crowds outside the Stöckli Bar. He got back to the Stettnerhof almost at the same time as Caporelli. The Italian's face was grim and as devoid of anger as if it had been carved out of the wood that lined the hall.

"He's gone," he said. "I forced the door. There were things all over the place. As though he'd slipped in and grabbed some clothes in a hurry and vanished."

"Then he *must* have been involved somehow."

Caporelli nodded. "He is Hofer," he said.

"How do you know? How can you be sure?"

Caporelli put his hand on his heart. "I don't know," he said. "Not from evidence on paper. Only here. I know now that all the time he must have been Hofer."

"But I thought he only belonged to the Volkspartei for the fun he got out of it."

Caporelli turned slowly. "Then why did he leave?" he said. "Because Dittli must have told him what I knew. He wasn't taking any chances. The game was up." He sighed. "It was a good disguise, wasn't it?" he said. "He was always so honest. Big, hearty Alois, everybody's friend. Nobody minded his politics. 'Sure, I'm a member of the Volkspartei. But I help the police all I can because I don't really believe in it. I'm only a member because the boys admire me and I can get some of the girls into bed. I'm not dangerous. I don't throw bombs. I've even got friends among the police.' "

Henry remembered the two policemen who had met them up the mountain, chaffing Stettner and pulling his leg about his customer, and realized just how good a disguise his honest attitude had been.

"That's what I thought, too, Aynree," Caporelli went on. "I was wrong. And so were the police."

"Where will he have gone?"

Caporelli shrugged. "Into the mountains. Where he's safe.

179

You could lose an army in the Catena di Saga. I could find him, but it would take months of searching. The police *never* will, because they don't know the mountains."

"Where will he head for?"

Caporelli shrugged again. "Perhaps over the border to Austria. He'll be safe there. Perhaps he'll stay in the mountains. Perhaps there'll be more explosions."

He was silent for a while, then he went on, speaking slowly as though he were tired. "I went into all the bars," he said. "I went to all his friends and to all the women I knew of. I even went up to Oswino's by the dam. He wasn't there. He's gone. He knows I will come.

"I don't understand why I never thought of it before," he continued in a bewildered voice. "These boys, these students, they weren't old enough to be leaders. It *had* to be someone older, someone with a knowledge of the mountains, someone with army experience, someone who knew the town. Who else could it have been but Alois? They admired him. He was a good guy. He was the best climber in the district and the best guide— or he had been. He could skin-dive better than anyone; he had more stories than the *Arabian Nights*. He could drink and had a way with women. There was everything in him that a foolish boy could want. *Of course he was Hofer.* I was a madman not to realize."

He struck his forehead with the heel of his hand. "But I shall find him," he said. "He'll come back. Perhaps to see Oswino's wife. They've been too close for too long. If not now, then next year or the year afterward. At the end of the season I shall go to Bolzano and Trento and Trepizano and ask after him among the students. They'll know where he is or where someone is who knows where he is, and sooner or later someone will feel he must tell me. I shall find him, even if I have to go all the way to Vienna for him."

He paused. "The police have set up an office in the basement

180

of the Municipio. They're already rounding up the students. Castelrossi tells me it's the same in Trepizano. The trains will stop again and the boats will not run. The lake will come to a standstill."

They were still standing there talking in low tones when the door opened and Maggie appeared. She had a heavy canvas bag in her hand which she put on the floor. She seemed to be in a daze, her eyes blank and shocked.

Caporelli at once went to the bar and Henry heard him asking for a brandy. He returned with it as Henry was helping her off with her coat. As they made her sit down on the divan in the hall, she looked up at Henry, her eyes wide and full of tears.

"Maggie," he asked, "what's the matter? What's happened?"

"It's Sister Ursula," she said. "She was at the police station returning the cross that Giovanni stole. They told me at the orphanage. They'd just heard. She was the one you saw outside the door."

Caporelli's eyes flew to Henry's and a spasm of agony crossed his face, then Henry remembered seeing the flattened figure in black with the parcel against the wall of the Questura. Sister Ursula! That calm, intelligent, clear-minded woman! She must have been just going through the door when the explosion had occurred.

For a long time none of them spoke, then Caporelli's throat worked, and his words came out jaggedly.

"I thought a great deal of Sister Ursula," he said slowly, and Henry could see the guilt for her death written clearly on his face. "I often did things for her children. She always came to me for help. It was Sister Ursula who told me about the dam."

It was impossible to say anything that would help him.

"What about the children?" Henry asked quietly.

Maggie lifted her eyes. "They don't know yet," she said. "Only Giovanni. He knows. They had to tell him because he kept asking if she'd taken the cross back."

"How is he?"

She made a movement with her shoulders, not a shrug, but as though she couldn't bear to think of it and was brushing it aside; her brows came down and she stood up abruptly and reached for the heavy bag she'd brought with her.

"I've brought you this," she said. "I've been down to fetch it. Nobody will ever notice. Not now. I didn't bring much."

"What is it?" Caporelli asked.

She ignored the question and went on in a flat voice as though she were delivering a lecture. "I hate the thought of Arcuneum," she said. "After this I couldn't bear to have any more to do with it. I shall be going home as soon as possible."

"Maggie—"

She shook her head as Henry spoke, trying to will him to silence.

"I want you to use it," she said. "I want you to do what you wanted to do. There's been enough unhappiness here since Lazzaro's cross appeared. God forbid there should be any more."

Caporelli stared at her and then at Henry; he crossed quickly to the bag and lifted it to the divan alongside her, feeling its weight in his hand. His fingers were trembling as he opened it, then he glanced inside and quickly closed it again.

His face had gone white as he stared at Henry.

"Plastic," he said. "Enough to blow the gate out of the stopper wall."

14

For a long time Caporelli stared at Henry, then he picked up the bag and nodded toward his office. Henry took Maggie's arm and led her, still dazed, after him.

Caporelli locked the door and drew the curtains, opened the bag again and examined the contents more closely.

"Pentolite," he said, as though he were reading from an inventory. "In two-hundred-and-fifty-gram packages. Eight of them. Lead azide detonators. *Madonna,* you could have blown your hand off! Wire. Everything we need."

He looked at Maggie for a second and she stared back at him, her eyes wide.

"Where did you get this?" he asked.

She sat down abruptly in the chair opposite the desk. "It's out of the old Customs House," she said. "We had to take the key every night to the police. You know about that. They insisted on it. It was my job. I had to sign for it. I never got there tonight. Nobody will miss it now. I expect everything was destroyed and nobody will think of it."

"They'll be looking for it tomorrow," Caporelli said.

"No." Maggie shook her head calmly, as though she'd thought of everything. "Nobody knows about it. There was no one there. Not even the policeman who stands guard every night. They'd been down for him to go up to the Questura." She paused. "I suppose he's needed more up there just now."

She indicated the bag on the floor. "They'll never miss it," she said again. "I only brought a little. There's so much in there, with the crates and the shavings and all the things we brought up from the lake, they'll never notice it—not for a long time."

"What are we going to do with it?"

Henry stared at Caporelli, suddenly caught by the wild impulse to suggest using it themselves on the dam, but common sense caught hold of him again. "Take it back," he said. "Take it back straightaway."

"No!" Maggie spoke explosively. "No! It was Dei Monti's fault. If he hadn't insisted on moving everything, the cross wouldn't have been stolen and Sister Ursula wouldn't have been at the Questura!"

"Maggie," Henry said, "if Lazzaro hadn't been drowned, *none* of it would have happened because that cross in the church would never have appeared and then *this* cross would never have been found. You might just as well blame it on Lazzaro."

She wouldn't listen and kept on shaking her head.

"No," she kept saying. "No. This is what I want."

Caporelli spoke quietly. "We can't take it back now," he pointed out to Henry. "Not now. Not after what's happened at the Questura. We can't risk it. They'd never believe she'd just taken it on an impulse. They'll still be too angry. They'll think she's had it all the time. They'll even think this is where the bomb came from, when"—he paused and his throat worked—"when it didn't, of course."

"Then, for God's sake, dump it," Henry said. "In the lake. Anywhere. Listen, Ettore, I know what you think of me, but I'm not just trying to keep my hands clean. It's a question of sheer sense."

Caporelli nodded. "Of course," he said. "I never thought otherwise. I quite agree." He placed the bag in the open safe behind his desk and locked the door and pocketed the key. Then he turned and nodded.

"Leave it where it is," he said. "It's safe there. I'll get rid of it as soon as possible." He nodded to Maggie. "You'd better persuade her to go to bed," he said. "She's suffering from shock. Get her away from Cadivescovo as soon as you can."

Henry nodded and took Maggie's arm. She rose without a word and allowed him to lead her out of the office. Several of Dei Monti's archaeological group were just arriving as they left but, although they glanced curiously at her, none of them spoke. Henry took her to her room and switched on the light.

"I want to go home," she said abruptly. "I'm going to pack."

She refused to go to bed, and Henry left her while she placed a suitcase on the bed and began to throw things into it, untidily, as though she didn't even see what she did.

Caporelli was still in his office when Henry reached the hall. "She'll not be allowed to go yet, of course," he said. "Not now. Not for a few days. There isn't a chance. The police were arriving from Trepizano when I came back. It'll be like getting through the eye of a needle. There's only one way out of Cadivescovo now and that's over the mountains. The way *he* went."

He looked up at Henry, his face concerned. "They'll guess," he said. "They'll find out he's gone before long and they'll guess he had something to do with it. Then they'll want to see *her*. They're bound to want to talk to her because she was always

185

with him. At least"—he managed a twisted smile—"until you came she was."

The town was sullen and angry the following morning. There were swarms of police about the place, and soldiers with steel helmets and machine guns, even a couple of light armored cars standing in the Piazza della Citta where builders were shoring up the front of the burned-out Questura. The boats had stopped. The Via Colleno was sealed off. The town had become a prison.

The rain had started again and was coming in flurries down the valley and along the lake, shutting out the view of Trepizano and giving the town an eerie, flattened old-photograph look that added to the oppressive feeling of gloom. Only a few disconsolate tourists were haunting the Municipio and the boat station in the hope of getting permission to leave.

The next day, with the town still patrolled by soldiers and everybody moving about silently, close to the walls as though they were full of guilt, the rain began to come down harder, so that the police and soldiers searched for doorways, standing out of the downpour with their guns sheltered by their rubber capes, their faces heavy with anger. Most of the tourists were either in their hotels now or in the bars, keeping out of the way, and still no boat had arrived from Trepizano.

Caporelli was watching the weather with a strained look on his face. He was bearing a heavy load of responsibility.

By the third morning the town seemed to have lost its power of speech. The police still filled the streets, huddling against the rain, and the damp air that was noisy with the wail of sirens as the police cars brought people to the Municipio for questioning. It was almost as if Cadivescovo had been occupied by a foreign power.

In the afternoon, however, in spite of the police, a few people began to make their way toward the Piazza della Citta. At first there were objections and a few muttered arguments, but the groups of people still kept pushing forward, not saying much, just moving forward all the time. In the end the barriers were pulled back a little and they were allowed to pass, watched carefully all the time by the uniformed men. By the time Caporelli and Henry arrived with Maggie, the Piazza della Citta had filled with silent watchers.

There was no trouble, however. The people had lined the walls quietly, making no attempt to stand on the steps of the Hoferdenkmal or the War Memorial. Many of them were in black and most of them had crepe-covered buttons on their lapels. It was as though they felt a sense of collective guilt and needed to show their sorrow. They waited silently, impervious to the rain and indifferent to the groups of policemen who stood at every alley end.

Father Anselmo was the first to appear at the head of the funeral procession, followed by Father Gianpiero and the acolytes bearing the incense. Then came the three hearses, all drawn by black horses with nodding plumes, two of the coffins draped with red, white, and green flags.

The hearses were followed by a long line of black-garbed men with enormous wreaths of mountain flowers and women who wailed and wept as they splashed through the puddles. Behind them there were a group of children from the Orphanage of St. Francis, scrubbed to the bone and painfully clean in their stiff threadbare clothes. Giovanni was among them, pale and strained-looking, and two or three nuns, Sister Agata weeping unrestrainedly. Finally there were a few grim-faced police officials and the Mayor. The number of policemen taking part was small because most of them were standing in the arcades or sitting in the lorries parked about the square waiting for the trouble that everyone knew was coming.

But still nothing happened and the procession, bowed against the rain, passed through the silent crowd. As it vanished into

187

the church and the high sound of boys' voices began, there was a long low sound like a sigh from the onlookers, then the mass of people began to crumple as it edged after the procession into the church. First one turned away after the silent file of black figures, and then another, until the piazza was filled with slow-moving, muttering groups.

As he moved away with Maggie, Henry was startled to see another procession coming out of the side streets near the boat station. It marched silently, almost mocking the slow movement of Father Anselmo, and some of the young men who formed it wore the black flowered waistcoats and knee breeches of the mountain. All of them had red-and-white rosettes in their buttonholes, and they were pale and defiant-looking as though they were trying hard to muster their courage.

"Oh, *Madonna*, no," Caporelli breathed.

They were students, more stupid than brave, marching to the statue of Andreas Hofer with a wreath draped in red and white ribbon. There were two large photographs attached to it, and Henry guessed at once that they were the pictures of the two students who had died in Trepizano, one of them choked by his own bed sheets in the jail, the other in the hospital from the injuries he'd received in the struggle with Sergeant Guidotti on the railway.

"*Mamma mia*," Caporelli said. "They must be mad!"

The dispersing crowd had stopped dead and turned. Henry took hold of Maggie's arm and began to push her away. She was watching with fascinated horror, her eyes wide, her mouth twisted in anger and disgust.

The procession continued to move forward, a splash of color in the somber square, and among the pale, nervous faces of the boys there were a few that were blank and stupid with idealism, and among the flickering, anxious eyes some that were blind with pride and arrogance.

"We'd better get out of here," Caporelli said.

188

The crowd, stupefied at the effrontery of the students watched them, motionless, shocked and horrified, as though something vile, that never normally saw daylight had come from the narrow streets. For a second longer, in an atmosphere charged with hatred, the students continued to push toward the Hoferdenkmal, their leaders rigid in their reckless lunacy, then the watching crowd seemed to step forward in one mass.

Henry tugged at Maggie's arm.

"Come on, Maggie," he begged. "There's going to be trouble."

There was another sound from the crowd now, a low murmuring that was sullen and angry. Henry saw a woman's face contort into fury and she shouted at the procession.

"Traitors! Murderers! Assassins!"

The police were moving forward quickly, but stones were already being thrown, and the procession was crumbling into frightened fragments.

As Henry pushed Maggie away, he saw one of the students go down and the wreath dipped, a student hitting back and a policeman's cap go rolling in the mud. Then the procession broke up into fist fights all over the square, with the crowd joining in willingly and the women beating the youngsters over the head with umbrellas. One boy, more hotheaded than the rest, fired an illicit pistol into the air. The crack of the shot seemed to stop everybody dead in their tracks. Someone stumbled against Henry and he almost fell as the crowd surged back, but he recovered his balance. Policemen, who had been mostly set on arrests before, now began to lay about them savagely with their rifles and fists and capes, and students began to go down like ninepins. Maggie and Henry and Caporelli watched from the steps of the Municipio, in the middle of a crowd of shrieking women, Maggie half behind Henry and crouching in fear.

By the time it was over, most of the students were in the old dungeons of the former Von Benedikt palace, and seven more,

189

who were unconscious, had been bundled not very gently into ambulances and carted off to the hospital at Trepizano. The wreath was lying in the gutter, where the rain had washed it against the bottom of the Hoferdenkmal, and there were only a few trampled red and white flowers and muddied leaves and a scrap of colored ribbon to mark the path of the procession.

It was afternoon before the police had restored order to the town and taken up their accustomed posts by the roadblocks, no longer polite as they asked for passports and identity cards, but brusque and rude, their eyes full of hate.

The Stettnerhof was gloomy in the rain which fell in an impenetrable curtain, tumbling out of the sky and sending the water draining off the mountains and racing in a thin sheet from the meadows across the road toward the lake. It was pouring out of the mountain lanes in thick torrents and washing mud and gravel into the road. Two streams met at the entrance to the forecourt of the Stettnerhof and leaped high into the air like a burst fire hydrant.

Pushing through the rain, huddled under an umbrella, the black figure of Sister Agata picked its way through the puddles that the explosion of water had caused, her glasses misted, her skirt spattered with mud.

She sat down in the hall to get her breath back while they all stood around her, waiting for her to speak.

"It's Giovanni," she said at last. "He's disappeared. He told Ercole Battista that as Sister Ursula was dead, the promise he made to her not to run away again was no longer any good. He disappeared after the funeral. I think it must have been during that awful fight in the square. It was only when we came out of the church that I noticed he was missing."

"Sister Agata," Caporelli said, "I owe that boy something. We must find him. Where can he have gone?"

190

"Last time it was Trepizano." She flapped her hands hopelessly. "I don't know why I came here. I've been to the police, but they're too busy. I suppose it's understandable. I could only think of you. He just disappeared."

"He couldn't get to Trepizano," Caporelli said. "They'd see him as he went through one of the roadblocks or onto a boat. Has he any money?"

"None. We can only think he might try to get to Bolzano. His mother came from the north. His father—I think his father was an American or a British soldier in Austria. I don't know. Only Sister Ursula really knew his background, and she's—she's—" She stopped and looked up at them, her myopic eyes puzzled and frightened, a plump ugly young woman who hadn't yet quite grasped that Sister Ursula was dead.

Caporelli took her back to the orphanage in his car while Henry and Maggie sat in the bar, waiting, waiting, waiting—that was all they seemed to do, Henry thought, wait for the next disaster. They were still there when the police arrived, their car turning into the forecourt with a rush of flung gravel.

There was a group of Dei Monti's archaelogists in the bar. They had continued to work in the rain at first, but without much enthusiasm, until the police had advised them to leave everything and go back to their hotels. The sight of them packing up Lazzaro's treasures to be carted off to Rome might well have stirred up further trouble.

They watched curiously as Caporelli led Inspector Castelrossi and a uniformed man into his office. Henry went to the door and watched them talking together, then Caporelli appeared, looking grave.

"They're here," he said. "They wish to see the Signorina Daniells."

"She's in the bar," Henry said.

Caporelli sighed. "Aynree, I wonder if you would tell her.

Perhaps it would be easier for her that way." He looked apologetic.

"Forget it," Henry said shortly. "What's it about? What she brought here last night?"

Caporelli shook his head. "They don't know anything about that yet. If they ask, I shall have to produce it, of course. But if they don't, I shall say nothing. It'll be better to let things calm down. They've discovered Alois is missing."

Henry nodded. "I'll tell her," he said.

Maggie was still sitting in the corner of the bar where he'd left her, under the carved eagle of Colleno, her hands folded, staring in front of her. She had the look of someone who'd been beaten; she'd been sitting like that since he'd left her.

"Maggie," he said gently, "it's the police."

"What do they want?"

"They want to speak to you."

She looked up. "Me?"

"I'm afraid so, Maggie."

"Why? Is it about the plastic?"

Henry shook his head. "Caporelli says they know nothing about that."

"Ought I to tell them?"

"Leave that to Caporelli. He knows what to do. He says they've come about Alois. He's disappeared. They think he was 'Hofer' and they know you saw a lot of him."

She stood up and he took her hand. "What shall I say?" she asked.

"Tell them everything. You're not involved. It's possible you might be able to help."

"Henry, I'm frightened. Will you come with me?"

"Yes, of course. If you wish."

In the office Castelrossi was sitting in Caporelli's chair and the uniformed man was standing behind him with an open

192

notebook. There were people in the hall, staring curiously through the window, and Henry saw Maggie go red as they had to push between them.

Castelrossi made no objection to Henry's presence. Caporelli was standing nervously opposite them, his mind full, Henry knew, of the knowledge that the responsibility for the explosion was always, even if indirectly, his own.

"I knew nothing about him," Maggie kept insisting, her face pale and strained as Castelrossi leaned forward and pushed his questions at her.

She seemed to have recovered a little, but she'd brought the dark glasses out again and Henry knew she found them again something to retreat behind.

"Surely he must have given some hint of what he was doing?" Castelrossi said.

"No. Never. Not to me."

"What was your relationship with him?"

Maggie glanced at Henry and blushed. "I went about with him," she said. "He worked on the boats with us, skin-diving for the group. Professor Dei Monti employed him because he knew the lake so well."

"I don't mean *that* relationship. We've got that information from Professor Dei Monti. I mean your personal relationship."

Maggie hesitated. "He got to know me very early when I first came here," she said. "I think he liked me."

"Is that all?"

"Yes." She spoke quietly. "That's all."

"What about you?"

"He made me laugh. We danced together. We used to meet at night."

"Go on."

"That's all."

"Are you sure?"

She glanced at Henry again and became silent for a while, and he could hear the clock ticking on the wall.

"He took me up the mountain occasionally when I first arrived. To the refuge at the bottom of La Fortezza. To show me the view, he said."

"Go on."

She looked agonized. "Do I have to tell you any more?" she asked.

Castelrossi stared at her and shook his head.

"Did he ever come to your room?" he said.

"Once. No"—she paused—"twice. The second time I made him go away."

"Did you ever go to *his* room?"

She nodded.

"Did you stay?"

Her head dipped slowly and she kept her eyes on the floor.

"Did you see anything?"

She flared up suddenly. "When you go to a man's room at night, you don't go to look for things," she snapped.

Castelrossi nodded. "You might have seen something," he pointed out quietly. "Something that might have linked him with what has been happening."

She shook her head. "No. There were a few pictures, that's all. Of himself taking part in parades in Bolzano. He liked pictures of himself. I saw Volkspartei posters, but everybody knew he was a member."

"Is that all?"

"I didn't know he was one of the Montanari, though once or twice I met people there who said they were members of the party."

"Who? Who was there?"

"Dittli. He was a waiter here. And another man with a beard."

"Did he say what his name was?"

194

"Yes, but I don't remember."

"Could it have been Carlo Wasescha?"

"It could have been. I don't know."

"Anybody else?"

"Nobody I knew."

"What else can you tell us?"

"I've told you," she said angrily, and she seemed to be crucifying herself in her own self-disgust. "When you go to a man's room at night, he doesn't usually fill it with his friends."

Castelrossi shrugged. "Is that all you can tell us?" he asked.

She nodded miserably and the inspector put on his hat. "Very well," he said. "We would like to have your passport, of course, Signorina. Just for a while. As a formality. It will be returned to you as soon as possible."

She looked up slowly. "Does that mean I can't go home?" she asked.

Castelrossi turned and nodded. "Yes, Signorina," he said. "It means exactly that."

When the police had gone Maggie sat with Henry alongside the big fire in the bar. Caporelli left them alone, but he quietly brought in two brandies and placed the glasses in front of them.

"What will happen?" Maggie asked. "What will happen now? Everything seems in such a mess. Giovanni. Sister Ursula. Now this. I feel so responsible for it all."

"It's nothing to do with you, Maggie. You weren't involved."

"It was my fault Giovanni disappeared. If I hadn't got them involved with what we were finding, he'd never have stolen the altar cross and then Sister Ursula would still be alive."

"Maggie," Henry said, "you can't dig too far back, or else everybody was responsible for everything that ever happened. Our ancestors were responsible for no other reason than that they gave birth to us."

She nodded. "What about me?" she asked. "Does it mean they'll put me in prison?"

"I shouldn't think so," Henry said, though he had to admit to himself that he wasn't any too certain. "At the moment, I imagine it'll just mean they'll ask you to leave the country."

"I see. I think I'd like to go home."

"I'll be going myself now," Henry said. "If you like, I'll hang on until they say it's all right for you to go, then we'll go together. You'll probably be glad of a little help."

"Yes. I've got a lot of luggage. You seem to collect it when you stay anywhere for a long time."

She spoke flatly, as though she were trying to make conversation to take her mind off the silence in the bar. After a while she touched his hand nervously, then he felt her fingers close and grip it tight.

"I'm very grateful," she said in a low voice. "I don't suppose I was always very kind to you, Henry, but I'm sorry if I said anything unpleasant. I'm sure I did."

"No," he said. "Nothing to worry about."

She looked up at him. "I'm glad you're going home too."

The rain came down harder than ever during the afternoon, turning the forecourt into a quagmire littered with leaves and twigs and small branches. The radio had started to draw attention to the weather, something Henry had never noticed before outside England. But there'd been flooding in the valley of the Piave, and a bridge had been washed out at Valli dei Signori to the south.

The low-scudding clouds drifted like smoke across the sky and the air was chilled and sodden with water after the steady drumming rainfall of the morning. The thunder had started again, too, and was crashing down into the mountains and echoing among the dripping crags. Caporelli was standing by the

196

door staring out at it, his face grim, his eyes burning, dark and agonized, in his pale face.

Maggie still sat by the fire in the bar, her hand in Henry's, as though she were deep in thought.

After a while she lifted her head and looked at him, almost defiantly. "It's all true," she said. "All I told that policeman. All of it."

Henry said nothing and squeezed her fingers.

"I did go to Alois's room."

Henry made no comment, feeling it was best to let her say what she wished. She'd probably regret it all later, but it didn't matter much just then. She'd gone through the process of becoming an adult painfully, and something, some small subtle expression, had changed in her face, and for the first time Henry felt the gap between their ages had closed.

Later he went out into the hall, leaving her by the fire, and stood with Caporelli, staring at the rain.

"I ought to tell them," Caporelli said slowly. "I ought to tell them about the box that came from my car. It was my fault. I was to blame."

"Don't be silly," Henry said. "You brought that stuff here for a peaceful purpose, not to kill people."

"You think it is peaceful to blow the gates off a dam?"

"The way you thought of it it was."

"It wouldn't have been peaceful if the Montanari had done it. It's only a point of view." Caporelli smiled slowly, a small withdrawn smile, as though he were mocking himself. "I wanted to make a bang," he said. "I was like a little boy with a firework. Others were making bangs and I wanted to make a bang too. I forgot I was over fifty. I thought I was still young and stupid. It's like a man suddenly leaving his wife and running off after a young girl. We forget we are old and go on trying to think of ourselves as boys, long after our bones have

197

grown brittle and our muscles stiff. Tomorrow I shall go and confess. It is my duty."

Henry wasn't sure how he fitted into it all. It was no responsibility of his, but he felt he had put the idea into Caporelli's head.

"I'll come with you," he said.

They were still standing there, watching the rain in silence, when they saw an old car turn into the forecourt. It was a battered Fiat with a torn canvas hood over the rear half.

"That's Oswino's van," Caporelli said. "What's he want?"

A heavily muffled figure was climbing out of the van and they heard a door slam. The figure passed in front of the car and appeared in the hotel entrance.

It was Dieter Oswino's wife and she looked like a plump drowned chicken. Her hair was hanging over her face underneath the hood of a gray rubber cape and her big eyes looked frightened. Henry had only seen them looking arrogant and challenging before, and the change made her seem smaller.

"Signor Caporelli," she said, "where is Alois?"

Caporelli's eyes narrowed. "I don't know," he said. "I wish to God I did."

"I must find him. I've been expecting him to telephone, but nothing's happened. The telephone's stopped working."

"Which one? Your own or Mornaghini's?"

"Both of them. The water's washed out the telegraph poles. I saw them at the bridge on the way down, hanging over into the river." Her eyes flickered about her nervously. "Signor Caporelli, I must find Alois. He has some things at the farm and he ought to come and get them. We'll have to leave. The water's coming down the mountain and cutting great channels in the soil. The pond's overflowed and it's making the barn start to collapse. It's washing away the foundations. Dieter tried to telephone. He's been trying to telephone for hours."

Henry's eyes flew to Caporelli's. He could just imagine the

198

wedge-faced, narrow-eyed farmer whom Stettner had apparently deluded for years, standing by the telephone, patiently trying to make contact with Mornaghini or the police, again and again and again, still dumbly trying when it would have been obvious to anybody else that there was no hope.

"Why?" Caporelli was asking. "Why did he telephone?"

"The water's coming over the top of the dam. They told us we had to let them know if it did."

Henry turned abruptly toward Caporelli's office, his brows down, his eyes angry, suddenly sick of the whole complicated setup, sick of the obstructions that had been put in their path, sick of Mornaghini's hesitation, sick of the threat of Stettner's Montanari. He had fought against involvement ever since he had arrived. He had told himself again and again that it wasn't his affair, that his concern finished with the opinion he had expressed. But somehow he was bound closer to Cadivescovo than he had realized. It was beyond his power merely to put the affair behind him and feel that he was finished with it apart from the report he would have to write. Caporelli had involved him, and so had Stettner and Maggie and Sister Ursula. A swelling sense of disgust and anger flooded over him, indignation mingled with contempt and a sudden new fear.

Caporelli stared after him for a second, then he followed him.

"Open your safe," Henry said brusquely.

Caporelli's eyes gleamed. "You will do it?" he asked.

Henry nodded. "Yes," he said. "Now. Let's go."

15

The rain was lashing down now, and they could hear it roaring on the glass roof of the veranda and trickling heavily into the puddles that had formed on the gravel where the gutters had overflowed.

Caporelli was taking Maggie's canvas bag from his safe and stuffing everything from it into a large leather brief case. "Here," he said, handing it to Henry. "Take care of that. And handle it carefully. I'll find some decent boots."

Henry was waiting in the hall with Maggie when he reappeared, dressed in a long rubber hooded cape, his legs heavily stockinged, thick *kletteschühe* on his feet. His eyes were bright and there was a new look in his eye. The stockings and boots and the cape had transformed him from a suave hotel proprietor to a mountain man, and he looked tough and capable and resilient, and he was enjoying every minute of it, even the urgency.

He glanced at Henry's light raincoat and shoes.

"Is that all you've got?" he asked.

Henry's face was pale and tense and the anger inside him, as unexpected and searing as the fury that had driven him once before in Egypt to defy authority and risk imprisonment for his beliefs, boiled up again. "There's no time for anything else now," he said brusquely. "We've got a job to do."

"Strong boots would help us do it better," Caporelli retorted.

Henry shrugged and looked at Maggie. "Stay here," he said.

"What'll happen?" she asked.

"Nothing." Henry shook his head. "Nothing will happen. We'll stop it. We'll stop it somehow. We must."

Caporelli picked up the canvas bag and took a big hand lamp and a long torch from a cupboard. The Alfa Romeo was in the courtyard, black and shining in the lights of the hotel as the rain water streamed off it. Caporelli placed the bag and the torches on the back seat, then dropped into his place behind the wheel. The interior smelled damp, and through his anger Henry became aware of the wetness of Caporelli's cape brushing against his trouser leg.

Caporelli started the engine and let in the clutch quickly so that the wheels spun before gripping, then the car shot off with a jerk. Unexpectedly he didn't drive on to the road but headed toward the garages behind the hotel. There he began to disconnect the battery of the Fiat van.

"We have everything we need," he said. "Explosives. Detonators. Wire. All we need is the electricity to fire it. That's all. We'll use this battery. It should be more than enough. If it fails, we've got the torch and the hand lamp. Both six volts. That's enough to crack any nut, so long as we keep them dry."

He lifted the battery off its platform and placed it in the back of the car with sacks and a pile of tools which he snatched off the wall above the workbench, then he found string and rope and a crowbar and adhesive tape, and for safety took down an ice ax that was hanging over the door. "We might as well be prepared," he said.

He nodded toward the car and they climbed in and he drove slowly out of the hotel grounds.

"We'll avoid the town," he said. "Because of the soldiers. They might try to stop us."

He turned right away from the town and began to climb the hill, the rain lashing against the windscreen and dropping in sheets across their view. From time to time the grayness of the mountain was lit up by lightning as it flared in great purple glows that were followed by the crashing of the thunder. Henry could see rain-whipped trees and a roadway that was littered with leaves and small branches that the storm had brought down, and the water running off the walls, bringing down silt and pebbles, and wet rocks glowing in the stormy light.

They followed the road until it narrowed, Caporelli flinging the car around the corners. Eventually the asphalt stopped, and they bumped savagely over a stony road, then that stopped, too, and became merely a track, then as the track steepened and the engine began to whine in difficulty as the wheels refused to grip any more, Caporelli fought the car into the entrance to a field by a group of houses and a small church.

"We'll not get it any further," he said. "We'll have to walk now. It'll be a hard climb."

"We can do it," Henry said shortly. "We can do it all right."

Caporelli opened the canvas bag in which Maggie had brought the pentolite and, wrapping the heavy battery around with sacking, he placed it inside the bag with the torches.

"That'll have to do," he said. "We still have the torches as an emergency."

He stuffed the tools and string and adhesive tape in after the torches, then zipped up the bag and slung the rope around his shoulders.

"Here." He passed the ice ax to Henry. "You never know. We might have to dig."

He managed a quick smile, but it was thin and cold and

202

unhumorous, and even through his anger Henry was startled by the change that action had worked on the man.

Henry was soaked within a couple of minutes of climbing out of the car. Caporelli handed him the brief case with another warning to handle it carefully and took the crowbar, and they set off up the mountain with the battery between them, bowed against the weather and the lashing rain.

Even with the driving rage inside him, Henry found it hard to keep up with Caporelli, who was sturdier, fit as a fiddle and used to the mountains. In addition, he had on heavy climbing boots and the cape, while Henry's light raincoat and shoes were worse than useless.

The path wound upward between isolated farmyards and the inevitable carved crucifixes and stacks of sawed winter wood. After a while the clumps of trees gave way to stunted shrubs and more sparse vegetation, and the wind, carrying the lashing sheets of rain, blew cold against them. Now that they were away from the shelter of the clumps of trees, it was harder going, with the bag containing the battery between them, and the path like a small river, the earth beneath it beaten into slippery mud.

They stopped once to get their breath. Already they could only just see the roofs of Cadivescovo below them, shining in the rain. The lake was almost invisible in the mist and there was no view of the mountains on the other side. Henry was already cold and wet but, in his smoldering rage, indifferent to his discomfort.

Caporelli adjusted his cape and pointed to his right. "This way," he said, giving Henry a little confident smile.

"How much further?" Henry said.

"Two miles, I guess."

"Come on."

Caporelli gave him a curious, admiring look and set off after him, his hair in his eyes, the water running across his cheeks and into his mouth, having to hurry to keep up with Henry's thin frame, bowed under his load and completely indifferent to the weather.

Eventually they saw the gray shape of Oswino's farm, and they plodded toward it through the rain and the torrents of water that were pouring off the mountain.

"Oswino'll help," Caporelli said. "I'll make him."

The door was swinging open. The huge fire had burned into a heap of cold ashes and the telephone receiver was hanging on its wire below the instrument. There was no sign of Oswino.

Caporelli's face was puzzled and angry as he splashed through the downstairs rooms. The water, coming in through the back door, was moving in a rapidly spreading pool across the flagstones.

The place seemed to be empty, and they were just on the point of leaving when they heard sounds from the back of the house. They scrambled through the back door, which slammed open for them before the gusts of wind as they released the catch, and through a river of muddy water that was roaring through the yard.

They found Oswino struggling in the mud at the back of the vast gabled barn. The pond just above the house had overflowed as the streams rushing from the mountain poured into it, and the water had washed away the foundations of the barn. Part of it had collapsed across his legs in a tangle of heavy timbers and he was lying face-down, trying to free himself, his clothes saturated, his face streaked with mud, half submerged in the rushing brown stream that flowed over and around him and down to the lake.

He looked up as they approached, and the furious, frustrated expression on his face changed to one of fright. The crowbar he had in his hands splashed into the mud and he strained upward toward a small handcart that stood hub-deep in the water alongside him, almost out of reach, trying to drag a tarpaulin across it.

They dropped their loads and ran across to him and, with the crowbar, managed to raise the timbers sufficiently for him to scramble free. He didn't bother to thank them, however, and through the misery of the lashing rain in their faces, they were aware of the oddness in his manner. Caporelli stared at him for a second, frowning, then he jumped forward and slammed him aside with a sweep of his arm. Oswino flopped down into a sitting position in the mud but, as Caporelli reached for the tarpaulin over the handcart, he scrambled to his feet again and leaped forward to stop him. To Henry's surprise, Caporelli swung around and in the same movement slammed his fist into the farmer's face and Oswino went down again, and Henry saw that Caporelli had a pistol in his hand.

Oswino was on his feet at once and Caporelli hit him backhanded across the mouth with the pistol. Oswino staggered back, blood starting from his split lips, slipped and flopped down again. Caporelli dropped the pistol and, reaching down for him, dragged him to his feet, half supported in his grip and trying to spit out a tooth.

Caporelli's face was contorted with rage, his eyes terrible in their anger. He slapped the farmer twice across the face with the flat of his hand, first one way, then the other.

"Look," he said to Henry, jerking his head at the handcart. "In there!"

Blinking the rain out of his eyes, Henry saw rifles and a sub-machine gun under the tarpaulin, and he realized that the accident he'd had outside Oswino's gate had been no accident at all. Caporelli had been dead right when he'd said that Henry might get hurt. Oswino had been in the plot. A lot of things were suddenly explained—even the calendar of St. Stephen's, Vienna, in the Oswinos' kitchen.

Caporelli was still hitting Oswino viciously. "You!" he was

saying. "You and that bitch of a wife! This is where you kept your guns. Under the barn floor!"

Oswino tried to struggle free, but Caporelli knocked him down again. At last he stopped and dragged the farmer to his feet, limp and bleeding from the mouth.

"Get going," he said savagely. *"Now,* you son of a whore!"

Oswino gave him a frightened look and started to run, his feet slipping in the mud as he scrambled away from them up the slope.

Caporelli started after him for a second, his eyes blazing.

"No wonder Alois was always up here," he said furiously. "No wonder that worm never objected! They were all in it together. This is what she wanted him to collect—before the water washed away the hiding place."

He gestured at Henry and began to load rifles into his arms.

"Into the pond," he snapped, indicating the little artificial dam Oswino had built, where a few ducks were swimming happily, indifferent to the weather, watched by a rooster and a few wretched chickens crouching under the dripping eaves of a broken-down shed.

The ducks squawked and skittered across the water with flapping wings and paddling feet as Henry threw the rifles in. Caporelli joined him and flung in the machine gun and pistol with a savage gesture.

Returning to the barn, he peered among the splintered timbers and kicked angrily at the mud.

"There'll be more in there," he said wearily. "There'll be a whole store of them. That's what he was doing when it collapsed. This is where they've been keeping them all this time."

He glanced around him through the curtains of rain, uncertain for a second, then he gestured angrily upward at the torrents of water that were rushing down on them and through the farm.

"It's all from the dam," he said. "And it's not coming

through the sluice gates, either. Come on. We can't stay here all day. There'll be plenty of time to sort out the Oswinos later."

He picked up the crowbar and they adjusted their loads, and they set off again, stumbling and falling in the rushing stream that the rain had made of the path to the dam.

After a while they came across a crude wooden shed, obviously where Oswino kept his cattle, and stopped to catch their breath. Henry's cigarettes were already only limp wet tubes, but Caporelli produced a packet from under his cape and they lit them and drew in the smoke gratefully, though it tasted sour in the damp atmosphere.

"We start really climbing now," Caporelli said.

Henry nodded and lifted the brief case, which was beginning to weigh like lead against his muscles now, impeding everything he did, and reached for the handle of the canvas bag. Caporelli hoisted the heavy crowbar to his shoulder and took the other handle.

"We shall do it," he said, flashing a grateful look at Henry.

As they went higher, stumbling and slipping, they began to meet rocks, their wet faces shining dully in the ugly light of the sky, and had to scramble around them and over them, clawing with cold fingers at the rain-wet surfaces, their feet sliding from under them on the wet grass and mud as they pushed their loads ahead of them.

"There it is!" Caporelli stopped, breathing heavily, and pointed upward. Through the mist Henry could see the gray stretch of the stopper wall, against the east shoulder of La Fortezza, and around the other side the gray curve of the main wall.

"It's up to you," Henry panted. "I don't know much about this department. You'll have to tell me what to do."

"The gates are in the tunnels," Caporelli said. "It should be dry in there, thank God. We can't afford to get the batteries wet. We can lay a charge and run off a wire and stand well clear." He glanced at Henry, noticing the fury still on his face. "Aynree," he said quietly, "this is going to be difficult. You can't afford to be angry—not even with anybody. You'll need a clear head."

Henry drew a deep breath and fought down the anger inside him. "O.K.," he said. "I'm all right. I shan't drop anything or start it off before you're ready."

Caporelli smiled. "Thank God the dam's still standing," he said.

Henry looked up. "It doesn't look as though it will for long," he commented.

The gray main wall was sprouting jets of water all along its surface. Henry could see them quite plainly through the rain, white against the gray-brown stone, and the center of the wall seemed more saddle-shaped than ever. There was a steady flood of water pushing over it, driving through the dip. The eerie light glinted on it, showing it clearly in a fifty-yard stretch like a weir. Over the noise of the rain they could hear another sound, low and moaning, like a huge animal whimpering in distress.

"It's the dam," Henry said. "It's going to give. Hurry, for God's sake."

Caporelli glanced up, his face twisted. "We shall fix it," he said. "We're not too late."

They scrambled the last half mile to the stopper wall, gasping and panting and streaming with perspiration in spite of the rain and the cold wind, and slithered along its foot to the entrances to the tunnels. Water was already pouring out of the first one they came to, as though the gate was leaking badly, and the tunnel and the gulley were choked with rubbish. They lay gasping against the wall, their feet in the puddles, fighting to get their breath, their muscles trembling after the climb. Even

Caporelli was beginning to look exhausted now, and Henry's legs no longer seemed to belong to him.

"Come on!"

As Henry struggled to his feet and pulled the brief case toward him, Caporelli grabbed his arm so that he fell back against the wall, feeling its icy surface through the thin clothes at his back.

"Wait!"

Caporelli's eyes were alert and his whole body was tense, his head on one side, listening intently.

"There's somebody in there," he whispered.

Then, above the gurgle and hiss of the escaping water running down the sluice, Henry also heard movement inside the tunnel, the occasional click of the metal heel of a shoe against a stone and the clank of a metal pan, as though someone were moving around alongside the sluice.

"Wasescha again?"

Caporelli met Henry's eyes and shrugged. "I don't know," he said. "Wait here."

Kneeling in the mud, he took the ice ax, then slowly got to his feet, edging toward the entrance to the tunnel, one foot after the other, the rubbed-soled boots making no sound on the rocks. Then, with the torch ahead of him, its powerful beam switched on and blinding, he jumped around the corner. There was a cry from inside, a thin, high cry that was quite unexpected, then silence.

Caporelli's voice came, slowly, as though he were startled.

"Aynree," he called. "Come in here."

In the beam of the torch, standing petrified over a fire he'd been attempting to build, was the slender, frightened figure of Giovanni, the missing boy from the orphanage, a pocketknife in his hand, his face taut and terrified, the hair laying in thick plastered curls across his forehead.

16

The boy was standing against the wall, his eyes wide and scared. Beyond him, Henry could see the old wood-and-iron sluice gate, black and slimy with age. He'd been trying to light a fire, but the sticks were wet and it was just a heap of smoldering twigs on the stony ground alongside the sluice. There was a dirty saucepan sitting crookedly on top, full of tepid brown water.

Caporelli put the torch down on a stone, placing it carefully so that it wouldn't roll, then he knelt and pulled the boy toward him, staring up into his face with a wondering expression.

"What are you doing here, Giovanni?" he asked.

Giovanni tried to meet his eyes but failed and his head hung. "I was trying to make the fire go," he muttered. "I was trying to boil some water."

"To drink?"

The boy nodded, and Caporelli's eyes were full of compassion.

"Listen to me, boy," he said gently. "Down at the orphanage

they are all in tears because you are missing. Down there they are praying for you because they don't know what has happened to you. Sister Agata herself came to see me. She couldn't speak for crying."

The boy's expression shut down at once, resentful and sullen, and he stood in front of Caporelli, his head low, the black hair hanging over his eyes.

"Why, boy? Why did you run away?" Caporelli's voice was soft and soothing, and Henry was surprised at the sudden change in him.

"Why?" he repeated. "Why did you do this to those good Sisters?"

Giovanni raised his head, his eyes glistening, his face full of desolation and bitterness. "Because there was nothing to stay for," he said. "Sister Ursula—Sister Ursula—" He choked on his words suddenly, and Caporelli swept him into his arms and held him against his breast, not speaking, holding him close while the boy sobbed out his grief.

"They killed her, Signore," he moaned. "They killed Sister Ursula and she loved me. I know she loved me. And I never had anybody who loved me so before."

There were tears in Caporelli's own eyes as he spoke. "But what did you hope to do, boy?" he asked. "What were you going to live on up here?"

"I don't know, Signore. I had some matches and I found an old pan and I was going to boil some water. I was cold and I thought it would make me warm. I knew it was all right to drink water if you boiled it first. I read it in one of Sister Ursula's books."

"That was very intelligent of you," Caporelli said. "But what were you going to eat?"

The boy's shoulders moved. "I don't know, Signore," he muttered. "Berries, perhaps. Something like that."

"Did you know *which* berries to eat?"

"No, Signore. I just hoped. I was going to try to get over the mountains to the north."

"But why, boy? *Mamma mia,* why?"

"I—I—they told me once that that was where my mother came from. I don't really know, Signore."

Giovanni broke down and sobbed again, bewildered and helpless. He had had no plan, no certainty about what he was doing. In his grief and anger he had fled in the only direction that was open to him, without any sure knowledge of his route, without clothes or food or money.

Caporelli held the boy against him, speaking over the top of his head. "I have no food with me now, Giovanni," he said. "Not now. But I'll find you something as soon as we get back."

Giovanni's face lifted to Caporelli's, thin and pale and like an old man's in its white weariness. "Did you come up here to look for me, Signore?" he asked.

Caporelli's eyes caught Henry's above his head, questioning and worried. "What are we going to do with him?" he seemed to be asking. "How can we go on with what we wanted to do now?"

He sighed deeply, looking into Henry's own hopeless face for help, then he pushed Giovanni away from him. "No, Giovanni," he said briskly. "We didn't come here to look for you. We came up here to do some work."

Giovanni looked puzzled. "Work, Signore? Up here? In weather like this?"

"Yes, Giovanni." Caporelli indicated the sluice gate behind them. It was spouting jets and leaks that shot water across the tunnel against the stone wall with the tremendous pressure behind, filling the narrow space with mist.

"Giovanni," he said gently, "during the war I learned how to use explosives. Here, in these very mountains. I learned how to blow things up. We have come up here today, the doctor and I, to blow that gate off. And more, if we can."

212

Giovanni looked startled. He stared at the gate, black and rotten with age, then at Caporelli, who tried to explain. "There are stupid men down in the valley," he said slowly. "In Cadivescovo. They are good men, you understand, but they are not very clever and they are lazy. They are not very big men, although they think they are, and they will not take responsibility for things that ought to be taken care of. Not because they are wicked, but because they are stupid. Now the doctor here"—he indicated Henry—"he is a very clever man. He knows all about dams and bridges and thing like that. He goes all over the world looking at them. He writes books about them and knows exactly when they are safe and when they are dangerous. *E bravo il Dottore,* and he says this dam is not safe and that with all this rain it is in danger of collapsing. You remember he spoke to you and to Sister Ursula about it? You had noticed that there were many leaks."

Giovanni nodded and Caporelli went on slowly, containing his impatience to get to work for fear of frightening the boy.

"We have tried many times to persuade these stupid people in Cadivescovo that the dam must be drained," he said. "Before the great wall collapses and washes away the town—and the orphanage and all the farms and houses and all the trees and flowers."

Giovanni's eyes flew to Henry's face. "Would it do that, Signore?"

Henry nodded. "It would do all of that and more, Giovanni," he said soberly.

"And what are you going to do then?"

Henry nodded at the gate behind the boy, the dripping slime on it shining in the light of the torch.

"There's only one way to drain the dam, Giovanni," he said. "We must blow that gate out. That one and others, too, if we can. If we don't, the main wall may collapse."

Giovanni stared from Caporelli to Henry and back again,

as though he were trying to assess their honesty. Then he looked at the gate and at the brief case in Henry's hand.

"Is that the dynamite?" he asked.

"Not dynamite, Giovanni," Caporelli said. "We have better things than dynamite these days. It's pentolite. It's very powerful. They mix it with oil to make it into a plastic that you can mold around things. Like putty. It's much easier to work with. That's what we've got."

Giovanni looked interested. "Signore, may I watch?" he asked.

Caporelli gave a sigh of relief and managed a brief smile at Henry. "That, Giovanni," he said, "was what I was going to ask you to do. We haven't time to take you down to the town and we just can't leave you to run away again. You must stay with us now until we've finished. Afterward I'll take care of you, I promise. You may stay at the Stettnerhof and eat all the food you can tuck away. I'll arrange it with the Mother Superior. Will you do that?"

"Yes, Signore. If I may watch the explosions?"

Caporelli grinned, as though all the tension had drained away from him.

"You may even be able to help a little," he said. "But you must do exactly what you are told and nothing more, because what we're going to do is dangerous." He gestured at the brief case. "The pentolite is in there and the energy contained in the small amount in that bag is released in the form of gas which reaches a speed of several thousand feet per second. The strongest steel is incapable of withstanding the splintering effect of this sudden expansion. You understand all this? It has to be set off with detonators and these detonators can blow your hand off if you don't handle them carefully. You see why I am telling you to be careful. I have told the doctor this, too, and he knows the dangers."

Giovanni nodded gravely. "I will do exactly what I am told, Signore," he said.

Caporelli patted his head. "Very good," he said. "And when it is all over, you must keep it a secret. Nobody is to know what has happened but us. You understand?"

"I understand."

"You may even have to lie a little in case people ask where you have been. They don't want us to drain the dam, so we have to do it in secret. I will tell them a story about finding you on the mountain, and you must remember it and say exactly the same. Do you understand that too?"

"Yes, Signore."

"It will perhaps mean lying, as I say, and Sister Ursula taught you not to lie. Would you for once lie for me if it is necessary?"

Giovanni nodded briskly. "Yes, Signor Caporelli. For you."

Caporelli pushed him away and, taking off his jacket, slipped it over the boy. "Very well then," he said cheerfully. "We've wasted enough time talking. Let's get on with it."

He caught Henry's eye as he turned away. "God help us," he said. "Making saboteurs of young children."

Caporelli flashed the torch across the gate and studied it for a second, his face somber as he stared at the cracks and the hissing jets of water. With the roaring rain outside and the gurgling water in the sluice and the misty dampness in the tunnel, it was icy cold under the stopper wall and they were all already soaked to the skin. Henry could feel Giovanni shivering alongside him.

Caporelli seemed to have forgotten the boy already, however, in his absorption with his task.

"It won't take long to blow that off," he grunted. "The water will do what we can't do."

After the delay Henry was itching with impatience, and the

215

way Caporelli opened the brief case and laid the tools on a stone one after the other seemed to be infuriatingly slow. He seemed to read Henry's thoughts and looked up and smiled.

"You need to know where things are," he said quietly.

He began to work at last, rapidly, moving surely as though he knew every trick and pitfall in the operation. Using the torch, he pawed across the leaking gate, standing knee-deep in the water of the gulley, saturated by the jets that played across his body as he felt through the green slime for the weak spots. Then, abruptly, he began to jab with the crowbar, digging into the crumbling cement and stone on one side of the iron frame.

"It won't take long," he said. "It's already eaten away."

He unpacked the charges next, and calling to Giovanni to pass him tools, he stuffed the first charge into the hole he'd made, while Henry stood in the sluice alongside him, his trousers plastered against his legs by the rushing water, and worked at the other side of the gate, making a second hole where Caporelli indicated, jabbing with the crowbar, indifferent to his trembling muscles and his skinned knuckles as he scraped them against the stone.

"Two charges will smash anything this size," Caporelli was saying. "So long as we place it sufficiently far into the concrete to contain the blast."

He was talking slowly all the time in an attempt to stop any sign of fear in Giovanni.

"This way," he said, "all the force comes outward and wrecks the gate. And we have to mold the plastic against the frame so that it works with maximum efficiency. We don't need much. We'll have enough to blow at least three more."

He moved back from the gate and, picking up the tin of detonators, carefully began to unwrap them. "This is where we have to take great care," he said slowly, peering down in the light of the torch that Giovanni held. "We have to insert these now. They will be linked so that they will fire instanta-

216

neously. This is a job that demands a cool head and steady hands, as a slip now could make a nasty mess. It is like an electric circuit and each separate element has to be in its proper place. When we've done this, we must lay out the wire to the battery. After that—whoof!"

He grinned at Giovanni and began to place the second charge, working quickly and methodically all the time, then he attached the wire to the detonators and pressed them firmly into the plastic.

"A strong charge across that," he said, talking like a lecturer, to hold the boy's attention as he fastened the wire to the gate with string and tape, "and up she goes. The way I've placed them, they'll blow the door outward. No chance of it jamming then—if there's any of it left."

He paused and rubbed his fingers, looking up at Giovanni with a bleak smile. *"Madonna,"* he said. "My fingers are cold. It's all this water. It's quite like the old days when the Germans were just around the corner."

He picked up the crowbar and managed a thin smile at Henry.

"Stay here," he said. "I'll fix some sort of shelter outside with my cape. Somewhere dry for the battery, around the corner out of the blast. Make sure nothing comes loose. Giovanni, bring that coil of wire. Once the gate's loose, the pressure behind will blow it out. We'll need to be outside then. Collect everything ready for the next gate. We'll not get back in here again when it starts."

Henry glanced at the rotten gate at the end of the tunnel. Water was still pouring through it in jets that splashed on the walls of the misty tunnel and bubbling out into the concrete sluiceway which carried it down the Val Caloroso and away around La Fortezza to the Punta dei Fiori. Crouching in the spray, he tried to visualize what might happen to him if the gate gave before they were ready for it. The immense pressure of the two million tons of water behind it would smash it to splinters that would be driven out of the tunnel like a shot from a gun, the fragments crushing the life out of him against the wall. His eyes flickered across the charges Caporelli had placed. Nobody would thank them for what they were doing, he thought, especially not Dei Monti, and if they were caught by the police, it would be hard to explain why they were there and where they'd obtained their explosive. It would probably have been much easier to let the dam go, he decided, and take refuge behind a smug "I told you so."

As he bent over the brief case, strapping it up again around the plastic, Caporelli picked up his cape and a pair of pliers. The crowbar was resting against the tunnel alongside him and Giovanni held the coil of wire, waiting for instructions, his eyes on Caporelli's face.

Then, as they started for the entrance to the tunnel, Henry caught a glimpse over his shoulder of a figure silhouetted against the pale light of the entrance, and Caporelli's exclamation made him whirl.

"Alois!"

It was Stettner. He was smiling, his gold teeth glinting brightly in the light of the torch. But he looked different from usual. Like Caporelli, he was wearing *kletteschühe* and a heavy cape that made him seem enormous in the choked entrance to the tunnel.

He grinned, and then Henry saw young Dittli appear behind him up the slope. He was carrying a rope and seemed scared and pale and without Stettner's ebullient self-confidence.

"The Montanari are here," Stettner said. "We saw you coming all the way. The refuge at the foot of La Fortezza makes a good shelter in this weather and a good point of vantage."

"*Cristo!*"

Caporelli lunged at once, his arm raised, and Dittli jumped

218

forward and swung with the heavy rope with all his strength. It caught Caporelli across the face and he staggered back, half blinded, trying to blink the sight back to his eyes, a livid weal across his nose and cheeks.

Stettner had a pistol in his hand now and he was gesturing with it. "Don't do that again, Brother-in-law," he said harshly.

All the eagerness and excitement Henry had felt as they worked had drained away into bitterness, anger, and frustration. He knew immediately why Stettner was there and he knew somehow they would never blow out the stopper gate now.

Another figure appeared in the entrance to the tunnel, wearing a bright green rubber cape, and Henry saw it was Wasescha, the bearded little man he'd seen with Dittli on the mountain.

Stettner was watching their expressions with a smile on his face, his eyes merry. "Do you usually bring children with you," he asked, gesturing at Giovanni, "when you get up to your dirty work?"

Henry swept the boy behind him, circling him with his arm, and he could feel his slender, trembling body crouched against his own.

"Because you *were* up to dirty work, weren't you, Herr Doktor?" Stettner went on. "You were going to blow the gate off, weren't you? You've been itching to do it ever since you came to Cadivescovo."

His smile vanished and he gestured at Giovanni. "What's he doing here?" he demanded sharply.

"Leave him alone," Caporelli said between his teeth. "If you touch him, Alois, I'll kill you!"

Stettner shrugged. "I very much regret there'll be quite a lot of killing before the day's out," he said. "When we've finished here, you're going to take a walk up to the dam. Later, perhaps tomorrow, someone will telephone the police to say there are bodies floating in the water. We had it all planned, though

219

we didn't expect to find a child here. He's a different matter and we may have to think of something else. An accident perhaps. A little plastic explosive that went off too soon. However, *Sie sterben für eine gute Sache*. You're dying in a good cause." He gestured at the brief case. "What's in that bag?" he demanded.

Dittli bent over the case and, as he began to unfasten it, Henry stepped forward to stop him. Stettner pushed him back against the wall.

"Don't do that again, Englishman," he snapped. "Your precious English passport won't save you. They can't send a gunboat up here to help, you know. I'll have to do away with you some time, so I shan't mind when."

He looked at the expression on Henry's face and sneered, his eyes bleak and cold with the dregs of a ravaged idealism, like the blue china eyes of a doll. "You should live here, Englishman," he said. "Then you might know something of the faith we have and the frustration that we've suffered. *We* shan't soil the joy of victory with halfhearted Socialism and collusion with the East."

He turned to Dittli, who was examining the contents of the brief case, and they began to speak in German.

"Who are they, Signore?" Giovanni whispered. "Why is the Signor Stettner here?"

Henry drew a deep breath. "They are Montanari, Giovanni," he said quietly. "They are the people who have been blowing up the railway bridges and the trains."

Giovanni's eyes narrowed and Henry heard him draw in his breath sharply. "Are they the people who killed Sister Ursula, Signore?"

Henry nodded. "Yes, Giovanni. They are the people who killed Sister Ursula."

The boy made a move forward, and Henry grabbed his arm and held him tightly. Caporelli's eyes were agonized.

"Be still, Giovanni," Henry whispered. "For the love of God, be still."

Stettner and Dittli had finished talking now and Stettner swung the pistol around to Caporelli. "Where's the rest of the plastic, Brother-in-law?" he demanded. "You've used some of it."

Caporelli glared back, his mouth tight, but Wasescha gestured toward the sluice gate and Dittli swung the torch around so that the spray from the jets playing on the wall became golden in its beam. Stettner nodded and Wasecha climbed across the rubble and stood knee-deep in the water as he began to detach the charges.

Caporelli swung around after him, but Stettner slammed him back against the wall with a blow across the face with the pistol. Caporelli shook his head like a wounded animal, and Henry saw there was a deep gash across his cheek. Even as he watched, the blood welled up in little beads and began to trickle down his face and off the end of his chin onto his shirt. Giovanni's eyes narrowed and glittered blackly, and Henry gripped his arm more tightly.

"Look, Stettner," he said savagely, as he saw Wasescha reaching up to the holes they'd dug, to remove the detonators. "That dam's dangerous. It's likely to go. That's why we were blowing off the gate."

Stettner gestured angrily. "*I* don't care if the dam goes," he snapped. "We've got better uses for plastic explosive than draining an old dam."

"What about the town?" Caporelli yelled, his fury exploding out of him at last.

Stettner shrugged. "It's filled with Italian police at the moment!"

Henry fought down his disgust and forced himself to speak calmly, knowing he'd get nothing out of Stettner in the black rage that was tearing at him.

221

"There are a lot of your friends down there, too," he pointed out.

"None that we shall miss. *Our* friends are in the mountains where they've been for months, some of them for years."

"Not Elena Oswino," Caporelli jeered. "She was down there looking for *you.*"

The laughter died out of Stettner's face. "Are you sure, Brother-in-law?"

"She was looking for you in the Stettnerhof. That's why we came."

Stettner's eyes flickered and for a second, as he looked uncertain, Henry thought they might dissuade him. Then he shrugged and grinned. "No matter," he said. "Elena knows where to go."

Wasescha was removing the plastic now, reaching into the holes they'd hacked out of the rotten cement.

"What else have you got, Brother-in-law?" Stettner jeered.

Dittli was examining the canvas bag now and he held it open for Stettner to glance inside. He straightened up and grinned at them. "We'll leave you your battery," he said. "We can soon get one of those."

Wasescha had removed all the charges now and was placing them carefully back in the brief case.

"Frau Oswino?" Stettner said, and grinned at Caporelli. "She'll be back. She'll know what to do with them. She's always known what to do. Right under your nose, Brother-in-law. All the time the police were looking. Even her husband did as she said. She wasn't born in Innsbruck for nothing."

Wasescha had strapped up the brief case now. He straightened up and looked at Stettner, still without having said a word, as though he had lived so long in the wordless silences of the Catena di Saga he'd forgotten how to speak.

"Schnell!" Stettner jerked his head and Wasescha turned

immediately and scrambled through the rubble and out of the tunnel.

"Listen, Stettner—" Henry began, but Stettner waved the pistol and pushed him back.

"Shut up, Englishman," he snapped. "I don't listen to you any more. Up here I'm not Alois Stettner, the guide, the tourists' courier, at the beck and call of every stupid English *Auslander*. Up here I'm 'Andreas Hofer.' These are *our* mountains, *my* mountains, and this is *my* country. There are streams in the valleys, Englishman, that you'll never see and those Italian policemen down there'll never see, and earth smells of warmth and good growth, and jays and woodpeckers in the trees and hawks over the meadows, and millraces that throw up water like a bow wave. These things are *ours*, not the property of some pious politician in Rome."

The pistol was jerking now. "I shall enjoy disposing of you," he was saying. "I have never disposed of an Englishman before. Only of English *girls*. You could have saved us such a lot of trouble if you hadn't been so infernally lucky. We had several tries, but they were hurried, and you had the angels on your side, and unfortunately we couldn't afford to be crude about them. They had to be accidents."

Dittli was watching them nervously. "Hurry, Alois," he said in English. "We can't stand here all day talking."

"No," Stettner agreed. "No, we can't. We must get after Wasescha and help him hide the brief case."

The hole in the pistol seemed as big as a tunnel. In a little while, Henry thought, we shall all probably be dead—if not in a matter of minutes, then in a matter of hours—and he had a terrible wish to be spirited away. He could feel his heart pounding, but he was somehow less afraid than angry and he put as much of a sneer into his voice as he could manage.

"You'd better hurry," he suggested. "Wasescha won't find it so easy to hide anything this time."

"What do you mean?"

"Because your hiding place has collapsed, Alois," Caporelli shouted. "We found it. We found Oswino trapped under it and pulled him out."

Stettner stepped forward and struck him across the face again with the pistol, once, twice, and he stumbled and fell against the wall of the tunnel.

"You're lying!"

Caporelli dragged himself up weakly and managed a jagged laugh. "Not this time, Alois," he said. "There were rifles and a submachine gun and a pistol, apart from a few other things."

Stettner's eyes flickered toward Dittli's, then he gestured at the wire and the scattered tools lying about the floor of the tunnel among the rubble. He spoke sharply and, as the waiter began to coil the wire, Stettner threw the cape off his arm with a gesture and glared at Caporelli.

He was obviously furiously angry now and began to kick the tools and wire toward Dittli for him to pick up, and as he did so, Henry saw Caporelli's hand creeping out toward the crowbar. The knowledge that Caporelli's mind was still set on action startled him because he looked gray-faced and sick as he leaned weakly against the wall. His nose was bruised where the gun had struck him and the blood was startlingly bright against his pale skin. But the eyes were alert in the drooping head, Henry saw, and the slow movement of the clawing fingers, stained with mud and green with the slime from the sluice gate, fascinated him and he had to jerk his eyes away to Stettner's face in case he should give him away.

Dittli was in the gulley with the wire now, his back to the entrance to the tunnel, and Henry moved slightly to place himself between him and Caporelli.

"Look, Stettner," he said, trying desperately to draw attention to himself. "Listen to me for a while. This is no quarrel of mine. I've got some money on me."

"Ha!" Stettner's head turned to Henry and the crawling fingers began to move again. "So the British Empire's pulled down the flag, eh? So! It's going to try to buy its way out as it has before." He kicked angrily at the wire. *"Machen Sie schnell!"* he snapped at Dittli. *"Schnell! Schnell!"*

"You can have all I've got," Henry said. "It'll help your party. I don't care what you do with it."

Caporelli's face was ghastly with the blood on it and the slime, but the moving fingers stopped as Stettner glanced at him and jerked his head at Henry.

"Perfidious Albion, Brother-in-law," he said. "They buy themselves out of everything."

He gestured at Henry with the pistol. "Give me the money," he said. "It'll not be wasted."

Henry fished in his pocket for his wallet, taking as long as possible while Stettner clicked his fingers impatiently. He knew there was very little money in it and he couldn't imagine it delaying Stettner for long.

He held it up at last and Stettner sneered. "It looks thin," he said. "As though the British Empire doesn't set a very high price on itself. That doesn't look enough to prevent your climb up to the top of the dam."

He clicked his fingers again and Henry tossed the wallet down in front of him. Caporelli's moving fingers stopped dead as Stettner's eyes swung across them all.

"That's too old a trick to catch me, Englishman," he said. "Pick it up and bring it to me. No"—he gestured as Henry moved forward—"not you!" He indicated Giovanni. "You!"

Giovanni backed behind Henry, and Stettner gestured angrily with the pistol. "Come on, you little Italian bastard," he snapped. "Come and do what your betters tell you! Pick it up and bring it here!"

Giovanni glanced at Henry, then he slipped out from behind him.

"Beeilen Sie sich! Hurry."

Giovanni looked again at Henry and then at Caporelli, his eyes questioning. Caporelli's lips twisted. "Do as he says, Giovanni," he said quietly.

Giovanni stooped and picked up the wallet, then he straightened up as Stettner clicked his fingers again. Somehow, from his manner, Henry knew his mind was working, and he could see his eyes were bright and quick, and he prayed that the boy would do nothing foolish.

Stettner took the wallet from Giovanni, the gun in his right hand, then, as his eyes dropped to it, Giovanni dived unexpectedly for his wrist, forcing the pistol away toward the sluice, hanging on to it with both hands and arms and every vestige of strength in his slight body.

"Quickly, Signore," he shrieked. "Quickly! Kill them!"

Stettner heaved, trying to bring the gun to bear, his mouth contorted and swearing, but Giovanni's arms were tight around his wrist and his legs were kicking wildly as he was swung into the air.

"Dittli!" Caporelli roared a warning as he grabbed for the crowbar.

The roar of the gun filled the narrow tunnel, deafening them as Henry flung himself across Dittli's back, hammering at his head with his fists in a savage explosion of rage. Dittli went downward into the muddy sluice among the rubbish and the sticks and the old tin cans, and Henry heard the high "whanng" of the bullet as it hit the stonework at the entrance to the tunnel and spun away into the mist. Then, as Stettner threw the shrieking Giovanni aside, the crowbar came down across his forearm with all the strength of Caporelli's shoulders behind it. Stettner screamed and the gun clattered to the stones at his feet, but with his mouth open, his eyes bulging with pain and fear and one arm limp and useless, he still tumbled one-handed toward Caporelli.

226

Henry saw the flash of a knife and shouted a warning, but the swing of the crowbar had almost carried the dazed Caporelli off his feet and he was at Stettner's mercy. As Henry leaped from his knees in a flat dive, his shoulder crashed against Giovanni, who was just scrambling to his feet, and sent him flying into the sluice, then his reaching arms had smothered the groping hand with the knife.

Stettner screamed with pain again as his broken bones were slammed against his side, but even in his agony he was strong and clearheaded, and as he ducked, Henry went somersaulting over his shoulders, cracking his chin against the wall of the tunnel. As he hit the ground, however, twisting around at once to regain his feet, he saw Caporelli recover and the crowbar come slicing around again in a great scything blow.

Stettner's feet were swept from under him as the steel crunched against flesh and bone, and he gave another cry and collapsed, half in the sluice, clawing with his one good hand for a grip, his eyes wild, his mouth working like a wounded animal's. Caporelli brought the crowbar down again in a gust of fury across his thigh, and he screamed once on a high tormented note and rolled back, unconscious.

Dittli was on the bank now, blood coming from his nose, his eyes wide with fear, his clothes saturated where he had fallen into the sluice.

"Aynree!"

As he dived for the entrance to the tunnel, Henry stuck out his foot and Dittli went flat on his face into the mud again. He stayed there, whimpering. Henry scrambled to his feet and yanked him up, one-handed, and slammed him savagely against the stone wall.

Caporelli had dropped the crowbar now and he leaned against the wall, gasping, his face gray. The blood had started to flow faster from the gash on his cheek.

"Ettore—"

Caporelli waved Henry away and indicated Dittli. "Never mind me," he muttered. "Watch him."

As Henry kept one eye on the sullen waiter, Caporelli stumbled across to Giovanni and pulled him out of the sluice, his face concerned, his eyes soft.

"Are you all right, my son?" he asked gently.

Giovanni nodded, but Henry could see he was shaking, as though shock had started to take effect on him.

Caporelli put his arms around him and held him close. "That was a very brave thing to do," he said.

Giovanni began to cry softly, his head down as though he were ashamed of his lack of strength. "It was because of Sister Ursula," he said. "Because they killed her. That's why. I'm sorry I'm crying. I can't help it."

Caporelli's mouth twisted. "That's nothing, my son," he said. "All brave men find the need to cry occasionally. It is the food of the soul—like grief and love. There is nothing to be ashamed of in it."

17

Caporelli pushed the boy aside gently after a while and made him sit down. Henry took off his coat and put it around him over Caporelli's.

"Soon," Caporelli said, "we will find you hot food and warmth. Be brave until then. Cry if you wish. It does no harm."

Giovanni nodded, his burning eyes on Caporelli's face as though, in the brief moment of savagery in the tunnel, he had transferred all the love in him from the gentle Sister Ursula to the strong and practical man.

"I'm all right, Signore," he said quietly. "I'm glad we beat them."

"So am I, Giovanni," Caporelli said. "And we did. Soundly."

He crossed to Stettner who was lying on his back in the sluice, with the water flowing around him, his mouth open, his eyes closed, the blood running across his hand from the crushed flesh under his sleeve.

Caporelli stared down at him for a second, his face expressionless, then he jerked his head toward Dittli.

"Better make sure he's not got a gun," he said.

Henry crossed to the waiter and began to search him. Dittli pushed sullenly at his hands and Caporelli stepped forward immediately and hit him across the face. Dittli staggered back, his mouth bleeding, and spat out a tooth.

"Now search him," Caporelli said.

This time Dittli didn't move and Henry found a small automatic in his pocket.

"Keep it," Caporelli said. "He hadn't the courage to use it. We'll decide what to do with him later."

Dittli's eyes flickered and he swung around in a sudden dart for the tunnel, his feet scraping on the stones. Caporelli gave him a violent push as he passed him—unemotionally, his face still devoid of expression—and he crashed into the stone wall with a cry, slid down and sat at its base, his mouth hanging open.

As he fell, Caporelli's pent-up fury burst out of him at last and he stood over him and, dragging him to his feet, hit him again, and again and again, cursing and panting and calling him every name he could lay his tongue to, punching and slapping and kicking until Dittli crouched against the wall, not attempting to stop him, his head covered with his arms, shrieking for mercy.

"You filth," Caporelli said in a cold, bitter voice. "You treacherous filth. You kill and murder and maim, and howl for mercy when it's *you* who's hurt."

Henry saw the startled shock in Giovanni's face and dragged Caporelli off at last, and he leaned against the wall, panting, his eyes wild with fury.

"Ettore!"

Caporelli spat at Dittli in a gesture of disgust that was as Neapolitan as Santa Lucia. Dittli looked up and began to shout back at him in German, and Caporelli hit him again with the flat of his hand.

"In Italian," he snapped. "In Italian, when you speak to me in my own country, you German murderer!"

He looked at Giovanni, whose thin face was pale and frightened but by no mean accusing. "Forgive me, Giovanni," he said. "I am only a man, with human feelings, and these men are wicked and murderers. They have stopped us doing what we came here for."

He took out his cigarettes and lit one with trembling hands, slowly drawing in the smoke as though he were desperate for it, then he went to the entrance to the tunnel and stared out in the direction of the main wall of the dam. Above the roar of the water in the sluice Henry heard that ominous moaning sound again. Until that moment he had forgotten it and he realized it was louder than before.

"We can do nothing," Caporelli said, swinging around, his eyes blazing. "These madmen with their stupid politics! God knows how many people might die now just because they want to blow up one policeman."

He picked up the ice ax and, jumping into the sluice, began to hack at the gate near the hinges, striking sparks as the steel clanged on the ironwork. For a second Henry thought he'd gone mad, then he swung around and, scrambling out of the sluice, dragged Dittli to his feet.

Dittli's eyes stared at the ax in his hand. "What are you going to do to me?" he yelled.

Caporelli suddenly became calm again. "I'd like to shoot you," he said bitterly, and began to push the waiter toward the sluice gate.

Dittli seemed to shrink, resisting against Caporelli's shoves as though he were being placed against a wall for a firing squad.

"You can't," he yelled. "You can't shoot me."

"No." Caporelli's eyes flashed. "No, I can't, because I didn't come up here to destroy such Tedescho scum as you. I've better things to do. Here—" He thrust the ice ax at Dittli. "Get going. Break that gate down!"

Dittli stared at him as though he were crazy.

"Get going!"

Dittli turned and stared at the gate, obviously knowing that if he succeeded and the gate gave, he'd be washed out of the tunnel himself by the pressure of water behind it, smashed by the heavy balks of rotten timber and iron. He turned again and stared wildly at Caporelli who quite calmly once more brought back his arm and smashed his fist into his face.

"Get going!"

Dittli heaved himself to his feet, staggered, and Caporelli went for him again with both hands, hitting out viciously until Dittli pushed him off and, jumping into the gulley, began to hack frantically at the gate. Caporelli stared at him for a second, then he picked up the crowbar and began to attack the gate alongside him like a madman.

"Why didn't you hit me with the ax?" he sneered at Dittli between blows. "When I had nothing in my hand. Why didn't you shoot us? Because you're a jackal who can only fight around corners in the dark."

Dittli stopped hacking at the gate and Caporelli gestured at him with the crowbar. "If you move away," he said, "I'll smash your skull in with this."

He turned to Henry and nodded at Stettner, who was just coming around.

"Get him outside," he said.

As Henry grabbed Stettner's shoulders and pulled him out of the gulley, he screamed, a rasping shriek of pain as the broken bones moved. Even in his anger, it seemed to shrivel Henry and he saw Giovanni go ashen and clap his hands, half hidden by the two jackets, against his ears. But Caporelli seemed unmoved.

232

"Get him outside," he repeated, and Henry realized just how hard a core partisan warfare had put in him. Caporelli had seen and done things Henry couldn't even imagine, and it had left an agate center inside him that eighteen years of comfortable living had not even touched. He could have shed his urbanity overnight and gone back without effort to the desperate living of the war years.

Stettner went on screaming all the time Henry was dragging him out of the tunnel, alternatively crying out in rage and begging in a whimper to be left alone. Shutting his ears, Henry jammed him upright against the stone wall, around the corner from the tunnel, and he sat there, half fainting, the rain running off his face. As he turned to re-enter the tunnel, Henry heard the whimpering, moaning sound again, and this time it seemed still louder. His eyes swung upward to the curve of that huge gray mass of stone and mud and rubbish.

"Ettore," he called, "it's too late!"

Caporelli came to the entrance to the tunnel and stared across the valley toward the wall. Among the trees in the dip they caught a brief glimpse of the green cape Wasescha wore as it moved toward the other side and the Oswino farm.

"No," he said. "We might still do it."

As he went back inside the tunnel, Stettner's eyes followed him. He had recovered a little now and was sitting hunched against the wall, one hand across his chest gripping his smashed elbow, one foot straight out, the other twisted in an ugly fashion to his left, the water streaming down his gray cheeks.

The moaning sound came again, then an enormous creaking sound like a door moving on its hinges.

"For God's sake, Ettore," Henry yelled.

The hacking sound in the tunnel stopped and Caporelli appeared again as he pointed.

"It's going," Henry said.

Caporelli's face was bleak and dangerous-looking. "We'd

better get down there," he said, "and try to warn them. We can do no more up here." His voice cracked. "We can't touch the gate without the plastic."

Henry indicated Dittli who had appeared in the entrance to the tunnel, his bruised face white, the blood livid around his mouth where Caporelli had punched him. "What about him?" he said. "And Stettner. We can't leave him here."

Caporelli blew the rain from his mouth and wiped the hair from his eyes. The look on his face was savage.

"Why not?" he said.

"He'll die."

"Dittli will take care of him."

"Aren't we going to hand him over to the police?"

Caporelli gave him a grin that, through the mud and blood, was ugly in its cruelty.

"Why?" he said. "Why waste time? He's finished. He'll do no more harm. *Ever.*"

He bent over Stettner who watched him with dumb-eyed sullen agony.

"He'll be a cripple for the rest of his life," Caporelli said, his voice harsh with satisfaction. "He'll never climb again or swim again or ski or sleep with girls. Perhaps someone will offer him a job. Sweeping the road or selling newspapers. And at night he'll sit in the corner of a bar and drink and get fat, and the boys will call him an old soak, and the girls he wants so much will jeer at his twisted limbs. That'll be worse than death to him. Perhaps it'll make up for the dead men and the grieving wives and mothers he's caused."

He turned to Giovanni and pulled him to his feet. "Can you walk, my son?" he asked.

"Yes, Signore, I'm all right now."

"Soon this nightmare will be over. Fighting and blood were never meant for children's eyes."

He never even glanced back at Stettner and Dittli as he took

234

Giovanni's hand and set off down the valley. For a second Henry hesitated, then he turned and followed him. Stettner watched them go, hatred and bleak courage in his eyes, while Dittli, looking worn and aged, stood behind him, leaning against the ancient stone, staring at the gushing brown water that came out of the tunnel.

They dropped quickly into the valley, heading back the way they'd come. Henry felt sick with anxiety. He'd been so certain that they'd succeed, and failure had left him drained and beaten. Ahead of them, on the opposite slope of the valley, he could glimpse the green cape of Wasescha as he climbed the hill toward Oswino's farm.

The groaning seemed to be growing louder now and, though it was difficult to see through the lashing rain, he felt certain he could see movement in the wall.

"Ettore," he called to Caporelli, who was below and ahead of him with Giovanni. "Wait! For God's sake, wait!"

Caporelli stopped and, turning on the slope, looked up at him. Then he stared up at the dam wall, his brows down. There was nothing up there that Henry could be certain of, but some instinct, some engineer's sixth sense that sounded a warning through his wretchedness, told him it was unsafe to cross the valley.

Caporelli gestured impatiently, but even as he turned back downhill, Henry saw a crevice the size of several barrels open in the face of the dam. As he stared at it, horrified, it crumbled into a V-shaped notch, ten feet wide, suddenly gouged out of the saddle-shaped stretch in the center.

"*Mamma mia!*" Caporelli's words came in a flat gasp, and he grabbed Giovanni's arm and began to retreat up the hill toward Henry.

As they watched, they saw Wasescha stop dead and stare upward at the dam, his face white in the gloom, then he whirled and started to scramble frantically up the slope again. A jet of water suddenly spurted from the wall, unexpected in spite of the crack, sprang thirty feet out into the valley below in a great arc, as though someone had turned on a giant hose. The spray from it leaped up as the wind caught it, and they saw more water welling through the very foundation stones as they watched in dreadful fascination.

Wasescha had stopped once more and, they saw him throw the brief case aside and start climbing again, his legs pumping like pistons as he struggled to gain height. The awful groaning continued, filling the air as though it came from all sides at once over the hiss and gurgle of the rain and the roar of the wind, as the twenty million tons of water beyond the wall were projected at the weak spot behind the break. A second jet spurted from the wall, and instantly grew thicker and deeper. The spray rose higher and they saw solid objects coming away with the water and realized they were lumps of earth and stones. The jets grew steadily bigger as the cracks grew longer; more jets appeared and finally the whole wall seemed to bulge.

"It's gone," Caporelli yelled.

The wall moved slowly, almost like an expanding balloon. There was a tremendous report like thunder that echoed against the slopes of the valley, and the wall moved away in front of the water as it leaped from its ancient artificial bed and plunged down the valley, pushing a three-hundred-foot segment of stone and earth with it.

They saw the water strike Wasescha, the first wave bouncing off him in a spray like a breaker against a rock on an open beach, then he was gone, engulfed in a brown muddy torrent and a mass of tumbling debris that smashed in a monstrous surf against the wall of the valley where he'd been climbing. Then Caporelli, who'd been slowly pushing Giovanni all the time back up the slope, was grabbing at Henry's arm and shouting in his ear.

"Run," he yelled. "Back up to the stopper wall. Run!"

The water was roaring toward them in a solid brown wall topped by foam and tumbling debris as the leading waves fought to get through the gorges to the lake and the following flood built up behind and spread across the narrow valley. They had swung around now and were running as hard as they could, heaving themselves over rocks and undergrowth, their feet slithering on the wet tufty grass. Several times Henry went flat on his face, his mind filled with horror at the thought of the racing bore of water rolling against the side of the slope, rising higher and higher all the time as the thousands of tons of water poured from the dam. He saw trees go down and huge boulders that had withstood all the ravages of centuries plucked from the valley face; his mind was numb as though he were in a nightmare, being chased by a monster and unable to make his feet move fast enough.

They had grabbed the sobbing Giovanni by the arms and were dragging him with them, his feet trailing behind as they stumbled and crashed over rocks and through the brushwood that beat against their faces with quick stinging blows that left livid marks. The breath was rasping in Henry's throat and the muscles of his legs were like jelly, his fingernails seemed to be torn out as he scrabbled for a handhold, his sight growing blurred, his chest hurting intolerably, and the blood pounding in his ears.

"Run," Caporelli kept shouting. "Keep going!"

The flood was a brown seemingly solid wall in which trees and boulders were moving. It was rushing up toward them like an express train, thundering and roaring higher and higher up the slope as the contents of the dam fell into the valley.

They stumbled headfirst into a ditch that had been dug for irrigation, probably by Oswino. The other side seemed too wet and muddy and too steep to climb out, and Giovanni was crying out, sobbing for them to help him as he clawed feebly at

237

the bank, all his strength drained away by the run up the hill. Caporelli was dragging himself up by the roots of a tree and he reached back for Giovanni as the first of the brown water came swirling up the ditch, forced along in a roaring, frothing, spouting cataract by the pressures behind it. In a second it was up to Henry's armpits and he could feel the force of it tearing him away.

He flung the boy up to Caporelli, who grabbed him by the shoulders and hurled him bodily higher up the slope in a tangle of arm and legs, then he reached down and grabbed Henry's arm, leaning back against the pull of the water as his strong fingers closed around Henry's wrist. A rock hit Henry at the side of the head and the water poured over him, thick and muddy, filling his nose and mouth as fought for breath. He could hear the awful roaring, gurgling sound in his ears and feel his heart pounding and the drag of the water at his limbs, but all the time he was conscious of Caporelli's strong hand still on his wrist. Then the water had gone again as suddenly as it had come, receding as the flood poured down toward the lake, plucking at stones and bushes and soil, and he was spluttering and gasping and half-drowned, with Caporelli above him, still holding on to his tree, and Giovanni sprawled like a corpse on the line of debris that the water had left behind as it retreated.

His head throbbing, Henry dragged himself slowly to the top of the bank and he lay with Caporelli, flat on his face, both of them covered with mud and twigs and gravel, gasping for breath.

"You saved my life, Ettore," Henry said at last.

Caporelli managed a weak shrug and blew a wet leaf from his lips. "You saved mine," he said. "But for you, we'd have been down there and we'd not have got back. But for you, Giovanni would never have got out of there."

The ditch had disappeared entirely under a flood of wreckage. There were trees and planks and two dead goats that had been snatched up from somewhere and were swilling back and forth among the rubbish.

They got to their feet and climbed to a spur of rock and threw themselves down, watching the brown flood roaring and smashing down the valley. The water seemed to leap, not touching the ground, bounding down the mountain, crashing everything down with it as the dam drained. The flood was literally treetop-high as it smashed downward, its speed diminished by the curves of the valley, rolling with it rocks that weighed tons. They saw all the crucifixes and little bridges go one after the other, snapping like pipestems as the water plunged down on them, and the piles of sawed winter logs exploding into the air as though they'd been hit by an artillery shell, and the trees leaning over under the tremendous pressure and disappearing beneath the flood as they were torn up by the roots. They saw the shed where they'd sought shelter climb the face of the great wall of water, rolled and tossed about like a twig, and finally dashed to splinters against a bluff of the valley.

As the water plunged down to Oswino's farm, Henry saw a small figure run out from the trees and head for the hill, driving pigs and cattle in front of it, but the flood caught up with them and they were snatched away, first the man and then the cattle, one after the other, and then the farm itself, in a tangle of timber and stones and exploding tiles. The pylons that carried electricity across the valley became surrounded by the eddying brown swirl and began to sway one after the other, and there were flashes of blue light as the huge cables bounded and twanged and finally snapped. Then they too had gone, smashed down by the awful force of the water roaring away toward Cadivescovo in a great solid wall, rolling, lashing, writhing in a hideous frenzy like a great brown monster, smashing great areas of rock face off as it passed and carrying a huge battering-ram of trees and logs and rocks and water.

The dam had literally melted away. At first there had been a hole big enough for a car to go through, then a few seconds later there had been an opening three hundred feet wide from the top to the bottom of the wall. Now, even as they looked, they saw what was left of the wall crumble slowly away and what was left of the lake fall into the valley.

"Gesu mio misericordia," Caporelli said in an awed whisper. "God have mercy on the people below."

18

By the time they set off down the mountainside, every last drop of water had vanished ahead of them, leaving a swathe of destruction half a mile wide so that they had to edge around the soaked debris and plow across the mud and silt that had been brought down.

The whole valley was full of wreckage as far as they could see, and it was impossible to make out where the road had been, let alone the car. There was still a river of thick, gluey water, the dregs of the dam, twenty feet wide in parts where the stream must originally have run, but now there were no banks, no trees, no walls, nothing.

They managed to cross it where the valley narrowed and a new small dam had been thrown up of logs and rocks and debris all piled in confusion with the bodies of cows and horses and goats and chickens. All his anger drained away in a hopeless feeling of failure, Henry felt numb and sick and cold as they climbed up the opposite slope, covered with mud to their waists. They had had to throw away the jackets Giovanni had been wearing as they became weighted with clogged mud and water and too heavy for the boy's thin shoulders. Henry had lost a shoe and Caporelli's shirt had been torn to shreds by the branches of the brushwood as they had raced up the slope away from the water.

They picked their way downward through the pouring rain, skirting the edge of the debris that had been flung aside and left behind, climbing flattened walls that were mere mounds of mud, pushing past wrecked farm cottages and outbuildings and the odd blank-faced farmer who was standing on the fringe of the destruction where the flood had brushed against his property and passed it by undamaged, leaving him shocked and numb and speechlessly thankful.

Here and there they came across survivors crowded around a shattered figure sprawled on the ground, and once they saw two or three men carrying a door on which there was a blanket-covered body. After a while Giovanni began to stumble and they had to take turns carrying him.

The group of houses where they'd left the car had completely disappeared, though the church still stood, its sides piled high with wreckage. The water had vanished except for the thick stream of mud still draining from the dam and the spreading cloud of brown dotted with driftwood and wreckage that stretched over the surface of the lake. There were no vineyards, no orchards, no meadows, none of the little inns and wineshops that had advertised their wares so carefully in Italian and Gothic German, no growing things at all in the path the water had taken. All the fields, all the grass, all the topsoil, the trees, and the people had been swept away, and the valley floor was a featureless expanse of pebbled mud, scoured and ground clean by the water in its rush for the lake.

"The hotel's still there," Caporelli shouted above the noise of the rain, as he peered downward.

The Stettnerhof was like an island on its little raised knoll of rocks, but on either side of it where the road had run, as though some massive bulldozer had swept past, there was a gouged channel and a swathe of debris as the island had parted the water. The whole center of the town to the east had vanished. They began to go faster, stumbling under the weight of the boy. Here and there as they descended they began to come across cars, hurled aside by the force of the water, flattened like tin toys against the rocks, and great banks of trees and bushes piled against the occasional stone building that had survived.

The debris that the dam had washed off the mountain had formed a moving wall of human beings, animals, trees, bridges, cars, a huge battering-ram of masonry, metal, wood, and flesh. The center of the town had been drowned in ten minutes, and it had gone like a picture rubbed off a slate. Houses had been crushed like eggshells, and the wailing cries of the injured were beginning to rise.

They began to see a few shocked people moving about on the slopes above the tide wrack of wreckage, and one or two more climbing to the piles of planks and splintered timber. Then they began to pass corpses, hanging in trees, half clothed, and protruding from shattered doors and windows, or impaled on ruined fences. Giovanni had fallen asleep now, his head bobbing over Caporelli's shoulder as he marched, step by heavy step, down toward the town, his face bleak and drawn and tragic.

They saw a couple of policemen, both of them without hats, bringing bodies out of a ruined house. They had already laid three in a row and were just bringing out a fourth. All the boats had disappeared from the fringe of the lake, and even the lakeside itself had gone, the trees, the flowers, and all the decorative bushes that had been tended with such loving care to attract the city tourists. Now there was only mud.

There was no sign of the boat station or the Stöckli Bar or

243

the Wolfhof, and there was no sign on the mole of the old Customs House, and it occurred to Henry in his dumb misery that Maggie's theft of the explosives would never be discovered now because what she'd left had gone too. The two boats the archaeological group had been using were lying on their side, half sunk against the mole, and even the wood and stone Church of Lazzaro di Colleno was gone in a tumbled heap of debris.

There was still the river of thick mud between them and the Stettnerhof, but Henry could see several of the archaeologists standing among the dark trees outside the hotel. Caporelli managed to find a rope and somehow, in the growing darkness, they got it across and made their end fast to a tree. Caporelli went down into the river of brown water, working his way across slowly. As he reached the other side, Henry took hold of the drowsy, whimpering Giovanni and followed him, groping for a foothold among the muddy boulders that shifted under his bare toes in the swirling water which broke in a wave against him and formed again in a vortex below. It was icy cold and Giovanni began to cry with misery, and Henry remembered it was all off the mountains and what wasn't rain was melted snow and glacier water.

There was no electricity in the hotel, but they could see one or two candles in the windows. As Henry heaved Giovanni up the muddy bank of the great fissure that had been carved out of the earth, he felt hands grab the boy and take him away, and more hands reaching down to him to help him up. He saw a face he recognized and realized it was Maggs. Caporelli was standing in the doorway, with Giovanni in his arms.

"Where's Maggie?" Henry said.

"She's here somewhere," Maggs said. "I saw her—or I thought I did."

He found her in the dining room and saw all the children from the orphanage were there, too, with the Sisters and the

Mother Superior, trying to find some comfort among the saturated, tumbled furniture.

Maggie saw him as soon as he appeared in the doorway. She was kneeling by a weeping child, and she jumped to her feet, the dulled misery vanishing from her eyes.

"Henry!" She pushed the child aside gently and ran across to him. Her hair was wet, as though she'd been outside in the rain, and her clothes were as plastered to her small body as his own.

"Henry! Oh, Henry!"

He put his arms around her as she flung herself against him, clinging to him, sobbing and trembling and shuddering, and he stroked her damp hair instinctively, as though he'd been doing it for years.

"We were too late," he said flatly. "Stettner was there. Stettner and his thugs!"

Her fingers were clutching at him, working nervously as they dug into his flesh. "I thought it must have caught you," she said. "I thought you'd gone."

"Not me. Thank God you're all right."

"It only took ten minutes. I ran up to the orphanage when you'd gone. At first they wouldn't listen to me, but they came in the end. And then the streets were full of people all running for their lives. The water seemed to—to lick them up, Henry, and the whole town just disappeared. Houses were tumbling one after the other, all pushed against the banks like packs of cards with everyone inside. The orphanage was one of the first to go. We watched it all from the windows."

She shuddered and her body was icy in his arms. "We heard it coming and I heard someone shouting, 'Run for your lives,' and then it all seemed to be noise and screams. I saw a wagon coming down the hill as the water came, but it lost a wheel, and everybody fell out and—and—and then they disappeared.

"Then the water began to come in at the back of the hotel and we felt the rocks and trees hitting it, and even houses. We thought it was going all the time. Henry—there's a policemen at the back there, and Oswino's wife. They're dead."

There was nothing they could do that night. Nothing at all. There were no lights and no doctors and no nurses and no police. Everything had vanished. All they could do was look after themselves as best they could until daylight.

Caporelli turned out every blanket he possessed, and they tucked the children up six or seven at a time in the beds on the dry upper floors with the worst of the shocked and injured. There were several people with broken limbs and one woman, whose hair had been caught in a tree, with the scalp almost torn from her head. There were so many people crowding into the hotel, there was nothing much Caporelli could give them in the way of food, but with a stomach full of soup and bread and with dry clothes on him again, Henry began at last to feel capable of thinking of others.

The town was black in the rain except for the small moving lights of lanterns and torches. Occasionally they could hear calls and cries across the dwindling strip of brown water, and all the time the wails and moans of injured people in the smashed houses around.

When they'd brought some organization back to the Stettner-hof, they collected a party of men and scrambled back along the rope to the other side, leaving the women and the nuns and the older people to look after the survivors.

Almost immediately, in the light of the torch Caporelli had given him, Henry saw a dead woman, practically naked, lying half covered with mud, on the bank, and he wondered why he hadn't seen her as they'd climb down from the dam. They dragged her up the bank and laid her on the grass and left her there. An old man was clinging to a roof where he'd climbed when the first flood had poured around him. In the dark and the rain he couldn't see to climb down and he was petrified with fear and cold. They rescued him with a broken ladder from a twisted barn, and he said he thought he could manage because his house was still standing.

As they reached the town, they began to meet people coming from the other side of the lake, clean people with dry clothes and rubber capes and stretchers, and they realized these must be the first of the rescue workers from Trepizano. There was a doctor among them, kneeling at the roadside, sewing up a gash in the arm of a girl who was leaning, white-faced and fainting, against a fence.

"They'll be bringing help from Bolzano," they were told. "There'll be more from Trento. Tomorrow. It'll be here tomorrow."

The wreckage was banked up in mounds thirty feet high, twisted around with barbed wire and telephone cable, wood, trees, stone, human beings, unbreakable and impossible to free.

"It'll take days to sort that out," Caporelli said.

The survivors they found, those who had been through the flood and escaped, were all shocked and helpless, with staring faces in masks of blood and mud. Where their homes had been there was now only bare ground. The whole town seemed to have been swept aside, with only an occasional stone building surviving. Those that were standing all had bodies in them, caught by the water bursting through windows and doors and rising to twenty feet in a matter of seconds, brown, choking water that had smashed the life out of them long before they were drowned. And everything, every single thing, seemed to be under a three-foot layer of slime.

The Piazza della Citta, which had taken the full force of the flood, was just a mass of debris and broken stone and scattered tiles. The old palace of the Von Benedikts still stood, but every door and window had gone from the first floor as the water had smashed through, and the dungeons contained the bodies of the students who had been imprisoned there the day before, together with that of a police sergeant who had tried to free them. The wooden houses in the streets behind had simply collapsed into piles of heavy timbers, where policemen and rescuers, directed by Castelrossi, were clambering about, trying to find the owners of the crying voices underneath.

They were stumbling with weariness when they got back to the Stettnerhof, and they congregated in the hall, sitting on the stairs, uncertain where to go and what to do with themselves.

Caporelli produced a bottle of brandy and filled glasses. They were all blank-faced and drunk with tiredness, and, seeking somewhere to sleep, Henry found himself in the dining room. The children had disappeared and there seemed to be nobody awake except for a nun sitting in the corner telling her beads among the silent mounds of sleeping people huddled on tables and under tables and in chairs. Then Maggie's head lifted and he saw she'd found a blanket and was stretched out on a goatskin rug near the door. Her face twisted into a smile that was sad and friendly both at the same time, and she lifted the edge of the blanket without speaking.

Henry stumbled toward her and stretched out beside her, feeling the young warmth of her body against his own cold limbs, and her lips against his cheek. Almost immediately, as she put her arms around him and drew him to her, he fell asleep and the last thought that entered his mind before he drifted into darkness was of Lazzaro's cross. Of the Church of Lazzaro di Colleno there had been no sign, and in his last conscious thought Henry wondered if the Cross of Lazzaro had gone, too, smashed to splinters among the wreckage, with Father Anselmo and Father Gianpiero and all the red cloth and the floodlights and the television cameras that it had attracted.

Daylight came with a bright sky that mocked the stricken valley with the first real promise of settled weather for weeks.

The first direct rays of the sun struck the upper crests of the Catena di Saga, so that they glowed dull red against the sky, then as the light strengthened, the red became orange and then gold as the shadows retreated from the screes. Then the gold was lost as the sun gathered strength until, in a sky of tragically beautiful ultramarine, the peaks standing out in dazzling cream and ivory.

The police started evacuating the survivors at first light, the injured first, and the long thread of people, many of them in black and carrying all that remained of their belongings on their backs, began to move out of the village, muttering and weeping and crying out to each other. The *Citta di Trepizano* lay just offshore opposite where the boat station had once stood, and the launches which had come across from Trepizano were ferrying people out for the ship to take them to relatives across the lake or to trains for the south.

Even the opposite bank had not escaped unscathed. The water that had smashed down from the mountain had created an artificial wave that had rushed across the mile and a half of lake and flung itself at Trepizano. The ferry had a set of smashed rails and twisted ventilators to show where she had been flung against the concrete mole, and other, smaller boats had been hurled twenty or thirty feet up the banks and onto the road. Cars had been snatched away, and there wasn't a chair or a table left along the water-front cafés.

The death roll in Cadivescovo was not as high as had been expected in the first shock of the disaster because, in spite of the old joke of shouting into bars that the dam had burst, everybody had guessed at once what had happened, the minute they'd heard the roar from the mountain behind. Fortunately, also, the valley was narrow and the debris that the flood had carried before it had formed a wall that had slowed the force of the water and given people a chance to run for high ground.

By the grace of God it had still been daylight, too, and they had been able to watch the moving wall of water and the plunging trees coming down on them long enough to understand what had happened. Only the laggards and those occupied in rescuing treasures had been caught. The rest had seen the advance guard of mist and heard the ominous sound of the water approaching behind the trembling horizon, and by the time the first wave had smashed into the houses, many townspeople had managed to reach the higher ground around the hotel or on either side of the artificial stream bed.

Henry said good-by to Caporelli who was waiting by the door of the Stettnerhof as he left. The children from the orphanage were going, too, to be evacuated across to Trepizano because the old sawmill was nothing more now than a flattened pile of timbers, stone, and tiles. They all had their little packet of sandwiches, carried in the small gay bags that Caporelli had been in the habit of giving to tourists in the summer for their outings up the mountains.

"We must have faith," Sister Agata was saying agitatedly in answer to a chorus of "Whys" as the children stared across the debris and began to ask questions. "We have our faith and we must lean on it. God moves in His mysterious way and we can suffer worse than this, far worse. If we cannot believe, we cannot live."

Caporelli looked up as Henry appeared. Giovanni was with him, still in his orphanage clothes, still pale and strained-looking, but with a new light in his eyes, a new alert look full of understanding and warmth that even the disaster could not touch.

"He'll stay here," Caporelli had said. "He's intelligent and sensitive and he's got plenty of courage. Sister Ursula would like that."

Caporelli couldn't speak as Henry put down his suitcase and just silently gripped his hand.

"Auf wiedersehen, Aynree," he said at last. *"C'i vedremo.* And thank you. We tried. We very nearly succeeded."

"Good-by, Ettore," Henry said. "I'll come and see you again some time."

"Yes, Aynree. Come back. I would like that."

They'd heard no more of Stettner or Dittli and, though Caporelli had taken the trouble to inquire at the little office the police had opened for people asking about relatives, nothing was known of either of them, and they'd guessed that somehow with the aid of sympathizers, Dittli had hidden Stettner and finally got him across the mountains and into Austria and safety, to live out his life in a bleak twilight as a cripple, cut off from all the things he enjoyed—women, climbing, swimming, laughing—tormented by the most appallingly cruel punishment that could have been devised for him.

As they moved down to the lakeside with the children in a long crocodile behind them, the rear brought up by the nuns, they could see cars along the Via Colleno—sight-seers and camera fiends who'd come to take pictures of the disaster. Bulldozers were at work in the town near the littered Hoferdenkmal, pushing the debris aside, while rescue workers examined it for the trapped bodies of the missing. The whole place had a soursweet stink over it, percolating through the smell of disinfectant and chloride of lime, and there were official vans from Trepizano, and men trying to bring some order back to the drainage and electricity and telephone systems.

The place was full of soldiers and there were tents everywhere, as well as a couple of helicopters circling overhead, one of them with United States marking on it.

Where they had buried Sister Ursula and the murdered policemen only a day or two before, there were no longer any cypress-shaded tombs, just a few smeared stone angels sticking out of the mud, and the broken slabs from the scoured graves, and the torn-off wall of a columbarium exposing the coffins inside. Soldiers were moving in a long line in the valley, searching, their faces stony, and there was a listlessness about their movements, because there was nothing to find. It was as if the valley had been scoured clean. All the homes had gone, with their flowers and the Gothic inscriptions that spoke of happiness and warmth which had been carved so lovingly over the doors, all their music and all their color—the church, the school, the brass band, the orphanage, the Municipio, the boat station, everything, leaving only a mud-covered expanse, with searching lines of dun-colored soldiers stretched across it.

The town was dead and without any kind of communication with the outside world. Food was short and water was short and there was a hysterical, unhealthy atmosphere among the soaked ruins because of the sudden danger of typhoid. Hundreds of people were still lying in the wet grass on the slopes of the mountains, afraid to come down, and nobody knew what was under the new floor of the valley.

A loudspeaker in the square was warning people to beware of cyanide washed away from the dye works, and the radio was full of appeals for blood plasma. A newspaper, brought over from Trepizano, had been thrown aside and lay in the gutter, saturated and muddy, and the headlines blared up at Henry as he passed—JUSTICE WILL BE DONE, the solemn promise of some clean, dry official from Rome. "It had better be," the newspaper had added in an equally solemn threat.

The birds were singing with heartbreaking happiness over the bell of Madonna del Piano tolling a Miserere as they approached the improvised jetty that had been thrown up. Knee-deep in the water of the lake, three soldiers were dragging out the corpse of a man, and there was a woman nearby watching, her face thin and ancient-looking with grief. Then Henry saw a television van and a boom lens directed at him, and a man with a flash camera stood up and half blinded him as the bulb went off.

He saw Mornaghini walking slowly toward the boats, his head bent, hatless and coatless. He had lost his home and his family, and his reputation had vanished. As he climbed into the waiting launch, someone called from the shore: "Murderer! Assassin!"

There had been no demand for an international rescue operation. There was nothing to find and the valley could never be restored. Nothing would ever grow again in the muddy subsoil and among the piled rocks—only the coarse mountain grass and stunted pines leaning toward the lake in the winds that blew down the valley, stark and gray as dead limbs. It was as bare and featureless as the higher slopes of the mountains and just as cold-looking, even in the sun.

Here and there he could see a tent erected in a garden, as the occupants of the house tried to clean out their wrecked home, and occasionally a shop with the inevitable *Business As Usual* sign in the window. Father Gianpiero was in the middle of a small group of people who stood with their hands together and their heads bowed. His face was white, his head bandaged, and his voice sounded thin and reedy over the noise of the bull-dozers and mechanical shovels doing rescue work by the lake-side.

"Troppo li abbiamo noi meritati avendo peccato contro di Voi—"

Of Father Anselmo nothing more had been seen. He had disappeared with his church in the first awful roaring of the flood.

Henry put his hand out to Maggie and drew her to him, and they stood aside as the nuns packed the children into the launches to be taken out to the *Citta di Trepizano*. Then they walked slowly hand in hand down the improvised jetty themselves. The launch was already full of people with pale drawn faces, all of them, with black-covered buttons sewn on their lapels. Maggie and Henry took their places with them among the archaeologists with their suitcases and packs, their shoulders draped with cameras and diving gear. There was no longer anything for them to do. They had offered to help, but the police had politely requested them to go home. There was not enough food for them, and no longer any work.

There was no Customs Shed and no boats, and no treasures from the bottom of the lake. No Church of Lazzaro di Colleno. Not even Bishop Lazzaro himself, because the church had collapsed across the crypt and even the bones had gone as everything had been scoured clean. There was not even any Dei Monti to complain because his body had been found in the wreckage of his hotel. There was nothing. Nothing at all—only Arcuneum on the floor of the lake at the Punta dei Fiori, untouched and undamaged by the flood.

Just Arcuneum—discovered, as everyone had wanted it to be, undisturbed, as they'd wanted it to be, still waiting to be picked clean when anyone had the courage or the stomach to investigate it again. One of the finest relics in Europe, they'd called it—as unharmed and unmarked as it had been a thousand years before, left there untouched in the disaster around it, like a symbol of the smallness of man.

Just Arcuneum, and by an ironic quirk of fate the cross of Lazzaro. It had been discovered among the wreckage of the church, protected from destruction by the collapse of a group of beams which had formed an arch above it and held it in place like a vise against the roaring waters, with the great oak timber from over the doorway, *Gebet Gott was Gottes ist,* jammed against it like a warning to interfering humans—Give to God what belongs to God. Apart from a few scars, the cross was as undamaged as when it had first been raised from the water, as though its own apparently magic properties had protected it. But this time there was no one to say it was a miracle, no one to produce red velvet and floodlights, and the cross remained in its splintered bower of fallen beams, almost forgotten, catalytic, stark and black and gaunt, like the stamp and seal of the tragedy that had followed it.

There was nothing else, just that long scar running up the side of the valley to where the Catena di Saga closed in, and the gap by La Fortezza where the dam had been, like a hole in a great gum where a tooth had been extracted. Nothing else but the magnificent sky and the pearly spires of the mountains.